LOVE YOU TRULY

STACY TRAVIS

FAST TURTLE PRESS

LOVE YOU TRULY

* * *

STACY TRAVIS

Cover Design: Wildheart Graphics

Copyediting: Jenny Sims, Editng4Indies

CHAPTER 1

ash

One Month Ago

The parking lot at Sunshine Foods market is jam-packed at seven in the evening. Typical.

After taking what seems like the last available parking spot, I weave through the sea of vehicles—pickup trucks and Teslas in equal numbers—and grab a shopping cart.

I know exactly what I need, so it shouldn't take too long.

Tortilla chips, avocado, chicken breasts, white rice, black beans. And a bag of powdered sugar mini donuts.

The donuts have nothing to do with cooking tacos for my family tomorrow night. They have everything to do with an after-work craving when I haven't had dinner and probably won't. Splitting a plate of wings at the bar hardly counts as dinner, but Lucas is as predictable as he is insistent that we keep our weekly guys' night ritual going.

In three years, neither Lucas nor I have missed a single Wednesday night, and I don't plan to be the one to break our streak. Let him be the one to fall for a girl and come crawling, telling me he just has to spend Wednesday night with her.

I'm stubborn enough to win any kind of showdown he throws my way, especially if it involves a woman.

Rounding the endcap of the cereal aisle, I try to recall whether I have anything left in my pantry that might qualify as breakfast tomorrow morning. If not, I'll double up on the donuts. For the past few days, I've slept in and skipped breakfast in order to make it to work on time. Bad habit.

The vast wall of cereal puts me in a temporary trance. Colors dance in front of my eyes as Cap'n Crunch's blue hat merges with the beak of Toucan Sam and morphs into the yellow of a Cheerios box. Organic cornflakes, regular ones... I wonder if they taste any different.

It should be a thoughtless selection. Any kind of cereal will do, especially if I end up shoveling it down from a coffee mug on the go, but the choice suddenly seems daunting.

Three days of worrying about vineyards and my fucking reputation have left me unable to make a basic decision. I should grab a box—any box—and move on, but my feet feel glued to the floor. I stare down the cereal as though it's Mt. Everest.

It's why I barely move out of the way when a frustrated "excuse me" sounds beside my shoulder. I feel it more than I hear the words—a lilt against my ear, a subtle hint of jasmine perfume, a warm sweep of air as a woman moves past me. My senses light up before I even get a look at her, as she nearly sideswipes me with her shopping cart.

The close call has my senses on alert. Same feeling I used to get when I played high school football, and I'd feel someone on my heels before I could see him running to tackle me. It allowed me to dart out of the way more than once and score a touchdown.

I'm interested enough to follow as she careens down the aisle like a drunk linebacker with a case of vertigo.

Her shopping cart is loaded to the top with box upon box of canned sparkling water and cases of bottled water, and the cart itself seems to have a wonky wheel. The bright flash of her red sweater calls to me like a toreador waving a flag. I'm the bull, unable to tear my eyes away as she weaves down the aisle.

The rogue wheel seems to be turning the cart in circles as the woman fights to keep it moving straight ahead, hanging on for dear life. The problem is that with a hundred pounds of beverages in the cart, she's fighting a losing battle against the laws of physics.

Instead of moving to help her, I stand frozen, watching the impending disaster unfold like a movie. I know it's terrible, but my feet won't budge.

I watch her long, dark hair swish against her red sweater, which highlights a tapered waist above tight black jeans, her legs long and lean. She works hard to control the cart, which nicks a box of Lucky Charms, sending it to the floor.

Swearing under her breath, she's loud enough for me to be amused by her choice of words. When she bends to pick up the box, she briefly lets go of the cart, which sweeps in a circle and dead ends into fourteen kinds of Special K. The weight of the cart keeps them in place, but freeing the cart isn't an easy job.

I can't help but wonder why she has so many drinks in her cart, but that's beside the point. Then I notice a jumbo bag of dog food on the lower rack. Probably weighs fifty pounds. I feel compelled to tell her there are delivery services for these things.

"Hey, can I help you with that?" I call after her.

She doesn't answer, instead yanking on the shopping cart, which hurls her backward into the center of the aisle. Digging in with her three-inch heels, she doesn't get much traction, but I admire the effort.

This is why I tell people like my uptight eldest brother that getting out of the office is important. Seeing people in their natural environments often tells me more about them than a résumé packed with qualities they think *I* think are important.

Hitting the gym and watching which guys are all about their own workouts—wearing headphones, refusing to spot someone who's lifting—tells me how they'd fare in a workplace. Selfish assholes. Seeing someone like this woman, determined to complete her mission, fighting a shopping cart goliath like David in a red sweater, tells me she has grit.

All of these things matter, and since I'm the one in charge of hiring new people to keep our winery afloat, I notice.

Finally unmoored from the linoleum tiles on the floor, I push my own cart after hers, determined to help if she needs it. I'm not being chivalrous; this now feels like a public safety issue.

I catch up with her in a few strides, but not before she tries to whip the cart around the end of the aisle. Big mistake.

The rogue wheel cuts too close to the end of the aisle, where an unfortunate pyramid of glass jars is stacked five feet high. Well, it was...

I abandon my cart as hers craters into the jars, and she goes with it. Her heels have no chance of digging in and stopping the cart on the slick supermarket floor, so she slides along like a kite surfer in a tornado.

The cart hits the display so hard that it forces a rebound effect, throwing her backward just as I reach her and put my hands out like it's fourth down and I'm alone in the end zone.

If it were a football game, I'd be the hero. In this case, I'm more like a punching bag, losing my own footing in a sea of pale green pickle juice seeping from dozens of broken jars.

"Whoa...!" she yells, punctuating my string of curses.

The air reeks of vinegar as both of us slip backward, me

holding her against my chest and throwing one hand down in an attempt to break our fall. More pickle juice greets my hand, which slips, dropping me to my back. My arm encircles the waist of the woman as her full weight lands with me on the floor.

Then, an eerie, still silence.

It takes a couple of moments before other shoppers appear, observing us down their noses like we're odd specimens who don't know how to grocery shop properly. "You guys okay?" A woman in a gray puffer coat down to her knees looks over her small round glasses and tilts her head to the side.

Since I'm pretty certain I took the brunt of our fall, I feel confident that the woman on top of me is probably okay.

"Yup. Fine. Clean up on aisle seven," I say, forcing levity into my tone when I'm halfway certain I've broken a rib. The other shoppers move around our two-cart pileup and go on with their days, and I do my best to push up from the floor with one hand.

However, the pickle juice has its way, and I slide sideways before righting myself. Meanwhile, the woman splayed on top of me wriggles out of my grip, but her heels slide in the pickle juice, and she has no luck separating her body from mine.

I have enough wherewithal to appreciate the warm feeling of her form against mine, the softness of her sweater under my hand, and the scent of jasmine, which I now realize is coming from her hair. Long tendrils dance across my face as she fails to push away.

Finally, I muscle my way to standing, holding tight to her body so she rises from the floor along with me. She's stiff against my rib cage, and her feet pedal against the floor as she struggles to stand on her own.

"I have it," she bites out right before slipping and almost taking both of us back down again. I hold on tight, bracing an elbow against a display of paper towels, which stays in place under my weight.

"Not quite, you don't." I push away from the towels and test my footing on the slippery floor. I feel steady, but I quickly realize I'm bracing this woman across the swell of her breasts. A part of me knows I need to move my hand—and quickly—lest she think I'm trying to grope her.

When she finally stops fidgeting in my grasp, she looks down at where my hand still grips her securely. I move it away gingerly, testing her steadiness before I take a step backward. I feel a whoosh of refrigerated air between us and fight the urge to pull her back against my chest.

"Sorry. You okay?"

She nods. "Yeah. Thanks."

I'm not a caveman, and I've never had a problem finding women to date. I'm not bragging. If anything, I wish my reputation as a ladies' man wasn't tattooed quite so insistently across my face.

"Once a man-slut, always a man-slut," Lucas says as women sidle up to me. I nod and fist-bump him like we're in on the same joke, an old habit. My friends seem to expect nothing less from me.

I'd like to be about as far from a man-slut as a guy can get, but old reputations die hard, and people see what they want to see.

Just to punctuate the moment, a jar of sweet baby dills teeters on what's left of the display, rolls off the top of the jar below it, and smashes on the ground a few feet away. Glass shards explode in all directions.

The woman sighs and turns around and surveys the damage around us—a dozen or so smashed pickle jars, tiny gherkins, and dill slices as far as the eye can see, and the pervasive smell of dill and vinegar. "Bet you didn't expect to become a human pickle when you came here tonight," she bites out.

But all I can think is that I know this woman. In fact, I've sort of known Mallory Rutherford half my life.

The fact that we've barely ever spoken is merely incidental. She was in the same grade as my older sister Beatrix, and I quietly worshipped her beauty like the testosterone-charged younger brother I was. Then, a few years ago, she had a brief fling with my brother. If I ever had any thoughts about asking her out, they died with the eye-rolling tales of what a nightmare she was.

It takes another few seconds for her eyes to sweep from the mess to my face, and I see the jolt of recognition halfway through her next sentence. "You landed hard—are you hurt?"

Her eyes go wide. "Dash."

"Mallory."

It didn't occur to me that the woman careening down the aisle a few minutes earlier was Mallory Rutherford because why would Mallory Rutherford be commandeering a stuffed shopping cart in high heels on a Wednesday night? Doesn't she have some expensive wine industry gala to attend where she can tease some poor vineyard owner into thinking she'll sell him a few acres from her family's sprawling lots?

Mallory Rutherford is a social butterfly, the daughter of land owners on the other end of Napa Valley, and arm candy to any man with a big enough pocketbook. As I said, I barely know her, so her reputation is all I have to go on, whether it's accurate or not.

The irony of that isn't lost on me, but sometimes reputations are correct.

Her face is a confluence of expressions and shades of pink. Lips colored with a rosy lipstick, cheeks drowning in scarlet, brow furrowed, eyes squinting. Then wide. Then squinting again.

She opens her mouth and closes it again as her cheeks notch a brighter pink hue.

"Are-are you okay?" she asks.

Her concern for my well-being strikes me as almost antithetical to everything I know about Mallory Rutherford—out for herself, only interested in a man if she can flirt her way into a business advantage, and ultimately, a woman with expensive taste who cares only about herself.

Again, the irony is real.

She looks me over from head to feet, and I feel the warmth of her gaze like the morning sun. Immediately, I shake myself back to reality because this is Mallory Rutherford, and I don't know whether she's sizing me up out of concern or because I might make a nice next meal.

My hand goes to my lower back, which took the brunt of my fall, but near as I can tell, I haven't broken anything.

"I'm fine. You?"

The embarrassment on her face is taken over by an icy stare. "Fine. Again, sorry."

She looks at her shopping cart, which has a few jars of pickles sitting on top of the cases of drinks, and begins removing them one by one. Her eyes dart around the floor for any jars that haven't broken—and there are a few—and she picks those up as well.

I stand there agog, watching Mallory totter around in her heels amid a green layer of pickle juice on the floor. She could easily walk off and flag down a supermarket employee to clean up the mess and be out of the store before the cleanup is finished. Yet she's trying to put the display back into its pyramid shape herself.

It makes me want to help her, so I chase the few jars that have rolled the furthest away and stack them back on the display.

"Thanks." Her voice is barely audible, and I can't decide whether it's because she doesn't like to ask for help or she doesn't like me, which is ridiculous because she doesn't know me.

But people have their opinions. I guess she's just another one who doesn't mind getting it wrong, and I don't care enough about her to bother correcting the misperception.

CHAPTER 2

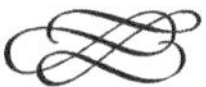

$\mathcal{M}$allory

Present Day

You know those days when it seems like you might actually escape without your whole life falling apart? Those days when it seems like everything will work out, and you actually take the first optimistic breath and start to believe?

I'm having one of those days.

The sun is high in the sky on one of those late summer afternoons that feels like it might go on and on without ever getting dark. Of course, I know better because day always melts into night eventually, but for the moment, I feel the optimism of an endless summer day.

Sitting at the small desk in my office that overlooks the acres of farmland my family calls home in Napa Valley, I stare out at acres of green. It's mostly wild plants and grasses where a handful of horses and sheep graze, but I see potential.

Even as a kid with long pigtails my mom curled into ringlets, I saw something more than what met the eye when I studied our land from this very window. Back then, it was a spare bedroom where the occasional visiting aunt or family friend would stay. The twin daybed is all that remains of that bygone era. I keep it because I occasionally take a power nap during the workday, and it's more comfortable than sleeping on a couch.

Otherwise, the room is all business with streamlined office furniture, file cabinets, an ergonomic desk chair, and bookshelves, all stained the pale natural color of light wood. The shelves are crammed with accounting books, financial planners, and corporate finance textbooks I've accumulated over the past four years of taking classes to earn my business degree.

The only people who know I've been learning about entrepreneurship are my professors and my fellow students, and that's the way I want it.

I inhale the fragrant air that slips through the open window and think about how I'd like to spend the rest of my day. Maybe a walk around the perimeter of the property, which sits at the foot of a sweeping hill covered in grapevines. Almost everyone around here is serious about farming grapes and producing wine —everyone except my parents.

Ironic that they own one of the largest pieces of land and have little interest in making wine.

Or just dumb.

But I'm about to turn thirty-three in a few months, and according to the trust they set up ages ago, I'll be the sole owner of Autumn Lake Cellars, which is currently two hundred acres of land and a barely-there winery they started a few decades ago. I don't intend to waste a moment of time when that happens.

Hence my business education and the whiteboard in my office with columns, arrows, and lists of big plans. Seeing my dreams for our property delineated on the board always calms me even though I've been chomping at the bit like a racehorse for ten years and the dreams have been nothing more than... dreams.

My eye catches on a plume of dust outside the window, indicating someone is driving up the unpaved road leading from the main highway.

Unlike most of the large wineries around here, I don't get a lot of visitors because we don't give tastings or tours. The only people who come up the drive are the workers who tend to the farmland, and they all finished their work hours ago, before the heat of midday.

There's no reason for anyone to be here, and when I see the dark blue of a Mercedes sedan driving through the haze of dust, my stomach lurches. I know that car, if only because the man driving it was here a month ago talking to my parents before their most recent trip.

I nearly blew my top then, and I'm about to do it again now.

Rushing down the stairs of the clapboard house that doubles as our business office and the main entry of Autumn Lake Cellars, I shove the loose strands of my long hair behind my ears and attempt to tame them. I have a habit of twisting my hair into a bun and securing it with a pencil while I'm working, but by the end of the day, it's a twirly mess.

Then I silently yell at myself for caring about how I look, especially in front of this man.

Yanking open the front door to the house, I see the dust settling around Felix Sutton's too-expensive car. Then I see the man himself shove open the driver's door and step out in his brown loafers and expensive suit.

I can't believe I ever looked at him and found him remotely attractive. Now, I just want him off our property before he decides it's his right to come any further.

His fake smile puts his overly white teeth on full display in the afternoon sun. They're like bleached seashells that have been left outside for too long. "Mal," he says, extending his hands.

I fold my arms over my chest and give him a blank expression like I barely know who he is.

He keeps advancing, and I hold my ground with my most agreeable face plastered on, unwilling to let him see how much he irks me because it only fuels him.

It's a game we've played for years, ever since our yearlong marriage proved to be a massive case of me getting played. He wanted me for my family tree—my position as the only heir to my parents' land fortune—and he was well-positioned to inherit half of what I inherit. Not anymore—thank you, divorce.

Basic stupidity on my part, thinking that love would last and he wouldn't turn out to be a snake in the grass.

Now I'm business-savvy and done with love. Smarter outlook, if you ask me.

"You're like a bad penny. Keep turning up," I say without changing my facial expression. I wish I could take the high road and pretend his coming here doesn't bug me, but I'm human. I'd like to turn on the hose and blast him off my property.

No, I'll get rid of him more quickly if I listen to whatever bullshit thing he came here to say, nod politely, and turn him away.

He smiles as though I haven't just insulted him. "Good to see you too."

High road, one. Me, zero.

"Right. What's up, Felix?"

He shrugs as though he's thinking about what he wants to say. He always knows, so it's a game.

Taking a step forward, he comes too close to me, daring me to step backward. But I don't. I'm not giving him an inch. Arms still crossed, I look upward and meet his eyes, which are a sickly shade of green. Like algae. Or poison oak. I can't believe I didn't notice this before we were married.

Guess love really is blind.

Most people find him utterly charming, seeing his inside jokes and handsy behavior as a sign that they've reached the inner circle. Inner circle of hell, perhaps. But other people's failure to read him is old news by now. It doesn't surprise me that Felix Sutton breezes through life, pulling the wool over everyone's eyes. It's just his way.

And yes, I fell for it too. Even before we started dating, he hovered close to me, massaged my shoulders, and put an arm around me in a slightly possessive way that I found harmless at the time. I even found it a little endearing.

Ugh.

"This is me coming with my hat in hand." He extends his hand, but it contains no hat. He doesn't seem to notice.

"Why?"

He leans even closer to me. I inhale a lungful of his cologne, which has a musky top note that makes me shudder at the memory of being with him. I can see his pores, which seem larger than they should be for a normal person, but maybe it's because he's two inches from my face.

I take a step forward so abruptly that he pitches backward and nearly loses his balance. He gives up on the physical intimidation and starts walking in a circle on the driveway. I'm about one minute from calling the cops and having them clear him off my property.

"We oughtta mend fences. I know you're not dumb, Mal. You see an opportunity when it presents itself, and I'm here. I'm an opportunity."

It takes all my self-control not to laugh in his face. "What kind of opportunity is that?" I ask calmly. I've seen his car coming and going from our property over the past few months, and I can't understand why my parents put up with him. But they've always liked the guy, and they've never seen him as the twat he is.

After we got divorced, he kept up a relationship with them, visiting monthly and sending them holiday and birthday gifts. It annoyed me because it meant I had to see him occasionally in passing, but it seemed harmless enough.

My parents are good people, but they have a blind spot when it comes to sussing out disingenuous turds, and unfortunately, this town is full of them. There's always someone trying to sweet-talk them into selling a parcel of their land, and they always smile and nod along.

Fortunately, what my parents lack in cynicism, they make up for with stubbornness. They'll never sell, plain and simple. Our land will always be our land, and it's worth millions.

"My parents aren't here. They're still in Europe," I tell Felix, even though I know he knows because I told him the same thing last week.

My parents, who live in a small house at the other end of our property, have been working at a farm in France for the past month. You'd think there would be enough for them to do on our own piece of land, but they're volunteering to pick produce for other people in exchange for room and board. They do it nearly every year during harvesting months, which landed them in Croatia picking olives last fall and in South America last spring. Different countries every time. My parents are more interested in doddering around on other people's farms and milking their cows than they are in talking business with people around here.

When I was younger, their granola hippie ways pushed me to go in the opposite direction, chasing fashion trends, burning up every credit card reader in town, watching makeup and hair tutorials, and styling my look before I knew what a look even was.

Thinking back, it was childish. It resulted in people seeing me as a hollow fashion plate, and I may need to change some minds when the calendar page flips on my birthday.

For years, I ran business ideas by my parents, trying to convince them to grow grapes on our land or lease some of the acreage to other wine growers. We're lucky enough to live on prime property in a sought-after appellation. We wouldn't have to sell any of the land, but we could still run a robust business and turn more of a profit.

But my parents would never hear of it. For all their counter-culture ways, they were traditional in one very inconvenient area —they believed that I should get married, have babies, and let my husband be the "career mind" in the family. I trotted out every Equal Rights Amendment piece of evidence to the contrary and made a strong case for "doing it all," but my mother had her doubts.

"I don't know why you'd make things harder on yourself than they need to be," she'd say when I floated my ideas about the business side of Autumn Lake. They wanted grandkids from me, not business ideas.

Then I met Felix. He too liked the idea of "being a part of the storied Rutherford family," as he put it, and he told my parents exactly what they wanted to hear. He'd be the squeeze-bottle ketchup to my crisp French fries, the lid to my boiling pot. They ate it up like a Thanksgiving feast.

When I married Felix, I convinced myself that maybe I could have it both ways. My parents would see that I took their desires seriously and partnered up with a man. And I lived with the delusion that my new husband would take my dreams seriously and help me achieve them like the blob of ketchup he was.

Wrong and double wrong.

He was in it for himself, and as soon as I realized that he'd never really love me, I sent him packing.

Except that here he is.

"I'm here to see you. I decided it's time we talk turkey."

"I have no idea what that means."

"It means that you have a birthday coming up, so we need a plan for how to run this place once we inherit."

I almost laugh because the idea of me including him in any sort of plan is nonsense.

"We? You sure you don't have your pronouns confused? *You're* not inheriting anything."

It happens so slowly, with such deliberate pleasure on Felix's behalf, that I almost don't see it. His face morphs into the most satisfied, shit-eating, buffoon of a smile. One second, he looks like his same boring self, and the next, he's grinning like the Joker.

"Of course I am. Unless you've been lying about your age."

"I haven't lied about anything. I'm turning thirty-three, and I'll inherit Autumn Lake. You will get your flabby ass off my property, and after that, my day will improve."

He stares at me as though he's waiting for me to flinch. Or let him in on the joke. Then his grin gets so big I'm afraid he might crack his lips and bleed all over my driveway, which would be irritating and messy.

"You don't know." He slaps his forehead. "You really don't know."

He's right. I really don't know why I haven't turned on the water hose yet.

But something in the self-satisfied way he's still hovering makes me a tiny bit nervous. We filed the divorce papers, right? I'd remember forgetting to do something like that. So what's he going on about?

"I give up, Felix. What don't I know?"

"That your parents love me. They know how good I am for you, and they know I only want the best for you."

"Questionable. But what's your point?"

"We're partners. Your inheritance is to be shared with me as your husband."

I laugh. Clearly, he's gone 'round the bend.

"You are not my husband."

"Not in deed, but in spirit. That's how your parents see it. They've explicitly retained me as supervisor for all the property you inherit."

"What the actual fuck?" I wish he didn't get my goat, but I can't help it. Even if he's lying, it's too much to bear.

"Partners, Mal. We're going to be partners."

"Okay, first of all, assuming what you're saying has any remote possibility of being true, what makes you think I need you as my partner?"

He runs a hand through his hair, or at least he tries. There's so much gel holding it in place that his hand gets stuck halfway through, and he has to extricate his fingers. "You're going to inherit a big responsibility, and you're going to need help."

"Says who?"

A laugh barks from him. "Anyone who knows anything about business."

"Great. I'll find one of those people if I need help."

"Be serious, Mal. This could really work. I'm good on the business end, and you could keep up appearances and be the face of the place."

"Wow, thank you for allowing me to be the 'face' of my own family business, one I can't possibly run without your help." My sarcasm and the slight shake in my voice betray my attempt to act like I'm immune to Felix's implication that I need help. I hope he doesn't notice, but from the way he licks his lips, I feel like the prey of a puma who just cornered his dinner.

That's the problem with being married to a person. Even though it didn't last beyond a year, our marriage allowed Felix to know things about me that other people don't. The guy isn't especially observant, but he eventually learned how to read when I'm bluffing my confidence.

It doesn't happen that often and shouldn't be happening now. I've put in the work, and I will soon have a degree to prove it, but if I breathe a word to Felix about my business chops, he'll find a way to sabotage me.

"Your parents are looking out for you. Making sure you have someone with your best interests at heart—and theirs—to help you manage all of this." He spreads his arms wide, and I vow to do whatever it takes to make sure he doesn't manage a postage stamp-size piece of dirt.

"If they told you that, you should assume questionable mental health. Nothing would be binding."

"I have it in writing. And they're fine. I should know. I spend enough time with them." He says that last part with an eye roll, and it hits me for the first time that this has been his plan all along—or at least since the divorce—to sweet-talk my parents into keeping him around.

"This isn't happening. I'll talk them out of it. You can forget about whatever little megalomaniacal plan you've concocted. The day we got divorced was the day you lost any claim on this land."

He tries again to comb his fingers through his hair. Again, they get stuck, and now his hair stands up like a cock's comb. Appropriate.

"I'm playing nice for now and offering to include you, but I don't have to be a good guy."

"You couldn't possibly be one, so we're on the same page there."

He licks his lips again, and I wonder why he's salivating over an opportunity he'll never get. If he fooled my parents with his cocky smile, I'll talk them right out of it. I'm their only child. They'll side with me.

Right?

Turning for the house, I leave Felix standing on the driveway without indulging this conversation further.

Grabbing my phone, I tap the app for our garden sprinklers, which I should have gotten fixed a while ago. They have a habit of spraying the driveway instead of hitting the flowers.

A second later, I hear an aggravated shout when they douse Felix's shirt and stupid hair.

A few seconds after that, I hear a car tearing away from the property. Good. Only place for a bad penny like him is under the heel of my designer stiletto shoe.

CHAPTER 3

 ash

I'M in a hurry because I'm late. Shocker.

Being late is how I roll because I get distracted by things that interest me, and it leads to all kinds of trouble.

Case in point, a food photo popped up on my social media last night, which led me to three different grocery stores before I found one that sold frozen yuca that I needed to make a jerk chicken potpie.

It didn't bother me at all that I needed to roll out my own pie crust and bake it for an hour. It was delicious when I scarfed down a slice at one in the morning before reading a quarter of a crime novel and remembering to water my indoor plants before crashing for six hours.

But now I've been running late all day. Skipped breakfast. Got to my office with my hair still wet. Caught hell from my overly punctual siblings because they had to wait for me to hear about who I've interviewed for new positions. We need to be the best, so it means we need to hire the best. Unfortunately, my short list was a bit too short for their liking.

It's been a struggle to find the sommeliers, viticulturists, and cellar masters we desperately need. The town is growing and competition is fierce. I'm a people person, and I've never had trouble attracting the best talent for our family business, but times are changing.

All at a time when Buttercup Hill has been losing key employees to competitors with big open checkbooks.

One last meeting of the day before I can blow off steam with my buddies at our weekly meetup at a bar in Calistoga. I need it tonight more than ever.

Archer sounded annoyed when I texted him after the family meeting, asking if he and I could meet separately. If anyone can convey annoyance via text, it's my older brother.

Me: Can we meet?

Archer: We just met an hour ago

Me: I know

I see bouncing dots on my phone. Then they stop. I wonder if Archer is going to respond at all. Maybe his non-answer is his answer. Then the dots return.

Archer: Fine. My office, 6

Me: 6 in the eve?

Archer: Ha. Yeah. Surprised you know there's another 6 in the day

At least he knows me.

The guy gets up at the crack of dawn and pounds out six miles before the bluebirds are awake. It's just the way he's wired. We couldn't be less alike in that way, but in other ways, I feel a kinship. We're both misunderstood. As much as people see me as the dopey golden retriever heartbreaker, people see him as irritable and cold.

Mostly, I think Arch is just unhappy. Getting laid would be a step in the right direction, but he'd have to be a little less growly in order to make that happen. He's tightly wound by nature, but he's been much worse since the entire brunt of being a winemaker fell on his shoulders with our dad's advancing Alzheimer's disease. On top of that, Buttercup Hill, our family's winery, is operating in crisis mode.

Part of it has nothing to do with me, and part of it…well…let's just say I could have made better choices.

On the financial side, we're in dire financial straits. Again.

Our father, who grew Buttercup Hill into the behemoth it is, took half a billion from company funds and gave it to Graham Garcia, a half brother we never knew about until about a month ago. He runs Duck Feather Vineyards, right next door to our property, and seems hell-bent on competing with us. As it is, he's hired away several of our key viticulturists right when we need to figure out how to increase sales. That means my ass was already feeling very toasty against a fire that keeps getting bigger.

Then, a few days ago, I ran into a local grower, Julia Soltero, at my favorite dive bar, and we got into a long conversation about the pinot noir grapes they might be willing to sell to the right buyer. *Us! Buttercup Hill! We're the right buyer.*

I saw an opportunity. I'm a people person, or at least that's what I've been told my entire life, so I bought Julia another round of drinks. We talked pinot grapes and professional soccer and whatever the hell else she felt like discussing. I wanted to bring in a win.

Problem is that Julia is married to Martin Soltero, and he's the jealous type. When word got back about us "huddled in a corner of the bar," he flew into a rage, accused me of trying to put the moves on his wife, and any chance we had of buying pinot grapes flew out the window like a trapped sparrow sensing daylight.

So now I have two problems. We still need more fruit if we're going to meet our growth targets and keep investors happy, and apparently, I've personally scared off any vineyard owner with a wife, girlfriend, or even a wandering eye. Saying my siblings are angry with me is an understatement.

Standing outside Archer's office, I try to gauge his irritability by looking at him. He has a baseball cap on backward and his shoulders are riding up near his ears. Not a good sign. He stands over his desk, staring at the schematics of our property.

"Hey, man. You good?"

As usual, he doesn't look up when I enter his office. He speaks more to the paper on the desk than to me, fanning his hands over it.

"Yeah. Even if the weather is perfect and we pick every damn grape, we still can't make the numbers we need."

"What if we do a special edition blend?"

He tilts his head. "That's an idea. Won't get us all the way, but it's a thought."

Archer holds up the page for me to see it, even though I know how the property is laid out and where every plot of grapevines grows. That's the problem. There aren't enough grapes. And without grapes, we can't meet our growth numbers. Archer could look at that damned map upside down and sideways, and nothing's going to change there.

"What's up?" he asks.

"Jose just gave his notice."

"Shit."

"Yeah. That's three in two weeks."

"He didn't tell me." He sounds almost monotone, but I know he's just covering. "He say where he's going?"

Archer picks up a metal tumbler from his desk and drinks water from a straw. I'm glad he downs so much water because sometimes the only reason he leaves his desk in a day is to use the bathroom.

"No. I pressed him, and he got a little uncomfortable, gave me some bullshit about spending more time with his kids."

"You thinking Graham?" Archer points over his shoulder in the direction of Duck Feather.

I shrug. "I don't know what he's offering them, but it must be pretty good. I dangled a raise in front of Jose, and he didn't even blink."

"We've got to get a grip on this shit show. Maybe we lock in current employees with year long contracts? We can't lose any more."

"I know."

"Okay, well, thanks for telling me."

I nod. "I'm scouring all of California for good people. We'll be okay. It's not the first time we've had turnover."

"I like your optimism."

Archer walks me out and raises an eyebrow when he sees my truck, a pickup that I've lovingly restored from its former junk-yard state. Painted a deep, shiny blue, it's a source of pride when I drive it through town, even if it still has a rattle deep in its bones.

"Where are you headed? There's still time in the workday."

"Grocery shopping. Then I'm meeting Lucas and the guys at the Dark Horse. Hoping to do some networking with the Calistoga growers." Maybe Calistoga was far enough away that I could find some fresh faces to replace the employees we've lost. Archer's eyes narrow, and he frowns at me. "The kind of networking you did with Julia Soltero?"

I shrug because there's no sense in trying to dissuade my siblings from thinking what they want about me. I suppose I come by my reputation somewhat honestly because I broke plenty of hearts during high school and college, and I certainly know how to have a good time. Or at least, I used to.

Old perceptions die hard. Hence my problem with Mr. Soltero.

And half his friends.

I need to do better, or at least convince my family I'm capable of it.

allory

My Jeep idles in front of my house, warming up before I take her on the open road. It's the only thing that will give me some clarity. That and yelling at my parents.

The first thing I do is calculate the time in Europe. Three in the morning.

The next thing I do is call my parents anyway. At least in the middle of the night, I know where they are.

"Mallory! We're just getting up to cook breakfast before we milk the cows." How my mother sounds this delighted when she should be fast asleep is beyond me. We seriously have nothing in common.

"It's three in the morning."

"Yes, I'm letting your father sleep for another hour. I think he was up late reading."

We make small talk for another minute before I can't stand it anymore and ask her what in the hell she and my dad were thinking.

"He has good business sense, and he's always looked out for you. I think he's still in love." She says the last part quietly, like she's divulging a secret.

"I highly doubt that. And I can't stand him, so there's that." I wish my mother didn't bring out the sassy teenager in me. It won't help convince her I can rationally manage a business.

"Oh, he's harmless," she says, which only proves how little she knows him.

"He's horrible, and he'll micromanage me, and he's not even that smart." As I'm saying the words, my mom hums back at me as though she agrees with my account. "On top of that, we're not married anymore!"

"Well, I know that."

A flickering sound on the other end of the line could be knitting needles or a piece of taffy. I try not to let it distract me.

"Great. So since we're no longer married, you can assume I don't want him to have anything to do with my life. Or our family business."

More humming. I assume she agrees.

"You see, I disagree. I think you can be helped by the support of a partner. A *husband*. The way your dad and I have each other. It would be different if you were married to someone else, but Mallory, you're all alone. That's why we made the deal with Felix. Like I said, if you were married, you wouldn't need Felix—"

"I don't need him now," I interrupt.

I hate the way she talks about my lack of husband like it means I'm sad and lonely. I'm not. I have a busy social life that includes lots of time spent wining and dining fancy winery owners who might make good business contacts. I spend so much time getting dressed up for industry meet-and-greets and galas that I wouldn't mind a little sad and lonely time. No reason to get married again. Ever.

"I know what I'm doing, Mom. I don't need a husband or a partner."

"Agree to disagree. Isn't that what people say?"

"Yes, but I don't agree. I really wish you'd see me as capable without having a ring on my finger."

"It's not about a ring. It's about the support a real partner can give you. A husband. I want that for my daughter. Is that so bad?"

"Yes. When you make a deal with my ex that keeps him in my business, it's bad. It's really, really bad."

I hear grumbling, which means my mom is now summarizing the past five minutes of our conversation for my dad so he can catch up. If he's awake, I know they'll be off to sheer a sheep in a matter of moments, so I need to say my goodbyes.

"When are you coming back? Can we sit down and talk about this when you're home?"

More mumbling, and then my dad picks up the phone. His voice is raspy and deep, and I'm not sure he's fully awake. "Do me a favor and check the mail, will you? It should be right in front of the house inside the—"

"Mailbox?" I interrupt because we've had this conversation before also. My dad is always afraid the mail carrier is holding out on him, not delivering valuable postal gems and keeping them for his own or something. "I'll check, dad."

My mom grabs the phone back. "Gotta run, sweetie. Sixteen cows need our help emptying their udders." Damn, she's cheerful as she smothers my dreams in Felix's smarmy brand of ketchup.

* * *

I GUN the engine of my Jeep, which seems to want an up close and personal relationship with every bump in the road. I love it anyway. When it's warm and I can put the top down, nothing makes me feel more free of worry than driving along the

Silverado Trail with the mountains fanning out on one side and miles of vineyards on the other.

Some of the mountains still bear the scars of a huge fire a couple of years back. It will take a while for the larger trees to repopulate the hillsides. I notice some new rows of grapevines crawling up a hill and wonder how long that new winemaker will persist before realizing the sloping terrain isn't right for growing grapes.

Often, it's wealthy newcomers who buy a piece of land with designs on being winemakers. They don't understand much about the business, only that having a vineyard in Napa is some sort of prize like owning a jet or a share of a pro sports team. It's easy enough to find people who will convince them they can grow grapes anywhere.

They mount fancy signs at the highway entrance to their property and take selfies in front of them for their social media. I swear, half of these people just want to own a sign with the word 'vineyard' on it.

The old-school winemakers know better. They've been here for generations in many cases, and they take pride in the terroir of their fruit. That basically means they spend a lot of time playing with dirt. It's the soil on the valley floor that gives the best grapes their ability to grow without a lot of intervention, and that allows them to make the best wine.

It's the minerals and stones left over from more than a million years of volcanic activity. Not something that can be reproduced with a machine.

Our property has only a small winery on acres and acres of land. We're pretty much the opposite of most vineyards around here, where there's always a scramble for more places to grow grapes. Winemakers are always jockeying to find a few more parcels of land so they can expand their businesses.

Land like ours.

But the system my parents have used all these years is barely keeping this place afloat. Our family business has generated losses for the past few years because the money we spend to keep up the land isn't covered by what we sell in wine. Nowhere close.

There are ways to change that. My business school education has helped me put muscle behind some of my ideas. I either need to sell some land, which I see as a last resort, or start growing a lot of grapes. We have one of the most sought-after appellations in the region, so we can sell grapes at top prices.

It will take some time to get vines grafted and producing fruit, and in the meantime, I need to curry favor with a lot of people around town and make deals that keep us afloat. I've been dancing that jig in my sleep for so long that I'm just about out of energy.

I shake my head, again thinking about Felix and his nerve.

As I pull back into the driveway of Autumn Lake, I let out a long exhale. Even though the place causes me stress, I'm still at peace when I arrive here. It's home.

Rufus comes bounding over and puts his paws on the window ledge. "Down, buddy. I need to open the door." It's a ritual between me and my giant newfoundland who still acts like a puppy at age two—he greets my car before loping away and circling the Jeep.

"Hey, was it a madhouse out there?" My friend Mary walks over with her arms crossed. It's then that I notice her red pickup truck parked around the side of my house.

She calls it Cherry and sometimes affixes a bow to the grill. Currently, the bow sits on the dashboard. The truck clicks and whirs as it cools down, so I know she hasn't been here long.

"It's a party," I say as Rufus trots over and licks Mary's hand. "Usual afternoon traffic on the highway, but I was just looking to drive. Wasn't going anywhere specific."

Swinging the Jeep door open with my foot, I grab my purse from the passenger seat. Before I have one foot on the ground, Mary starts giving me jazz hands. "It's pub night."

I blink at her and force a smile. "Right. Yay."

"You forgot."

"Because you switched days on me." Normally, we go out on Monday nights because most places are empty.

Her shoulders slump, and she tries to pout, but she's too excited to pull it off. "No matter. We're still going."

I nod. No point in trying to dissuade her, even though going out is the last thing I feel like doing. I just want to slink upstairs and spend an hour soaking in my tub. Maybe that'll get the Felix smell off me.

I look down at my wide-legged jeans and oversized, pale yellow tee. They're fine for the pub. I spend most of my time dressed to the nines because I'm trying to develop relationships with anyone and everyone who could be a potential business contact. People—yes, by people I mean men—seem to like it when I show up looking like a hot date. I used to hate using my looks to get what I want, but after enough years of being judged for them, I leaned in. The same way some men use their bank account and their swagger.

Once I turn Autumn Lake into a thriving business, I plan to give twenty percent of our profits back to the community of workers who can't afford to live in the area. They're the reason our town is thriving, so they deserve it. If I can accomplish that more efficiently by wearing makeup and flirting a little bit, so be it. No one needs to know who I am underneath the facade.

The only person I've let in a tiny bit is Mary, and that's only because she's a newcomer in town who doesn't judge. The gossip mill gave her an earful about me, informing her I'm desperate for a husband and willing to offer false promises about selling family-owned land as a way to seduce the men around here. To her credit, she decided to get to know me before believing everything she heard.

Mary arrived a year ago from England, where she spent her entire life in one small town. Her brother plays soccer for the San

Francisco Strikers and lured her across the pond after their dad passed away. He expected her to live near him in the city, but she decided she liked small-town life better.

She found an au pair job with a family that lives next door to our property. Her hours vary, so she spends a lot of her free time at Autumn Lake, helping me with the food garden I'm trying to establish. It's off the back of my house, which separates it from the rest of the land my parents basically ignore when they're not chasing a sheep through a meadow.

Mary has proven to be a far better gardener than me, and I've learned a lot from her instinctive sense of plants and what they 'want.' If I'm going to grow grapes, I need to understand their needs and desires, according to Mary. For some reason, coming from her, it sounds less loony than when my parents wax poetic about some bean they harvested in England.

For years, Mary worked in a pub and did a lot of their cooking. She claims she misses it and pops over here regularly to cook meals for our small team of workers. And she refuses to let me pay her.

That makes her the best of all worlds—labor I can afford and a friend I never knew I needed.

She checks the back of the Jeep and sees a giant bag of dog food I've been avoiding lifting for days. She's half a foot shorter than me, but she hefts the bag like it's full of cotton, and I wipe the sheen of sweat from my forehead. "Long day?"

"Nothing I can't handle." I fake a smile and twirl a lock of my hair. I'm so accustomed to these habits that they come without effort.

Mary crosses her arms again and nails me with a stare, shaking her head. "That's a bloody lie if I've ever heard one. You can tell me all about it at the pub. First pint—or four—is on me."

There's no use trying to fool her. She'll see right through me if I try to pretend I'm not frazzled. It's the beauty and the curse of Mary Cheltenham. I can't lie to her.

"Felix stopped by again…" I say.

Mary's face twists into a scowl. "That bloody cocksucker?" Her accent makes even those words sound charming. Mary detests Felix almost as much as I do. "Man responsible for you losing faith in love, bloke has no business stopping by," she mutters.

She's exaggerating.

Felix is the reason I'll never trust my heart to make decisions for me again, but I haven't lost faith in love. Not entirely. Just mostly.

Casting a look across the vast field of untended farmland that abuts the main house on our property, I see a flat expanse of dirt and wild greenery. At moments like these, I imagine what that farmland could be someday—acres of vineyards growing cabernet grapes and more acres of sauvignon blanc, all under the Autumn Lake Winery label. I envision a sea of staked vines growing in neat rows, the soil beneath them ruddy and dry.

"Fine. I'm not going to get any more work done at this hour anyway." I haul a case of canned dog food out of the back of the Jeep, and Mary follows me, chattering all the while.

"Great. Can we go to that cowboy bar? I really liked it the last time we went…"

It's a good choice, I decide. Understated, definitely not trendy. It's the last place in town I'll run into my ex.

CHAPTER 5

Mallory

A HALF HOUR LATER, we're in a back booth at the Dark Horse, which Mary says reminds her of home. "I used to cook meat pies in a kitchen half that size," she says, pointing at the kitchen, which she insisted on seeing the first time we came here.

"Like, meat in a pie? Or is it really something else like sweetbreads?" I can't help wincing at the memory of my first awkward bite of that particular dish on a trip to England.

She laughs. "I take it you were one of those tourists who thought sweetbreads were a dessert, then?"

"Honest mistake. I was just a kid when we took a family trip to London, and my parents didn't know any better, so they couldn't warn me."

She nods. "Meat pies are how they sound. Meat in a pastry dough." She inhales a deep breath and closes her eyes. When she opens them, she scans the bar menu hopefully.

"You won't find those here, I'm afraid. It's pizza and wings. Basic bar food."

"I'll make do with some chips." She shoves the menu across the table to me, but I slip it between the salt and pepper shakers and a bottle of ketchup on our dark wood table.

Taking a wary glance behind me, I survey the crowd. So far, so good. No sign of anyone I know, which is what I expected when we chose this place. The crowd is small. A few people play pool at the one table in back, and three guys sit at the bar watching a baseball game on the big screen TV. The easy beat of old-school rock plays in the background, and a steady hum of voices makes the place feel packed yet anonymous.

"You want a dark beer or a lager?" Mary asks, signaling to the bartender with a raised finger.

"Dark."

Mary holds up a second finger. It didn't take her long to get in tight with the owners of this pub and everyone who works here. If I didn't know better, I'd say she's angling to supplement her au pair salary with a few shifts at the bar, but she denies that she's being anything other than friendly.

Unlike most of the bars around town, where visitors sample glasses of local wines and angle to spot celebrities, this place is homey and rustic. Some might even call it shabby.

I'm happy to sit with my back to the door and tune out everything but Mary.

A few of the other tables are occupied by couples or groups, and I notice no one is lined up to play darts. "One game," I tell Mary, pushing my chair back.

"Hell yeah." She trails behind me and swipes our two pints of beer from the server. She hands me mine and keeps moving to the chalkboard, where she writes our initials.

"There's no point in keeping score. You're a ringer." Last time we played, she got six bullseyes and eventually conceded to playing with her left hand. Even then, she beat me.

"My town didn't have much to do," she explains, plucking the darts from where they stick out at awkward angles and holding them with the little blue flags facing my hand. "Here. You go first."

I back into position behind the painted line on the scratched wood floor and focus on the board. Raising the dart in front of my eyes, I move my hand back and forth a few times, lining up my aim. Then I throw the dart and watch it sail straight into the pie shape above the six.

Mary marks my score on the chalkboard and I throw the next dart. Closer to the center, but not great. Mary marks an eight. The rest of my darts hit various places on the board. It's a respectable first round for someone whose opponent didn't grow up in a pub.

Backing away, I get ready for the drubbing that will occur in a matter of seconds.

Mary takes a swig of her beer. Then another. "Helps my focus," she explains. She spends far less time than I did surveying the board before throwing her first dart. It hits the largest ring outside the bullseye.

"Bollocks."

"Are you kidding me? That's great."

"Not great, but I'm just getting warmed up." She squares her shoulders and takes aim again, squinting at the board. The dart flies straight and hits just to the right of the center. "There we go. Getting closer."

I mark her score, which is already so much better than mine. If I don't hit some big numbers or if Mary doesn't cramp up in the next couple of minutes, this game is going to be over before it starts.

Mary looks at the floor, then stares at the target with such focus I'm surprised it doesn't burst into flames. She takes another sip with her left hand and proceeds to hit the bullseye before she even swallows. "What are we playing to?" Her smile returns.

I'm going to get my ass handed to me in this game, but I'd rather be here than almost any place else.

"Does it matter?" I sound grumpy, but really, this is the happiest I've been all day. Here, in this grubby bar, I don't have to be Mallory Rutherford, super social party girl who's always looking for a new man. I don't have to prance around in fancy shoes with red soles and taunt the vineyard owners all over town with the idea that I might have land to sell in order to stay relevant in this small community.

I can just be myself, a shy girl who gets excited about darts and would rather drink beer than wine sometimes. This place is my own little haven.

Or at least it was.

The door swings open.

"Speak of the devil."

My heart sinks because there's only one devil, and I've already dealt with him once today. I don't want to speak of him or think about him. I especially don't want to see him.

I feel his breath against the back of my neck before he says a word. It's like a Saharan wind slapping my skin, and I bristle at his presence.

"Mal." The way he says my name feels more like a command than a greeting. His voice lacks any warmth, and for the millionth time, I ask myself how I ever fell for him in the first place.

I debate just not turning around. I could pretend I didn't hear him and continue throwing darts at the board. Or I could turn and throw darts at him. My fingers twitch at the idea of that.

"Babe…" My shoulders rise at the term of endearment.

Slowly, I turn around. "'Babe?' Really?"

He smiles. Hair slicked back, perfect teeth, a smile that looks like a puma who wants a meal. Felix shrugs and tilts his head to the side, fixing his dark eyes on me. They used to seem soulful.

Now I know the man has no soul. He just wants what he wants, and in my case, he wants our family's land.

"You are still a babe," he says. "But if you want, I'll call you something else."

"You don't seem to understand, Felix. I don't want you to call me at all."

Now his smile bends into the smirk of the devil that fits his face so much better. "You keep saying that..."

"Because I mean it. What did you do, follow me here?"

Felix fondles his chin in a way I found sexy for a brief insane moment, and when his eyes finish their sweep around the interior of the bar, they land on me. He tilts his head and furrows his brow. Doesn't make him any less of a stalker.

"Maybe."

I feel my blood pressure rise at the idea that he did, in fact, follow me. "Do I need to take out a restraining order, Felix?"

He holds up his hands and takes one step back, but the smirk on his face makes it clear he thinks this is all a joke.

Mary, who's been watching our exchange, takes a couple of steps closer. She stands in front of Felix with one arm crossed over the other, a handful of darts in her extended hand. "We're in the middle of a game, if you don't mind. You should sod off."

Felix laughs. "I don't mind. Finish your game. I can wait." Signaling at the bar, he mimes the size of a rocks glass. Ordering his usual bourbon, I assume.

"Restraining order sounds like a decent idea," I tell Felix, grabbing one of the darts from Mary's still-outstretched hand. I hold it in throwing position, and if he doesn't move, it's going to hit him squarely in the chest. He wisely sidesteps and lets me take aim at the board.

The dart flies wild and barely makes it onto the board at all, scoring me a measly two points. Damn him. Not only is he ruining my anonymous night out, he's ruining my darts game.

"Do you mind?" I take the remaining darts from Mary, and she goes to the chalkboard.

Felix looks from me to the dartboard and takes another step back. Crossing his arms, he smirks as though he's getting ready for an epic fail. Even when we were together, he loved it when I fell short of any objective. Brownies overbaked? He smoothed the hair off my forehead and told me it was okay that I wasn't a chef. Plants underwatered? He gave me a condescending smile and said he hoped I'd do better at keeping our future children alive.

Secretly—or not so secretly—he seemed to enjoy my little failings. They provided proof that I needed him more than I actually did.

I hone my focus. Hell, if I'm going to lose with him watching. I line up my next dart and let it fly.

It hits the bull's-eye like it has a homing device stored in its little feathers. The success of the first bull's-eye fuels three more, and now my score on the chalkboard rivals Mary's. Okay, not exactly because she's trounced me in the past four rounds, but if she throws blindfolded, I have a fighting chance now.

I turn back to Felix with a plastered-on smile. "Nice seeing you, but I'm going to enjoy the rest of my evening with my friend."

Mary gives him a little wave. "Bye, Felicia," she says in her clipped accent. But Felix doesn't take the hint.

In fact, he steps closer. I feel the rush of air when the door to the place opens and closes again, but I don't look away from Felix.

"Just when we were getting along so well, you have to go and be rude."

"I'm not being rude. I'm asking you to leave me alone."

He takes another step closer crowding me. His finger reaches out and he boops me on the nose. It's a too-familiar gesture, but Felix takes liberties, inserts himself into situations by referencing some tiny past interaction like it was an intimate moment.

"Sorry, babe. Not until we talk."

Shuddering at the sound of the word 'babe,' I exhale a long breath and close my eyes. As I count backward from five, I calculate the odds that Felix will be gone when I open them. Pretty close to zero, and I'm good at math.

"She told you to go. I'd listen if I were you." The voice is deep, gruff, threatening.

When my eyes open, I'm surprised to see Dash Corbett nearly burning a hole through Felix's face with his fiery glare.

Oh god.

As if the day weren't going horribly enough, I'm pummeled with another level of humiliation, one I've successfully blocked for the past two weeks.

After our run-in at the grocery store a month ago, something kept nagging at me. Something about the gentlemanly grace of a guy who kept me from plummeting to certain injury in a sea of pickle juice, mixed with something so hot that my skin still reacts from the mere memory.

I couldn't explain it at the time and I still can't. I've known the Corbett family most of my life and I even dated the middle brother, Jax, briefly a few years ago. Or more like I hooked up with him. *Potato, potah-to.*

No doubt, the Corbett siblings have the impression of me as a snooty, man-crazy socialite. In fact, I acted haughty and gossipy when I ran into PJ with a billionaire in a movie theater a month back because I'd gotten a bad grade in one of my accounting classes, and it was easier to hide behind a mask than let my disappointment show.

It's how I roll. Feelings are mine and only mine. Perceptions offer a safe hiding place for things I don't want people to know.

But after my collision with Dash, thoughts of him disrupted my days. Two weeks later, I couldn't make them stop. So after losing one too many dart games one night and consuming one too many black and tans, I sent him a text.

And asked him out.

Then, crickets.

Yup, he ignored the text. Didn't merely turn me down. He didn't respond at all. And now here he is in all his glare-y splendor, facing off against my ex for some reason. It doesn't excuse his failure to reply to a text in a timely manner. Ignoring me is just plain rude.

I wish I didn't notice the way a lock of his dark hair falls over his forehead like he just finished shoving his hands in it and a stray piece fell loose. His pale blue eyes are arresting this close up, begging me to stare, but I force my gaze downward, snagging on the rough stubble that makes him look like he just rolled out of bed after having sex for forty-eight hours straight.

For a moment, my mind wanders to what that would be like. Then I shake myself out of the trance I've somehow fallen under and remind myself that asking him on a date was purely a business move, which is irrelevant now anyway.

If he simply forgot to reply, I'm guessing he remembers now. He offers me that lady-killer smile of his, only I'm not falling for it. Well, I'm trying not to, but it's difficult.

It's even harder when he turns and fixes an icy stare squarely on Felix. My insides twist and heat at how much I like it.

His glare emphasizes the tiny crinkles around his eyes, which narrow in a way that should not be this sexy. His chest, muscular under a worn tee, heaves with anger similar to what I feel. And his scowl makes his boyish face look so much more serious. Menacing. Hot.

For a second, I imagine him hovering over my body after stripping off every last stitch of clothing. I picture the same intense expression on his face as he contemplates all the ways he can pleasure me, leaving me aching…

Jesus. What?

I shake myself out of the momentary reverie and refocus. Clearly, the ire I feel toward Felix has affected my sanity.

Glancing back at Dash, I see him looking at my ex like he's the pond scum he is. I appreciate it, though it surprises me because Mary is the only other person I've ever seen with the same look of disgust when she beholds Felix's annoying face. And she's used to kicking drunk guys out of pubs.

I wonder if Dash knows Felix well. He must, based on the distaste he seems to have for him. I mentally add that fact to the tally of things he and I have in common. So far, the total is one, but it's one more than we had a month earlier in the grocery store.

"She asked you to leave her alone." Dash's voice is deeper than I remember it sounding just hours earlier. There's a growl that makes him sound dangerous. Also so incredibly sexy.

Stop it.

Now is not the time for me to be thinking of Dash as anything other than a temporary saving grace who allows me to take a couple steps away from Felix. The area around me feels cooler now, and I inhale a gulp of air.

Felix turns to stand toe-to-toe with Dash, and I notice for the first time how small Felix looks. Unimposing.

Or maybe it's Dash who looks especially tall and built like a lumberjack.

"Not your business, fella," Felix says.

"I'll decide that for myself."

"I'm not joking. This is between me and a friend."

Felix attempts to return Dash's angry stare with the same ferocity, but it's a waste of effort. He looks outmatched, even as a server shows up by his side and hands him a small tumbler of bourbon. Felix takes the drink but ignores her.

"It's polite to say thank you," I can't help saying.

"Jesus, are you serious?" He makes an exaggerated turning gesture toward the server, a diminutive blonde with black eyeliner who looks like she could kick Felix's ass with a hand tied behind her back. She also doesn't care enough about him to bother.

"You wanna pay now or open a tab?"

With a grimace, Felix shoves a hand into his pocket and retrieves his wallet. Without looking, he yanks out a twenty and shoves it at her. "Thank. You," he breathes in her face. Then he downs half his drink in one pull. It feels like dramatics—tough cowboy trying to scare off the local boy with his drinking ability. Dumb move when the local boy owns a winery.

"You should go. Respect her wishes," Dash says, positioning himself between Felix and me.

"Who even are you? And why do you care so much?"

I appreciate him going to bat for me, which drives home the idea that some part of me was right when I asked him on a date. Looking back, I should have worded my request differently. I should have asked for a meeting. As a fellow vineyard owner, he'd have been more likely to say yes.

Instead, a new idea starts bouncing around in my brain. It's a crazy idea, but I've tried normal. Crazy is all that's left.

So I look at Felix dead in the eyes and grab Dash's hand.

"He's my fiancé."

ash

IT'S a good thing I'm so engrossed by the weird showdown with the douchebag in front of me that I haven't ordered a drink.

Because if I had one in my hand and had taken a sip, I'd have spewed it all over the bar at the word *fiancé*.

It's also good that the one who uttered the word is Mallory Rutherford, a woman who's grown more intriguing to me over the past month, starting with a full cart of drinks and dog food and an out-of-the-blue text asking me out. Sort of. I believe the exact wording of the text was, "It's Mallory Rutherford. Are you free to meet for dinner?" I wasn't sure if she wanted a date or a business meeting.

And now this dude who's puffing his chest out like a territorial rooster.

Or at least he was.

The word fiancé has shut him up and turned his swagger into

a series of stammered syllables. He finally decides to slug down the rest of his drink in response.

"Really." Sarcasm drips from his tongue like maple syrup drowning a pancake in its god-awful sweetness. "You expect me to buy that? I saw you two hours ago, and you didn't mention it."

It shouldn't make my pulse tick up a notch when he refers to seeing her earlier. I shouldn't feel possessive enough to run my hand up her back. She stiffens at first, but when she relents, I run my fingers through her hair and feel her shiver beneath my hand.

"Yes. It's been a whirlwind. I've been...*distracted.*" Mallory's eyes heat and linger on me. It leaves no question about exactly how I've been distracting her, and it makes my dick twitch in my pants at the things I could do to distract her for real.

This is a woman I spent the better part of my teen years fantasizing about, after all. Now, up close and personal, she's every bit as fierce and lovely as I imagined.

And also possibly delusional.

"Bullshit," he says, finally, his shocked expression morphing into a fake smile.

"Hey." Instinct takes over and I get in the guy's face. I don't like how he's talking to Mallory, even if I'm still doing a double take after her pronouncement that we're...engaged? "Watch your language."

The guy casts me an annoyed glance and returns his glare to Mallory. "I'd have heard about it if you had a boyfriend."

"Really? Do you have little minions reporting back on everything I do? Because that borders on creepy stalking."

I could insert myself more into the middle of this, but something tells me I'll learn more and get farther if I observe. Mallory grits her teeth and balls her fists at her sides, but she seems like she can hold her own. For now.

"Face it, Mal. I'm not the outsider I was when we met. I know a lot of people in this town. People who are very aware of our *history.*" He looks at me when he says it, maybe hoping for a reaction. I give him nothing.

Mallory shrugs.

"People talk is all I'm saying, and no one's said anything about you and a new boyfriend, let alone a fiancé."

"Maybe because they have better things to do than blab about me to my ex-husband."

Instead of a snappy retort, the reference to him as an *ex* seems to shut him up. He clears his throat and looks around the room as though something or someone will give him an excuse to linger.

And now I have my explanation for why he feels like he has any right to talk to her the way he is—not that it excuses his rudeness.

The pieces click into place, and I realize why I'm the sudden object of Mallory's affection. This is a revenge play, plain and simple. Or at least a fuck-you sendoff. Well, I can get on board with some good, clean *sayonara* fun.

"If you don't mind, I'd like to enjoy my time with my *fiancé*," Mallory says, emphasizing the word. "Gosh, I'm still getting used to calling you that, but I do love it." She locks eyes with me, and there's a pleading in them and also an intensity that mesmerizes me. For a second, I allow myself to believe it has nothing to do with her ex.

Her look makes me sweat with discomfort and charges my veins with a fire I've never experienced.

"Better get used to fiancée, because soon I'll be calling you *my wife.*" Nothing wrong with adding a little fuel to this blaze she's started.

I watch her ex swallow down his irritation. It seems to stick in his throat, and he coughs and turns away.

Hearing myself say the word *wife* should send a petrified chill down my spine, but, shockingly, it doesn't. I even like it a little bit, which I attribute to how much I already hate her ex, if surface impressions are any measure.

Mallory's eyes widen, but she quickly schools her expression, and the broad, fake smile returns to her face. I wonder how her ex doesn't recognize it when he's obviously spent a lot more time with her than I have, but some guys just aren't that observant. He seems ruffled by her whole act.

I wrap my palm around her waist, enjoying the feel of her warm skin where her yellow shirt rides up an inch. I rub my thumb over the bare skin and feel her shudder under my touch. Her body melts just a little bit into my hand, and I pull her closer.

Meeting Mallory's eyes, which seem to blaze with desire, I hope mine convey the exact same thing—game on.

If she's going to drag me into whatever charade this is in front of her ex, I am one hundred percent in, but I'm going to give just as good as I get.

"I-I guess that will take some getting used to as well." She recovers enough of her composure to nail me with her full smile —plush, ruby lips, straight white teeth—and I nearly lose my mind.

I lean in close, making sure my breath feathers across her neck as I speak in a low, growling tone her ex can hear. "You won't just get used to it; you'll love it. I'm sure of that."

As long as we're both putting on a show, I might as well swing for the fences. I give this guy another five minutes of discomfort in the situation before he bugs out of here. Fine by me.

My friends wait at a table across the room, where a cold beer gathers condensation in front of my empty chair. They'll love this story, especially from the guy voted least likely to get married— ever.

I haven't given much thought to marriage. I'm the youngest of three guys in the family, and so far, only one is engaged. There's an order to things, or so I always assumed, and with Archer still holding the mantle of oldest single guy in the family, I figure I have plenty of time before I need to settle down.

Besides, this little stage play is simply that. As soon as her ex blows out of here, we can go back to what we were—not friends. Not a couple. Barely acquaintances, even if bonded by a pickle mishap and an unreturned text. And now this. Not sure what that makes us, but I'm open to ideas.

Yet hearing Mallory refer to me as *her* anything, let alone her fiancé, has unleashed a sudden urge to throw her onto one of the wooden game tables in the pub and tear her clothes off. Slowly. Luxuriously…

"Sure, yeah. Okay, well I still need to hash things out with you. Time's a-ticking and we're in this together…" her ex says, jutting his chin out but taking one step backward.

"Send it in an email. I'll look at it when I'm at work." One warm hand wraps around the back of my neck, and she drags a finger from the other hand down my chest. "Right now, I want to play. Okay, honey?"

I feel my cock twitch in my pants, which surprises me because I know this is an act. She could barely stand the sight of me a month ago in the grocery store, and the only thing different now is her ex in the room.

But my body responds to her touch nonetheless. It's purely physical—I have no illusions about that. But in another minute of letting this little fantasy play out, everyone within ten yards of me will know I'm not acting by the wood in my pants.

"I'm all yours." I am nothing if not a good sport, so I carry the ball all the way over the goal line. Pulling Mallory's body firmly against my hip, I caress the side of her face with my hand. She watches me with a slight look of fear, more because she doesn't know what I'm planning to do than because she isn't willing to go along for the ride.

The corner of my mouth lifts, my partial smile reassuring her we're in this together. She nods ever so slightly and lifts her chin.

I don't have to glance to the side to see her ex's eyes glued to us. Even if it pains him, he can't look away from the car wreck that is his lost relationship with this woman.

I feel bad for him there. I may not know Mallory well, but this guy was outclassed when he had her.

Then I go in for the kill, showing him that he should seriously regret whatever he did to screw up the relationship because I know without asking that he was the one who screwed it up.

Dragging a finger down Mallory's cheek, I stare into her eyes like a soldier coming back from a year at war. I let the sounds in the room fall away and listen for her breath, which comes a little faster as I touch her skin. Pre-performance nerves, I'm guessing.

Her eyes stay locked on mine, focused. We have a job to do. Even if her heart is beating like a snare drum under the pale skin of her throat, she's here for the show. I won't disappoint. "Been waiting all day to see you." I make sure my voice has plenty of growl, enough to make sure her ex knows she drives me wild.

"Aw, I missed you too," she coos, nuzzling against my hand.

"Jesus, Mal, enough already. You're not even into public displays." Her ex sounds bored, but the crimson at the tips of his ears says otherwise. He's pissed. Or mortified. Or both. He stares at the two of us like he just might hire a hitman.

"I am now." Her voice is breathy and soft, more audible to me than him.

But really, it's all for him. I remind myself again.

"Whatever. I call bullshit on this whole charade. I'll send you an email." He moves toward the exit, but he still has the drink in his hand. I stay focused on Mallory's chest rising and falling, but I can see her ex pause by the door. Watching us, nosy.

So I lean in and brush my lips over hers. They're softer than I expect, and I catch a whiff of cherry, which only makes me need to taste them. Her eyes drift shut and I deepen the kiss, cupping her cheek.

I need to keep this real, even for a zealous boyfriend, so I pull back only slightly and linger. Her breath melds with mine, and I tip our foreheads together. Then I kiss her once more, softly. And once more, like I can't get enough.

I keep her tight against my hip and move my arm up to her shoulders. Possessive. Unwilling to go a second without having her close. She tips her head up and kisses my neck, and I have to fight to keep from carrying her into the nearest closet or the back of my truck and tearing her clothes off.

I feel the breeze when the door opens with a wheeze, bringing a little more air in from outside and letting her douche of an ex out.

Other than the woman I gather is Mallory's friend, who's been staring at us with her mouth agape, not a single person in the room seems aware of what just happened in our corner of the bar.

People make out in bars all the time, and even more people get into fights in bars. Probably as a result of making out with the wrong woman. It's all connected, from where I sit.

Mallory's interaction with her ex barely qualifies as a scuffle, and our kiss barely tips the radar on public displays. But it was a hell of a good kiss.

I can tell by the color rising in Mallory's cheeks and the slightly dazed look in her eyes that she agrees. She refocuses quickly and takes a long swig from a glass of amber beer. I wouldn't have pegged her as a beer drinker. She seems like a champagne or rosé gal, based purely on perception, but that's changing by the minute.

"Thanks for that," she says nonchalantly. She goes to the board and plucks the darts out one by one.

"Oh no, you don't." I cross the space in two strides and stand in front of her so she can't easily evade me. "What the hell was that all about?"

She shrugs. "I'll tell you in a minute. First, I need to make a phone call." She hands the darts off to her friend, and a second later, I'm watching her tight little ass sashay through the bar in the direction of the restrooms.

"She means she's got to use the loo," her friend explains helpfully with a cackle.

"Yeah. I caught that."

It's the only part of the conversation we just had that makes any sense.

ash

I HOVER next to the round table where my friends have ordered a pitcher of beer and have already finished half of it. Lucas hands me a full pint glass and toasts it with his.

"Just when I thought you couldn't outdo yourself, you managed to be lip-to-lip with a lady within two minutes of entering the place. I thought you weren't seeing anyone. You holding out on us?"

Just like that, three pairs of eyes size me up, and each friend sits eager to give me shit or congratulate me or both. Lucas nudges the fourth chair away from the table with his foot and nods for me to sit.

"Not holding out on you, but I'll be back in a minute, and you can ask me whatever you want. Not saying I'll answer, but you can ask."

I take my beer and walk in the direction Mallory went.

People have their opinions about me—some call me a playboy,

lady-killer, man-slut, while others think I'm as lazy as they come —but whatever their assessment, most would probably agree that I mind my own business.

I can't speak to people's opinions because they tend to be formed based on rumors and old reputations, so I mostly ignore what people think and go about my affairs. No sense in encouraging the irony of putting in a lot of work to convince people I'm not lazy.

Minding my own business seems like good sense, and it's one of the few lessons I recall my dad instilling in me when I was a kid. "Stay out of other people's way and don't go looking for a fight," he said one afternoon while I sat at our kitchen table trying to scrub the word 'loser' out of the fabric of my school backpack.

With two older brothers, I rarely got picked on, but that particular year, I was still in elementary school, and both of my brothers had graduated. So there was no one to defend my scrawny ass against a group of kids in the grade ahead of me when they decided I was 'too small and too stupid' to join their game of kickball on the schoolyard.

I made the mistake of sticking up for myself, which is what I told my dad. "I wasn't looking for a fight. I was trying to avoid one."

My dad stirred milk into a cup of coffee and watched me scrub the black ink so hard that it formed a muddled gray patch on the fabric. He didn't offer to help, but from the way his sharp blue-eyed stare assessed me, I had the feeling he knew a better method for removing ink. He just wasn't about to tell me.

"There's power in observation." He leaned back in his chair and ran a hand over his cheeks and chin as though checking to make sure his clean shave hadn't missed a spot. "You don't need to be the loudest one in the room. You need to be the smartest. And sometimes you can do that best by being unseen and unheard until the time is right."

At the time, I didn't understand his meaning because I wanted to unleash ants into the lunchboxes of every one of those kids. It took me several more years before his wisdom started to make sense to me.

My dad was rarely unseen or unheard. His loud voice bellowed through our house and put the fear of God into employees at Buttercup Hill. Sometimes I wondered if he forgot to take his own advice.

But I digress. The point is that I normally mind my own business. I observe. I plot my moves and execute them when the time is right. It allows me to work under the radar and avoid a lot of drama.

However, walking into the Dark Horse and finding some asshole trying to shove his tongue down Mallory's throat obliterated my bystander instincts. Okay, his tongue wasn't actually involved, but still. He was in her face and in her space, and I could tell she was uncomfortable—partly because she looked just as pissed off as she did after taking down the pickle display last month.

Seeing that expression directed at some other dude could mean that she always looks annoyed, but I chose to trust my powers of observation. She didn't want him anywhere near her, and as soon as I intervened, she seemed relieved.

So relieved, apparently, that she concocted a lie of mammoth proportions. Well, fine. I've been with enough women for enough years that I knew how to bring it home. Now, I want a little payback in the form of an explanation.

In case Mallory plans on slipping out the back door of the bar without coming to find me, I plant myself in the hallway where the restrooms are.

"You the bloody stalker, now?" The clipped British accent throws me at first, and I'm not sure it's directed at me. When I turn, I find Mallory's friend staring me down. She's a good foot shorter than me and wears no makeup. Her brown hair is tied in a ponytail, and she's drowning in a baggy beige sweater. But there's no mistaking the sharpness of her stare, which could wilt a pot of daisies in one go. Based on that, I can see why she and Mallory are friends.

"I didn't catch your name. I'm Dash."

She huffs a laugh. "I didn't tell you my name so there was nothing to catch." Salty, this one.

"You want to tell it to me now, English?"

Her eyebrow notches up. I lean against the dark wood-paneled wall and glance toward the restrooms, wondering if it's possible that Mallory has already slipped out a back door. I tend to doubt it, given that her ex could still be lingering outside.

"Mary. Nice to meet you." She looks me over from head to toe and matches my stance. "That was…interesting back there."

"Yeah, well, I didn't start it." I hold up my hands like a caught thief.

"Nope, but you sure ended it. I didn't think there was any kind of repellant for that wanker, but it turns out, you're it." The sound of an electric hand dryer hums behind us.

I laugh because her surly demeanor is a strange mix with the compliment. "You know him well?"

She shrugs. "Not really. I've only been in town for a bit, but he's come around a few times trying to get Mallory to talk with him. She shuts him down every time. Easy when you have a front door to slam in his face. Harder here."

"True. But not impossible."

She nods slowly. "So you've proven." Mary perks her head up at the sound of a toilet flush behind us. She gestures toward the restrooms with a tip of her head. "I'll leave you to it, then. Send her back with fresh pints when you're done talking."

She leaves before I can ask what kind of beer they're drinking, but I assume Mallory knows. A moment later, I hear the pop of a lock and accompanying shoulder against a door. Waving her hands to finish drying them, Mallory looks surprised to see me there.

"Oh. Hi. Were you waiting for that?" She gestures behind her, and I watch the mask of confident nonchalance return to her face. It's exactly how she's looked every time I've seen her in the past, which is why I had the impression of her as a manipulative socialite. Her demeanor always seemed practiced and polished to a sheen designed to get her what she wanted—usually a man.

But now I've caught glimpses of what lies behind that mask—vulnerability, disappointment, maybe even unease—I'm intrigued to know more.

I'm the last person who should be forming assumptions about a person when I know how few of the perceptions of me are actually true. That would be zero. Maybe I should wipe the slate clean when it comes to her, but I can't until I understand her better.

"No, I was waiting for you."

That seems to surprise her. "Oh. Okay." She crosses her arms and hits me with a broad smile.

"Don't do that."

Her smile falters only slightly. She's good at keeping this shit going. "Do what?"

"Pretend to be happy to see me. Or smile when you'd rather not."

She doesn't relent. The smile stays, and she assesses me in a way she didn't have time to earlier. Her glance runs from my face to my shoes, then back to my face, where her gaze lingers.

"You wear glasses."

Not what I'm expecting her to say. "Yeah. It helps when I want to see things."

"You didn't have them on at Sunshine Foods that day." She looks away and snaps her lips shut. Like a confession slipped out. I tuck that nugget of information away, interested that she remembers something from a month ago so clearly. It would be like me remembering the color of her sweater that day.

Red. Crimson red like a fucking fire truck.

I shrug. "Probably why I didn't recognize you at first in the store. Sorry about that."

"You don't have to be sorry. I think we're even now."

I can't help the canary-eating cat grin that's spreading across my face. "Oh, we are so not even. First of all, I want details. *Lots* of details. And second, is this the only time you'll be requiring my services as fake fiancé?"

A tiny bit of the facade drops, and her practiced smile fades into one of actual amusement. "You're serious."

"Damn straight."

"No thanks. This was a one-time, get me out of a bind thing. And I appreciate it. I'll buy you a beer, okay? Good enough?"

I hold up the one in my hand, which I've barely sipped. "Don't need a beer."

"What, then?"

"I want answers. What happens when word gets out we're engaged? What if you need my help getting rid of the douche nozzle in the future? Why was he bothering you, anyway?"

I get only a shrug, so I ask the question that suddenly seems most important.

"Why'd you marry such an ass hat in the first place?"

"Long, not-very-interesting story. You'd be better off with the beer." The plastic smile is back. Does she really think she can dissuade me from getting what I want with that? Now that I've glimpsed a peek at a different side of Mallory Rutherford, I'll be damned if I'm going to settle for what she gives everyone else.

I shake my head. "No way. You asked me for a date. And granted, I'm a bit calendar-challenged and waited a week to respond—"

"Two weeks," she corrects.

I hold up a hand, then lower it to where hers are balled into fists. Taking one of them in mine, I straighten out her fingers and see an almost imperceptible drop in her shoulders. "Two weeks. I apologize even more. But this is me saying yes."

She takes a step backward. "You can't say yes. The offer isn't on the table anymore."

"Mallory, please. I'm sorry. I'm an attention-compromised individual who forgets a text the minute the next new shiny thing beeps on my phone."

I take a step forward. Now we're closer than we were a moment ago. She lets out a long exhale. I know I can be frustrating as hell sometimes, but it's hard to stop when I'm having fun.

"Can you forgive me?"

"No." Her response is a bit less forceful.

I put a hand over my heart and give her my most earnest, serious expression. "Please?"

She rolls her eyes. "Two weeks, Dash. Two weeks."

I laugh because I'm enjoying this night far more than I planned and it has everything to do with her. "Fine. Then I'm asking you out instead. Dinner. Tomorrow night or whenever you're free."

She shakes her head and takes another step back. I step forward.

She steps back again. I step forward again. "We could do this all the way to the door, and I'll take you to dinner right now if you want."

Mallory glares at me. Finally, the fake smile is gone, and I see a glimmer of the woman at the grocery store who's frustrated as hell. Even though I'm the one frustrating her, I like the look of it. Maybe *because* I'm the one frustrating her.

"Come on, let me take you to dinner."

Without asking, she reaches for my beer and takes it from my hand. She drinks several gulps and hands it back. "Thank you. It's hot in here."

"You didn't answer my question."

"What question?"

"About dinner."

"You didn't ask a question. You just told me to let you take me to dinner. Rude." But I catch the faintest hint of a smile, a real one this time. It's barely there, but it's so much better than the plastic shit she wears for everyone else, and I feel gratified to have earned some honesty.

"Will you have dinner with me Mallory?"

"Will you drop all discussion of my ex and promise that we're even-Steven if I do?"

"Your odds are infinitely better if you eat food with me."

Letting out a long, exasperated breath, she shakes her head and mutters, "Needed a fiancé, and I got a debate captain."

She extends her hand, and we shake. There's no mistaking it —the zing of electricity at the contact with her skin that tells me this is no ordinary interaction with another person. And even though I just implied we'd be even after one dinner, a big part of me feels certain I won't stick to my end of the deal.

She's the most interesting woman I've come across in a long time.

CHAPTER 8

allory

IF IT WASN'T SO nice out, I'd have a better excuse for waking up in an irritable mood. It's hard to open the window shades, see a bluebird sky, smell the late summer roses on the vines, and declare that life is crap.

But boy does life feel like crap right about now.

Doesn't mean I can stay in bed wallowing, but it means I'll have to put even more effort into seeming cheerful when I go into St. Helena this morning. I'm bound to run into someone, and it could possibly be someone who I'll need to have in my corner when Felix comes around again. And I know he will.

That has to be the reason I'm in a mood. Two interactions with him in one evening would push anyone over the edge. Fortunately, Dash played along and that seemed to loosen Felix's barnacle-like hold on me, at least temporarily.

The memory of how my skin flamed hot when Dashiell

Corbett joked that I'd one day be his wife sends a new shot of warmth down to my bones. It irritates me.

I don't want to feel anything around Dash, especially when he seemed to enjoy our charade a little too much. Almost like he was mocking me. That has me edging past irritable and into downright pissy.

The harder I tried to hide my mood, the more makeup I put on this morning. I spent extra time choosing an outfit that would act as my game face because anyone I see could be someone to work with when it's time to grow our wine business at Autumn Lake. It's smart to have friends instead of enemies.

As it turns out, the first person I run into is a pair of moms who used to be high school friends of mine. That's right—we're not friends anymore, mainly because they got married and stopped inviting me to dinner parties after my short marriage to Felix ended. Some married people only like to spend time with other married people, I guess.

They're dressed alike in black workout tights and zippered jackets, blond hair in matching high ponytails. It's irrelevant whether they're coming from a workout or going to one—the point is to tell the world that they care about fitness.

"Mallory! What are you doing in town?" Meadow asks, pulling Jackie to her side and linking arms.

"Picking up a few desserts for the workers. They've been putting in long hours, so I want to keep them happy." My glossy lipstick frames my teeth when I offer a full smile and hold up my bakery bag.

"Oh, good for you." They look me up and down, eyes snagging on my Moncler puffer vest, dark-washed skinny jeans, and Blundstone boots. "How do you always look so put-together, even running errands?" Jackie says, clutching a to-go cup of coffee.

I don't bother telling them that the boots are seven years old and because I've polished them and treated the leather well, they'll last another seven. I don't bother saying that I got the vest at an outlet store and saved money by buying the largest child's size instead of the more expensive women's medium. All my clothes are designer-perfect, and that's the point.

"Aw, thanks. You're sweet." I smile and take a step back, fishing my keys out of my purse as a hint that I don't have time to linger.

"Though I guess it's what you have to do when you're still single, right?" Meadow gives me an upside down smile that I hate.

"Totally," I say with my brightest smile. "You guys are the lucky ones." I hope my singsong tone sounds convincing since I'm lying through my teeth. Running around in yoga pants trying to fill the day until school pickup sounds awful to me. And then shuttling the kids to playdates? No thank you. I'm good.

"Oh, if you only knew. Tommy had hand, foot, and mouth disease last week, and Maggie spent half the night in my room because she had a bad dream. I'm exhausted," Jackie says. Meadow nods.

"Well, you make it look easy," I say. This time, my smile is genuine because her description of motherhood sounds harrowing, and I salute her.

We air-kiss goodbye, and I make a beeline for my car, desperate to get back to the farm before running into anyone else, least of all Felix, who seems to turn up at every pass.

On my way home, I stop next door with a bag of chocolate chunk cookies for Mary and the kids. Hearing those moms talk about the trials of raising kids makes me appreciate Mary, who does it for someone else's kids.

I pull my Jeep into the driveway of the house and turn off the ignition. The first sound I hear when I pop the door open is the trill of children's laughter coming from the backyard. Even with the white clapboard house between me and the kids, I hear them loud and clear.

I follow a path alongside the house to a gate that opens to the backyard. There I find Mary crouched behind twin toddlers who stand at small easels. The kids paint with gusto, each armed with a row of multicolored paint dishes and wearing oversized tee-shirts over their clothes to keep them clean-ish.

"You start with the face and then add the eyes and mouth," Mary tells the three-year-olds.

"I don't want to do it like that. I want to start with the eyes." One of the tow-headed toddlers pops out his lower lip and sulks. "He's not even painting a face." He points at where his sibling uses both palms to swirl paint on the hanging piece of paper.

"Okay, it was just a suggestion. You're the artist. You do it how you want."

I can't help but laugh at her attempt to reason with him. Mary spies me and widens her eyes in a silent plea of "help me."

"Hey guys. What are you painting?"

The twin who is anti-paintbrush turns around and eyes me suspiciously until he recognizes me. "I'm painting a soccer player. I don't know what he's doing." He gestures to his brother's painting which is a swirl of color. His twin is too absorbed in mixing the paint on the paper to stop for commentary.

"Soccer player, huh? Did Mary tell you they call soccer players footballers where she comes from?"

The twin lets out an exaggerated sigh. "Like a million times."

"A kid has to learn." Mary puts her hands on her hips and ushers me over to a picnic table a few feet from where the kids are absorbed in their art. "What's this?" She gestures to the bag.

"Brought you some reinforcements." Holding the bakery bag up, I lean on the edge of the table.

Her eyes dance. "I assume some are for the lads, but I might not tell 'em and eat them all myself instead."

"You do you." I'd never begrudge her a dozen cookies.

A bluebird flits in and out of one of the small wooden houses perched atop the old fence that separates the backyard from the field behind our property. Autumn Lake spans a couple hundred acres and abuts the backs of homes on the street running perpendicular to us. So even though we're technically next door neighbors to the twins' family, we don't live on the same street, and it's a fairly long walk from door to door.

"You want some coffee? I'll make a fresh pot."

"No, I can't stay. Just dropping off your afternoon sugar rush, and then I need to get back to plotting world domination. Or at least finishing up my business plan." I unroll the bakery bag and realize I've had the top in a death grip, though I can't imagine why. The paper is smushed and mangled, and Mary notices all of it. Fortunately, the cookies have been spared.

Mary nods. "Is this when I tell you what I think about your little charade from last night?"

After Felix left, I told her to zip it. The whole episode left me so worn out that we agreed to just throw a few more darts and enjoy the night. Of course, I couldn't get a darn dart anywhere close to the bullseye. That's how rattled Felix makes me. To say nothing of my fake fiancé.

"I don't know what I was thinking. Seriously, it must've been the beer. And now I somehow agreed to a date with the guy who already blew me off once. Clearly disinterested and now he's just preparing to rub it in."

"I disagree with that last part. He fancied you. That was obvious."

I stop fidgeting with the bakery bag and sink into a cushion atop one of the benches flanking a picnic table. Mary takes the bag from me and rips it open down the center, turning it into a placemat for the dozen cookies that spill out. Glancing in the direction of the twins, who are still absorbed in working on their paintings, Mary swipes a cookie and takes a large bite.

"Oh, this is a proper biscuit. Thank you." She takes another bite before swallowing the first one, and I realize she probably skipped lunch.

"Lemme guess. You didn't eat with the boys?"

She makes a face, somewhere between disbelief and a wince. "I don't fancy peanut butter, and that's all those boys eat." She pops the last of the cookie into her mouth and bustles off to the house, calling behind her, "Gonna be the death of me."

I break off a corner of one cookie and pop it into my mouth. Even the delicious bite of the dark chocolate chips and the bits of sea salt sprinkled on top don't improve my mood. Mary returns with a pitcher of water and a stack of plastic cups. She pours for each of us.

"I need to get back to work." I say the words, but somehow my body stays fixed at the table.

Mary grins at me through chocolate-stained teeth. "What you ought to do is find a man. Marry a bloke just like your mother wants and it'll invalidate Felix's claim on you and your property. Your parents can pin their hopes on a new guy, and meanwhile, you'll be free to run the business. Like in that show."

I'll never be able to keep up with Mary's obsession with classic American TV shows.

"Which show?"

"The one with early Pierce Brosnan. Remington Steele, I think it was? She wants to run a detective agency, but no one takes her seriously so she invents a front man and names him Remington Steele. Then a real dude with that name shows up, and he's lovely to look at, so she keeps him as the man candy and does all the real work herself."

"I feel like there's something sexist and sad about that."

"Of course there is. That's the beauty!"

"And you think I should use this as a model for my life."

"Edit as you see fit. You already convinced Dash to be your fiancé for a night. Just take it to the next level. With him as your husband instead of Felix, you'd be trading up."

"I don't even know him." I say it as though that's the only problem with her ridiculous plan. "Not to mention, he might've been okay messing around in a bar in front of Felix, but I doubt he wants a wife. And I don't want a husband."

I'm drawn back to when he said the words "my wife," and my nerve endings caught fire.

Maybe it's the stress of the situation or the idea of being hitched to a man I barely know, but the idea makes me laugh so hard it brings tears to my eyes. "Ah, thank you for that. It's so nice to feel an emotion other than stress for a hot minute."

Mary watches me dab my eyes and nods slowly. "That's what makes it perfect. The relationship won't get in the way of the goal. I'm serious."

"You don't need to marry me off. But thank you for the idea."

"It's a good idea. The men will be lining up a mile long."

"No way. It'll land me right back where I started, linked at the hip to a man who puts his own interests before mine."

"I'm done." One of the twins waves Mary over with two hands covered in paint. She hauls herself up from the table and looks longingly at the cookies before dashing over with a container of wet wipes.

"Oh, that looks beautiful!" she exclaims, unpinning the painting from the easel. It's covered from end to end with paint, every color in the palate blended together in swirls. Just witnessing her Mary Poppins energy makes me tired.

"I'll see you later, Mare," I call, heading around the side of the house and back to my car.

I hear her cheerful voice behind me. "Let's get those hands cleaned up, and we'll all eat some biscuits. Yeah?"

As I'm sliding into the front seat of my car, the three of them start to sing a song about a hungry moose. It makes me smile. Then I think about the crazy idea Mary proposed. It makes me smile a little wider. That's when I know I'm in trouble.

CHAPTER 9

ash

OUR NEXT FAMILY meeting takes place at a back corner table inside Sweet Butter, the café on the Buttercup Hill property, because my sister is hungry.

"Stop saying that," PJ whines, right before taking a huge bite of an egg and bacon croissant.

"You're the only one here who's eating," I observe, pointing at where our eldest brother Archer stews over a cup of coffee and Jax sips from a metal water bottle. I rolled in late because I slept late.

No one ever acts surprised when I'm late, just like they're not surprised by my penchant for going out to bars and having a very active social life. It barely registers as an event if I have a late night. But for the last few nights, I haven't been out at all. I've been up late with thoughts churning through my mind. Thoughts about a woman I never gave two brain cells worth of worry about until we ran into each other—twice.

I'm almost grateful for a family meeting, normally the bane of my existence, because it will force me not to think about Mallory Rutherford. And I need to stop thinking about her for fuck's sake.

"They ordered. They just haven't gotten their food yet." There's no point in arguing with her—or with any of my siblings, for that matter. I was born into a family as stubborn as it is loving, and each of us has a tendency to dig in when we think we're right.

Beatrix comes in last and sits at the table without going to the counter to order anything. I'm about to point at her as an example of someone who clearly isn't eating when the server brings over a latte and a croissant she'd apparently been holding for my sister.

PJ follows my gaze and gives me a smug nod.

"Fine, whatever." I get up and go to the counter. If everyone else is eating, I'll take my sweet time picking out something tasty from the case. No sense working on an empty stomach.

"Almond croissant's always a good choice." Jax's voice over my shoulder sends a creep of dread down my spine. I didn't mention anything to him about the fake boyfriend charade the other night, mainly because he can't hear Mallory's name without wanting to spit nails.

I never really understood where all the bad blood came from after what seemed like a harmless hookup, and I never cared enough to ask. Jax was a grumpy asshole for the year or so after his wife left him with their newborn daughter. In fact, he was a grumpy asshole right up until he met Ruby, our sommelier who talked her way into a job here by offering to be Jax's nanny.

I will always have respect for Ruby, knowing what she had to put up with from Jax before he settled down and fell in love with her. Sometimes I wish she was our sibling instead of him. Kind, easygoing Ruby wouldn't be growling in my ear.

Turning to face him, I see that my brother doesn't have a scowl on his face for once. Having Ruby in his life really does agree with him, even if she did somehow allow him to grow the beard he's currently sporting.

"Have you looked in the mirror today? The werewolf next door wants his razor back."

"Fuck off." He says it with a smile, which means I haven't annoyed him nearly enough. And I feel the need to rib him more —it's a little brother thing.

"Big words for an old man. Didn't know you still had it in you."

He smiles and I swear the guy has gone soft. So much so that I can't even think of a way to taunt him. Maybe it's me who's gone soft, and I hate to think it has anything to do with Mallory, even though I can't stop thinking about her.

"Did you know Mallory Rutherford was married?"

"She is?" Jax looks shocked.

"No, I mean, she was. She has an ex-husband." It's then I realize the barista has been waiting for me to pick out a pastry while I've been standing here gabbing about nothing. "Sorry, I'll have a chocolate croissant."

"And an almond one for me," Jax pipes in, lowering his voice again when he tells me, "I didn't know that. Was it a recent thing?"

"Not sure. I just know she has an ex. Met him, actually. Guy's a super douche." As the words leave my mouth, I realize there will be questions I'm not sure I'm prepared to answer.

"Yeah, that figures. She's a lot to put up with."

A defensive surge moves through my chest, and I find myself wanting to tell him he's wrong about Mallory, even though I don't know her well enough to say for sure.

"When did you meet him?" Jax asks. The blue of his eyes matches my own, but somehow, I doubt mine leave the piercing impression his do. I heard a woman once describe me as having bedroom eyes, whatever that means. If anything, I doubt she meant they had the discerning focus of the blue staring me down now.

"He was at the Dark Horse earlier this week. So was she. Seemed like there's some bad blood there, made me curious whether you knew anything about him."

"Nah, she never mentioned an ex. Not that we spent a whole lot of time talking the one drunken night we were together."

"How can you hate her as much as you do based on that? I wouldn't even think you'd remember a drunken night all those years ago."

He rubs his hand over his face, and I wait for him to tell me to stay the hell out of his business, but he blinks a couple times blankly as if thinking back through time. I make a mental note to buy Ruby a gift because she's toned my grouchy brother way down, and I like this guy more than the old version.

"It wasn't the night we were together—not even sure I remember so much about that, if I'm being honest..." He blinks hard and the corner of his mouth hints at a smile. "It was what came afterward. She wanted it to mean something, and I just wasn't in the headspace for that."

"Seriously? That's why you've badmouthed her all these years? Because you weren't in the "headspace" to date her after your hookup, and she had the gall to suggest it?" It can't be the whole story. Jax is a grump, but he's not that much of an asshole.

The barista hands us matching white plates with our pastries, and we take them to the table where the rest of our siblings are already sitting. "Look, I don't know what to say. I wasn't in a good place after Annabelle left, and Mallory wants what she wants."

"Which is what?" If there's something to all the rumors I've heard about her latching onto any man she sees because she wants a husband, I need to know.

"It's all about business with her. It may seem like she's there for a good time, but there's always something else at play.

Whether it has something to do with Autumn Lake or her parents' money or something else, she's working an angle."

Picking up my chocolate croissant, I let the buttery scent wash over me before taking a bite. "That's what you thought she was doing after your one-night thing? Working you for something?"

He demolishes half his almond pastry in one bite and talks through the crumbs, shrugging. "I did at the time. Who knows? Maybe it just seemed that way because she kept on hinting to anyone who'd listen that she had some kind of claim on me." He wipes the crumbs from his mouth with the back of his hand and takes a seat next to PJ, who has all but demolished her breakfast. All that remains on her plate are pale flakes of croissant and a dab of ketchup.

"Could it be that your general foul mood until you met Ruby gave you a skewed perspective?" I'm needling him, but I also want to see if he'll revise his prior take on Mallory. Again, I check myself when I realize that I care about what he thinks of her more than I should.

Jax picks up a white ceramic coffee cup and fills it from an urn on the table. "Yeah, I'd allow that. She did come with me to an event a while back and it was sort of okay. Maybe she's not so terrible. Why the sudden interest?" He raises an eyebrow.

"No reason. Like I said, I ran into her, so it got me wondering."

He locks eyes on me, assessing. My brother may be irritable, but he's not dumb. I just hope my game face is good enough to persuade him there's nothing there.

I'm saved from further questioning when Archer passes out stapled copies of financial reports, accompanied by a map of our property and the surrounding land.

"Why the map?" Beatrix asks, pushing her long, dark hair off her shoulders. It's one of the few times she doesn't have her hair in a clip or a bun or whatever, and she can't stop fidgeting with it.

After re-tucking the loose strands behind her ear, she gives in and twists it into a knot and points accusingly at the page we all have in our hands.

"Look at it and you'll see," Arch says calmly like a school teacher who's willing to wait for us to get the point of his lesson.

We each study the map in front of us. PJ doodles on hers, connecting the squares that denote different types of grapes we grow and drawing circles around some areas that Archer has marked outside of our property.

Beatrix and Jax study the map silently, but I notice Jax's knee bouncing next to me. He hates it when Archer tries to make him guess what he's getting at because he hates being wrong.

"I see our property and a bunch of squares of stuff we don't own," I contribute, ready for one of my older siblings to jump down my throat and tell me I should stick to human resources issues. But we're all in the family business together, and it's as much my future as it is theirs. If Archer's asking what we see, I'm going to tell him.

It surprises me when he nods. "Exactly. If we want to grow the business, we need to buy land to grow more grapes or buy them from growers in the same appellation. That means taking on new debt when we're running on a shoestring until the new crops start producing. And now that Dad's seen fit to buy our half brother a vineyard down the road, our options just became much more limited."

"Why? We have funds, now that Colin invested in Buttercup Hill." PJ looks sheepish as soon as she says it. She's still not used to the fact that her fiancé, an astrophysicist tech billionaire from Silicon Valley, is now a large shareholder in our business. But the truth is he rescued us after our dad took half a billion dollars out of our winery and gave it to the half sibling we never knew about. Without Colin, we'd be up a creek and in debt.

As it is, none of us is certain how to handle the new family member who may have designs on the very same grapes and land we do.

"It's not about funds. It's about scarcity of resources."

"Land," I confirm.

Archer nods. "Look at this map and you'll see that all the available land where we can either grow grapes or buy them is accounted for. None of it's for sale and only the smallest growers have fruit we can buy."

"Can't we just cobble together a handful of small players until we have what we need?" Jax asks. Seems logical enough.

Archer takes a long sip of coffee. "You really want to juggle the finances on thirty small batch vineyards?"

"Thirty?" Jax swallows hard and grimaces.

"And we need to stay within our appellation so we can keep selling the same product at the same standards."

"Maybe it's time to branch out. Maybe we get into a different appellation and market it like a special edition. Peej can make a big push in that direction with the media. We make it a good thing instead of a bad one." Beatrix always makes her ideas sound so logical and convincing that I'm ready to take out a pen and sign on the dotted line.

It falls to my more persnickety brothers to come up with all the reasons she's wrong. And they always do.

"If we go outside to other regions, the soil is different, the microclimates are different. It's not just about producing a special edition wine. It's about knowing what we're doing. I'm just getting my brain around the wine making here. I can't add another appellation to my plate, or my brain'll explode."

He's taken on the lion's share of responsibilities since the five of us took over all the day-to-day running of the business from our father. His Alzheimer's made it impossible for him to stay at the helm, and I'm grateful Archer jumped in with both feet.

"Is there an option three?" I ask.

Archer points at a few blank areas on the map. "Here and

here. This is the land that could work if we can work out a deal with the owners somehow."

I feel a pit in my stomach when my brain catches up, and I realize that one of the properties on the map is owned by the Rutherford family. Mallory's parents are a couple of the original San Francisco natives who moved to the area and turned a small farm into an enormous one, but they're notoriously against growing grapes on their acres of land. And they've turned down multimillion dollar offers to sell.

"So we're trying to get into business with the Rutherfords?" Beatrix asks, turning her attention to me. "Hey, did you ever end up going out with Mallory?" Beatrix asks, tapping a pencil against the map right in the spot where the Rutherford property lies. I had the poor judgment to mention it to my siblings that Mallory texted to ask me out a couple weeks back, and now they'll never forget it.

"No, not yet." I feign disinterest as my stomach roils with discomfort. I could tell her about my upcoming date with Mallory, but I don't want to. I'm not sure how I feel about the scrutiny when I'm fighting to keep her from taking over my every waking thought. It makes no sense after the little time I've spent with her, but she's under my skin.

"Well, maybe you should," PJ suggests. When I meet her eyes, I find her studying me with a serious expression.

Jax smirks and takes a slug from his coffee cup.

I fidget with my cup, which I've already drained, wishing I had something to distract everyone from their sudden fixation on me.

"You're suggesting I take her to dinner and try to convince her to sell us some land?"

"Doesn't just have to be talk." Jax winks.

"Doubt he wants your sloppy seconds," Archer says. A jolt of anger pierces my chest. I know it's just locker room banter, and they probably expect me to join in, but I can't.

"I'll meet with her and see where her thoughts are." I shrug and lean toward the middle of the table to refill my coffee. This doesn't have to be a big deal. I can float the question over dinner and report back that she's not interested in selling. No reason to make an issue out of it or let them know I haven't been able to stop thinking about the woman since I kissed her.

"Who owns this land?" I point at the other large space.

"It's parkland. Getting the government to sign off on commercial use might actually be easier than getting the Rutherfords to agree to sell, but first things first."

I nod. First things first.

And the first on my list is deciding what restaurant to go to with Mallory.

allory

"Who does this?"

I can tell from his reaction that Dash expects me to say something different. And maybe it has something to do with the fact that I'm standing here with one hand over my heart like he scared me to death. Not so far from the truth.

When I heard a knock on my door, my stomach sank because I figured it might be Felix. The guy can't take a hint—or a direct instruction, apparently.

When I fling the door open, ready to tell him to take a hike, I find a shocked-looking Dashiell Corbett who takes two steps back and nearly falls off my porch.

"If looks could kill..." he mutters, eyeing me warily.

"At least you know how to take a hint. More than I can say for my ex."

Dash's expression changes on a dime. Now he looks focused

and territorial, stepping forward and squaring his shoulders as if readying for a fight. "He here?"

"No."

"But he's been bothering you after we had words the other night?"

I shake my head. "No, but I thought maybe you were him."

Dash's shoulders drop, and he lets out a long breath. "Oh. Well, I'm not." He puts a hand on one of the painted posts that hold up the roof over my porch and leans against it casually. I wait for him to tell me why he's here. Instead, his eyes trace me from head to toe and land back on my face.

"I can see that now," I say.

"Glad you can tell the difference. And even more glad that he isn't bothering you." Dash's gaze makes another trip over my form, and I feel it like he's using his hands, not just his eyes. Weird. That's never happened before.

Granted, I came to the door in a pink yoga bra and tights because the abrupt knock at six in the evening caught me in the middle of an online yoga class I do almost every night. There's a yoga studio in town, but I never go. This works better for my schedule.

But now I'm regretting not throwing a sweatshirt over my top. It's not because I dislike Dash looking at me. It's because I do like it.

I need to stay objective about him, so I push the feelings away and cross my arms over my chest. "How can I help you?"

A slow smile spreads over Dash's face as though I've just offered to give him a briefcase full of money and a blow job on my porch. "You can tell me when our date is. I'd like to put it in my calendar."

"That's why you came over here? There's this thing called the cell phone. You can make calls on it and even text." The irony hits me. "Oh right, I forgot you don't know how to do that."

"When are you going to let me off the hook for that?" The smile hasn't dimmed and it's distracting me.

"Never."

"Even if I beg?"

The idea of that sends a shot of lust straight to my core.

"*When* you beg," I correct.

"What makes you so sure I will?" His smirk tells me he definitely will.

"One of my superpowers."

A dimple pops, and his smile tells me he's not put off by my sass, and it's refreshing. It makes me feel like I can peel back one more layer of the mask I normally wear. Part of me hates that he's making me trust him. Trusting people hasn't turned out well for me in the past. It makes me weak, which in turn leads to poor decision-making. I can't have that, especially when my future business interests are at stake.

"Please, Mallory. Please allow me to take you out," he begins. "I hope to learn about some of your other superpowers."

"You're bargaining now? I wasn't offering anything up in exchange for dinner, just so we're clear."

"Oh we're clear." The smirk edges into dangerously sexy territory, and I wish it didn't make my veins thrum. "Only thing that isn't clear is the time and date. Can we settle on that, please?"

"You're polite, at least."

"I wasn't raised in a barn," he says. I laugh because I've seen the big brown barn that once housed the entire Corbett family, and he absolutely was raised in it, but I don't bother to correct him.

Rufus comes bounding outside and gives Dash one throwaway bark before going to investigate a bush.

"That's Rufus. Thinks he's a lapdog."

"Don't change the subject. Our date," he insists.

"Fine. When do you want to go?"

"Tonight."

His quick response makes me laugh again. Twice in under a minute? That doesn't happen unless I'm watching stand-up comedy and even then, it's rare. What is it with this guy? How does he keep getting past my defenses?

"Not tonight," I tell him, unsure whether he was serious anyway.

"Why not?"

"It's already tonight. If we were going out tonight, we'd have needed to plan it before right now."

Now it's his turn to laugh. "Oh, really? Is that a universal rule of dinner dates, or do you just make this shit up on the spot? What kind of advanced planning is required?"

"I'm fairly certain it's a rule. There should be *some* planning. Or at least a shower." I indicate my workout attire, and he looks me over with wolfish glee.

"Shower. Noted." He grins. "Blow dryer too?"

"Stop," I demand, even though I don't really want him to stop. The way he makes my body hum with desire is not something I'm quick to part with, but I don't want him to sense how much he affects me. I realize I do need some planning before I go anywhere with him so I can lock these urges down tight beforehand.

Sneaking a look at his still-smug grin, I puzzle over how this man—or any man—could stir this reaction from me. I should have the upper hand in this conversation. I should be able to tell him exactly when and where he can put his swagger and leave him feeling extremely grateful when I do agree to a date in the distant future.

Instead, I find myself wanting to jump in his car and take him up on his offer.

Dangerous territory. I need to stay in control because any interaction I have with Dash needs to be about business. Eyes on the prize.

The other prize.

"Fine. Tonight. But give me an hour." I tilt my head and take him in, liking what I see. "Girl's gotta make herself pretty if she's going out to dinner."

He shakes his head. "Honey, you don't need to do a thing where that's concerned." My heart flutters at his endearment even though I know it doesn't mean anything. "When we're talking pretty, you don't just rewrite the rules, you *are* the rules."

My stomach bottoms out and I feel a hot blush flood my face. I will not survive dinner with this man if he keeps saying things like that, and the idea should unnerve me. Instead, it lights me up.

As he slowly turns away, his eyes stay locked on me, lingering, flaming the surface of my skin. It's the sexiest damn thing I've ever experienced in my life. An orgasm wrapped in satin and sealed with a hot kiss.

I turn back toward my house because my heart has just rammed into my throat and my blood's turned to lava.

Flirting with Dashiell Corbett is the most dangerous game I've ever played. I should stop right now. Or I should sashay into my house to get ready for dinner.

allory

"Why'd you ask me out?"

I'm not expecting the question, which has the effect of making me choke as I'm taking my first sip of wine. I manage to recover and swallow, rather than spitting it all over Dash's snug black Henley.

I suppose I knew the topic might come up, but I didn't think Dash would be so direct. I certainly didn't think it would be the first subject he'd want to discuss after the server filled each of our glasses with cabernet sauvignon.

"Um. Just…no reason. It was just an idea. A passing idea." Let him think I was going down my list of men in Napa Valley and happened to pause at his. For all of a millisecond. And now I barely remember what possessed me at all.

I don't intend to tell him the real reason now.

"Bullshit." The deep rumble of his voice cuts through the ambient chatter in the restaurant, and I look around to see if he's caught anyone's attention. No one seems to notice him. But my body notices, and I curse it for the thrill that races through my gut at the velvety sound.

"Excuse me?" I'll just play dumb.

"You had a reason. Tell me what it was. You already dated my brother, so I refuse to think you'd go double dipping in that pool. Although the charm of the Corbett men would get anyone all hot and bothered."

He leans back with a knowing smirk. This is the Dashiell Corbett I expected when I texted and asked him out. He's a player. He likes women. It doesn't take an engraved invitation to get him to sign on for a night of fun, and he had no reason to think I'd want anything else.

"You got me. I'm still not over Jax, and I thought maybe you'd give me the dose of Corbett man I was craving."

I meet his gaze, challenging him to dispute my explanation. Knowing he won't.

"Again, I say bullshit. Excuse my French."

"It ain't French, just so you know," I say.

"*Non? Tu parles francais?*"

"I do, actually. Studied it a little bit in school, then spent a year there."

He nods and his eyes travel over my face, fixing on my eyes for a moment and ending at my lips. He picks up his wineglass and swirls the liquid inside. I find myself staring at the swoosh of deep burgundy as though I've never seen a glass of wine before.

Or maybe it's his long fingers wrapped around the stem of the glass. Something has me mesmerized, and it takes a moment to shake myself free.

He takes a small sip and puts the glass back on the table. My eyes follow his graceful hand to where it rests on the white tablecloth. He taps his index finger on the heavy linen, and I can't stop thinking about what else he could do with that finger. A jolt of awareness shoots straight to my core, and I shift on my chair.

"You studied abroad during college?" he asks, bringing my thoughts back to the present. When I meet his gaze, I find him assessing me, and I feel stripped bare, like he knows exactly what I was thinking when I looked at his hands.

I shake my head. "No."

"You went after college?"

"Yes." I can't have a conversation with this man. I feel tongue-tied, and that's never happened before. I can't understand it because I didn't have this problem in the grocery store or in the bar. But we weren't alone at a fancy restaurant with a tiny glowing candle on the table and easy jazz playing in the background.

This "date" is throwing off my mojo, and I need to get it back.

His mouth twists into a smirk. "Are you really going to make me keep guessing? Spill, Marshmallow."

I'm about to come up with some words, but he leaves me speechless again with the odd nickname. I blink a few times and manage to close my gaping mouth. "What did you just call me?"

He shrugs and his eyebrows bounce. A dimple flashes in one cheek. Over the years, I've seen Dash from a distance, but I haven't spent this much time in proximity. Now that I'm here, I can admit that he is a very attractive, extremely hot man, and I can feel the heat rise in my cheeks just from looking at him. Yet there's a more important matter at hand, so I try to focus.

"Marshmallow."

"Is that your favorite dessert or something?"

"No, I prefer a chocolate tart, if I'm honest, but it just might be my favorite nickname for you." I roll my eyes, but there's no getting rid of that grin. "You don't like nicknames?"

Now it's my turn to shrug. "I've never had one before."

"Well, that doesn't surprise me."

I can't decide whether I'm offended or not. "Why do you say that?"

He leans in and speaks more quietly and deliberately, his deep baritone setting my nerve endings on fire. "After spending two minutes with that ass-wipe you were married to, I knew for damn sure he didn't have the creative impulse to give you a decent nickname. You deserve better, Mallomar."

I can't stop the frown from settling in. He nods. "You don't like it."

"It's not that. Just…" I debate cutting off the conversation and going back to why I spent time in France. It would be easier. He doesn't need to get to know me any better than he already does. We're here for one date. One and done.

"Tell me."

His grin is persuasive. It's probably lured countless unsuspecting women into his man cave for a night of debauchery. I have to push down the rogue impulse shouting that I want a night like that. I don't.

But there's an innocence about Dash. Unlike Felix who tips his head and looks like a dumb dog, Dash looks like an adorable golden retriever who only wants to please. What the hell? I might as well be honest with him. I'll probably never see him again, so what's the difference?

"Those sweet desserts are a little…cute. And I'm not like that. I'm…harder to like than that."

His expression loses the playfulness, and his mouth settles into a hard line. "Not from where I sit. And if you don't mind me saying, I dislike that anyone has ever made you feel that way in the past."

I'm so surprised by his pronouncement that I have nothing to say—none of my normal rebuttal and evidence to prove that I am, in fact, unlikable. In the face of his extreme distaste for that idea, I find myself feeling overruled.

That has never happened before.

He holds his wineglass up to the light. I expect him to take a sip, but instead, he holds it toward me for a toast. "To our first date."

I huff a laugh. "Ha. First and only, don't you mean?" I lift my glass to clink with his, but he withdraws his hand, studying me quizzically.

"That wasn't what I meant. If I'd meant it was our only date, I'd have said."

A succession of noises erupts from my throat, but none of them turn into actual words. My face heats so much that I start fanning the air around me with one hand and slurp down a big swig of wine with the other before putting the glass down.

"Surely there won't be a second date. This is just us, you know, making good on the date I asked you on and the whole thing in the bar and all that."

"Well, I might ask you out again, and then there will be a second date."

"But...we're even now. Why would you want to do that?"

He smiles, and I'm momentarily blinded by his straight teeth and that damn dimple. "Because I like you, Marshmallow. You're different than I expected in the very best of ways. That's why."

"But-but..."

Dash reaches his finger out—that long, gorgeous index finger —and places it over my lips so I stop protesting. He brings his glass to the space between us and hands mine to me. Our fingers brush, and I feel the hum of electricity at his touch. It's enough to calm me down and send my blood racing through my veins at the same time. An addictive combination.

"One more time... to our first date."

Obediently, I clink my glass against his. "To our first date."

He gives me a closed-lipped smile that's full of knowledge or promise about what might follow this first date. And I want all of it. Heaven help me.

ash

"YOU WANT A TASTE OF THE EGGPLANT?" I stab a noodle from my Penne alla Norma. "Or are you not into eggplant?"

"Eggplant?" Mallory coughs, and her face turns pink. "Um, I'm into it."

Swallowing hard, I realize the double entendre. Her blush deepens, and I know I should steer the conversation back to G-rated territory, but I wouldn't dare. Not when it makes her skin look like that.

I put some penne onto my fork and heap on a chunk of eggplant and smoked mozzarella before extending it toward Mallory. "Bite?"

Her eyes go wide at the suggestion of eating from my fork, but her hesitance lasts only a second. She nods and opens her mouth. Sliding the fork between her lips feels intensely personal, and I try to convince myself it's not because I'm imagining my cock there instead. I'm a shitty convincer.

I'm also a shitty spoon-feeder because I manage to leave a drip of sauce at the corner of her mouth, so I lift my napkin to dab it away. She follows my motion with her own, dabbing the now-clean spot and looking almost self-conscious as she chews. This isn't the brash, snooty woman I'm used to seeing at industry events. This one is softer, more real.

Much, much more interesting.

She's similar to the woman I encountered in the grocery store who was flustered and surrendered to the inevitability of pickle juice. I like this version.

"Good, right?" I'm talking about the pasta, but my question could be generalized to this whole evening. I came here with an agenda, prodded by my siblings, but I'm finding it hard to focus.

"Mmm-hmm." She swallows the bite and looks down at her plate of spaghetti Bolognese. "Want to try mine?"

"Yes, please." Again, my words feel like they have multiple meanings.

Mallory twirls some strands of pasta onto her fork and holds it out with the handle facing me. As I take it, our fingers brush, and it feels like we both pause. I know what I feel—stirring ripples of electricity pulsing across my skin where it grazes hers. Her eyes dilate slightly, and I notice tiny flecks of gold in the gray.

Taking the fork from her, I keep my eyes fixed on hers. Somehow, this is even hotter than when she ate off my fork.

"Good," I confirm, my voice a rasp. She nods. I pour the last of the wine into our glasses and swirl mine around before taking a generous sip. I need something to cool down the flames I feel licking the back of my neck.

"You like the wine?" she asks. I realize then that she's been watching me each time I take a sip and gauging my reaction.

"I do."

She turns the bottle so the label faces me, and I can't resist running a finger along the inside of her wrist before she pulls it away. Her jaw goes slack, but only for a moment. She regains composure and clears her throat. I tell myself to knock it off—I don't want to be a handsy jerk like her ex, but I can't resist touching her.

Instead, I study the bottle. "I don't know this wine. Is it a favorite of yours?"

It's not unusual for me to come across a winery I've never heard of. Even living in Napa and surrounded by wine, there are too many upstarts in California alone to keep track of them all. Besides, that's more Archer's domain since he's the one in charge of the wine making.

"It's one I've been studying." She picks up her glass and swirls the dark red liquid before taking a sip. From the way she blinks and smiles, I get the feeling she tastes more than grapes with a hint of oak barrel, which is all my unseasoned palate recognizes.

"Why's that?"

She presses her lips together and looks around the restaurant, where other diners sit at similar tables for two and four, sipping their wine and eating Italian food from white ceramic dishes. No one seems the least bit interested in us or our conversation.

Once Mallory seems reassured, she continues. "I have a business idea for Autumn Lake."

"Ah, are you thinking of expanding your wine production?" It wouldn't surprise me since they have acres and acres of fertile land and a tiny winery. From the time I was a kid, people have talked about what a "crime" it was that the Rutherfords didn't make better use of their land.

After a while, I stopped listening because broken-record conversations aren't my thing. What's the point?

"That's one part of it. The other part is even simpler. I'm sure you know our property sits on prime acreage in an appellation lots of people want. With the demand from other wineries as high as it is, I could run a thriving business just...growing fruit."

She says the last part like it's a dark secret. Like it's blasphemy, and she might get hauled off to prison for it.

I laugh. "Kind of what people around here do with their land. I assume the fruit you're talking about is grapes, not oranges. But no judgment if you want to water a hundred acres of strawberries every day."

"That would be silly in this region, don't you think?"

"I think we're particularly well suited to grow grapes, so yeah."

"Okay, then."

If I was looking for divine signals from the universe, they're falling at my feet left and right. I should use this opening in the conversation to suggest she lease us some land so we can grow the vines we need. All part of the conversational flow. Like I just thought of it this minute, rather than chewing a hole in the side of my cheek all night waiting for the right opportunity.

I hate this. If I just enjoy myself and forget about turning tonight into a power play, I'm the weak, pretty boy everyone thinks I am, and my family will be disappointed I couldn't close the deal.

On the other hand, if I make a sweet deal to snag some land, I'll feel like I'm using her. And right now, I like the way this evening is going. Just two people getting to know each other and enjoying each other's company. I guess that's why I date women instead of doing business with them. Only lately, I haven't done either one.

"Okay…" I wait for the second part of the story. I must be missing something because I can't figure out why she's being so secretive about doing the obvious. The only thing I can't figure out is what took her so long to get started.

"I assume this idea didn't just occur to you. Your family has had that land for years."

She looks around the room again, and I can tell this conversation is making her uncomfortable. And yet she brought it up.

Tipping back in my chair, I hold my wineglass and watch her. Her long dark hair frames her heart-shaped face, and her cheeks glow a pale pink as though she's just run around the block in brisk air. She's excited, but from the thrumming of her pulse beneath the pale skin of her neck, she's also nervous.

I'm dying to know why. Dying to understand why she's guarding a basic assumption of most land owners in Napa Valley like it's a national security secret.

"You want to get out of here and go for a walk?" I look down at both of our plates, where we've demolished all of our food, and tip my head toward the exit. "We can find a place for dessert or coffee and keep talking where it's quieter."

She nods, and I ask for the check. She fishes around in her purse for her wallet, but I've already put my credit card into the folio and handed it off to the server before she extracts hers. Looking from me to the server who's retreating into the distance, she scowls like I've pulled a fast one.

The color rises in her cheeks, and she holds up her credit card. "Didn't we agree that I owed you?"

"I never agreed to that. I asked you out."

"I asked you out first."

"You snooze, you lose." The server brings back my card, and I add a fat tip and sign the check. "Shall we?" I stand and offer her my arm.

Still scowling, she shoves her credit card back into her purse. She doesn't take my arm, so I rest a hand on the small of her back as she moves in front of me and heads for the door. "You should really put your credit card back in your wallet so it doesn't get lost in your purse," I say softly over her shoulder. I watch her eyes squeeze shut and her hands flex, and I know I'm cracking her attempt at an icy facade. And I plan to keep going.

If she only knew how much I like baiting her, she wouldn't give me such a reaction. It only encourages me.

* * *

FIFTEEN MINUTES LATER, we're the only ones sitting at the outdoor tables behind Lalaland, an ice cream shop in St. Helena. Mallory starts talking the moment we're alone with our twin scoops of lemon cake ice cream. "I have big plans."

It's like someone loosened the cork on a bottle of champagne, and Mallory's energy sent the thing sky high. Once she starts talking, she can't seem to stop. "I want to develop our land and sell to some of the growers who need additional fruit for their wine making, plus I want to expand our own winery and make it commercially competitive. I'm also looking into leasing some land or…"

She stops and licks a drip from her ice cream cone before it can run down her hand. One second longer, and I'd have licked it from her skin.

I know I sort of coerced her into this date as payback for helping her with her ex, but my brain, my pulse, my skin…no part of me has gotten the memo. She mesmerizes me with every gesture and every thought.

I lean a little closer, testing her. The space between us feels intimate and electrically charged all at once. She doesn't back away, so I lift a finger as though I plan to trace the outline of her cheek. Her gray eyes heat, and the soft skin of her throat quivers as she swallows.

But I don't touch her. Instead, I back away. "Sorry. I thought you had a bug on your cheek." I tap the apple of her cheek softly, and her lips press together before she swats me.

"I did not have a bug." She frowns as though I've insulted her.

"Not anymore. But I had to get closer to be sure." I lean in as though checking again. I'm flirting shamelessly, waiting for her to fight that fake frown. Eventually, a corner of her mouth betrays her, and she smiles.

"Okay, can you tell now? No bug."

She leans closer, getting in my space, and I fucking love it. I inhale her jasmine scent before backing away.

"Sorry. My mistake." I can't help the grin from spreading across my face.

We reassume our positions, leaning back in our respective chairs, but I feel an invisible filament connecting us now that wasn't there before. I don't know exactly why I'm pushing her. Maybe I am just a flirt like everyone believes.

No, that's not it. It's her. I like her.

"So why now? Is there a reason your family has never developed the land for wine growing before now?" I ask the question calmly, but I can hear my siblings' voices in my head telling me that we need any advantage we can get. If I'm the first one she's telling about her plans, maybe I can get first dibs on the future harvests, which we desperately need.

"Yeah. The reason is my parents. They were never interested. But they made a deal with me about ten years ago that they'll cede control to me on my thirty-third birthday, and that's coming up in a few months." The softness in her voice would feel like satin if I could touch it, yet I sense sadness there too.

"This is a good thing, right?" I know I'm no financial wizard like my older brothers, but I'm smart enough. Yet I feel like I'm missing the point here, and I hate it.

My eyes snag as her tongue slips out to lick the melting yellow ice cream. Watching her, I feel my dick jump in my pants. Her eyes flit around, and she takes a few more swipes at the ice cream, seemingly lost in thought.

"I thought so, but now...ugh."

Still not understanding, I get up and pace around the patio. My ice cream is nearly gone and I bite into the cone before chucking the remains in the trash.

"Did you just...?" Mallory has her hand on her chest as though she's witnessed a car accident. "The cone is the best part."

Laughing, I return to the bench next to her. "Sorry. I thought the ice cream was the best part."

"Nah, the ice cream is just a warm-up before the waffle cone. I can't believe you threw yours away."

"Sorry. Won't happen again."

I expect her to say something about how it won't happen because this is the first and last time we'll ever eat ice cream together. I'm well aware of her assertion that this is a one-and-done situation, even if every fiber of my being resents that idea.

"Good. Better not."

"So tell me about the 'ugh.' What was that about."

"Oh, just that my ex convinced my parents to put us both in charge of the business. Like I need a babysitter. They've always liked him, and they want me to get married and have babies. They think I can do both if he's here to share the burden of the business."

"They're *your* parents. Just convince them otherwise."

"You don't know my parents. They're…unconventional. And Felix figured out how to work them. He's an asshole, but he's smarter than I realized."

"There has to be a legal loophole that would keep him out. He's not a blood relative, and you're the rightful heir."

"My mother said the only thing that would keep him out of my life and out of my business is if I have some other husband to help me run the place. Which isn't going to happen because I'm done with marriage. Felix saw to that by being the delightful human he is. I'm done with a capital D."

I don't know why it disappoints me to hear her say it. It's not like I'm looking for a wife. But there's something resigned and sad about the way she rules out love. Someone like her—feisty, gorgeous, smart—she should have everything.

"Families can be tough," I agree.

She tilts her head. "Speaking from experience? I always thought you Corbetts were damn near perfect."

"Hardly. What makes you think that?"

Mallory shrugs. "I remember back when I was friends with Beatrix, you all seemed so close—there was always commotion and friendly bickering at your house. I envied it, being an only child."

"You got the bickering part right. We're still like that today, only the barbs are more real. Mostly them telling me I fucked something up."

I swallow hard, unsure why I'm admitting this to her, but I've watched her drop her facade tonight and it makes me want to show her who I am beneath the shell of what people see.

"Are they hard on you, or are you hard on yourself?" She asks the question quietly, innocently, like it doesn't pierce through nearly thirty years of truth.

When I meet her gaze, I see a look of understanding that can only be based on experience.

"Both. I guess. I don't know." I inhale a full breath of air and let it out. "I just feel like the pretty face who isn't smart enough to do anything but network and hire people, the job no one else wants."

"That's not how I see you, for what it's worth." She shrugs, but I want to tell her it's worth a hell of a lot. Instead, I just nod.

The night sky is dark all around us—not just overhead. That's the beauty of the vast area of open land where we're lucky enough to live. It means I don't even have to look up to see a shooting star drop right out of the night sky in front of us.

"Did you see that?" Mallory gasps. There's no denying the magic of something bigger and brighter charting a path through the sky. I'm grateful for the change of subject.

"I did. It's good luck."

She lets out a long exhale. "I'm gonna take your word for it. I need a little luck right now if I'm going to get things straightened out so I can do what I know is right for Autumn Lake."

She brings her fingers to her temples as though the conversation gives her a headache. Reaching for her, I grasp her fingers and lower them so I can see her face. I don't let go of her hands. Looking down, Mallory studies our connected fingers, but she doesn't pull away.

"Maybe you shouldn't be so quick to dismiss the marriage idea." I say it before I can talk myself out of it. And I should have talked myself out of it.

"What?"

I don't explain my thoughts about her being deserving of love because we barely know each other. Instead, I offer brevity. "Don't let Felix spoil the ideal of what marriage could be, is all."

She nods slowly. "Yeah. Maybe." Her expression is wary, and she withdraws her hands. "Anyhow, Mary—you met her at the pub—thinks I should play hardball and marry someone else so Felix will have no choice but to buzz off."

She rolls her eyes. Maybe it's petty jealousy, but the idea of her marrying someone else grates at me. And getting rid of her ex feels like the Holy Grail.

The situation is almost too perfect. She needs someone to get between her ex and his plans to butt in where he has no right to insert himself. I need to secure land to grow grapes or establish a preferential land agreement with someone willing to sell to us.

It's a moonshot idea, but I feel emboldened to take it. "Fine. You concocted a fake engagement easily enough to get Felix off your case. Sounds like you should just get married. To me."

ash

"Wʜᴀᴛ?" Mallory stares at me.

I have nearly the same response to my own idea the second the words leave my mouth. "I know, it's crazy, but we haven't detested each other too much tonight, so maybe it could work."

"Did you just hear yourself? I think a marriage should be based on more than just 'not detesting' the other person."

"I know. And yes, I did. Forget it. The idea is crazy."

I'm about to go back into the ice cream place and order a plain cone just to appease her when she holds up a finger. Slurping the last of the ice cream from her cone, she lets it melt in her mouth while looking at the same shooting star sky that made me come up with such an insane plan.

She crunches into the cone and stands. "Really is the best part," she says through a mouthful of waffle crumbs. "Hang on. Lemme think this through. Maybe we should get married."

"Wait, what? You just said it's crazy."

"So did you."

"Because it is." And I shouldn't like the idea even a little bit. I'm not the marrying kind. Then again, it sure would dispel all the talk about me being a man-slut. Maybe then I'd have better luck making deals with new growers and convincing the best employees to work for us.

I look back at the sky because it's clearly doing weird things to our brains. All I see is darkness with pinpricks of light where the stars flicker a million miles from here. They look so harmless, and yet we both seem to be losing our minds.

She starts walking away from the patio, so I follow her because I think she's saying words. When I get closer, I realize she's actually quietly singing a Taylor Swift song, which is equally troubling. I think I liked her better when she was angry and feisty. That, I could handle. This is scaring me a little.

"Why are you…singing?" It's not the most important question, but it's still one I'd like her to answer.

"What? Oh, it's just something I do when I need to think."

"Always Taylor Swift?"

"Mostly." By now, we're in the gravel parking lot behind the string of shops, and my car is the only one in sight. "Just so I'm clear, did you just say we should get married to keep my ex out of my business plans and satisfy my parents' need to see me married off? I heard that right, didn't I?"

I gulp oxygen instead of breathing it. This is my chance to backtrack and tell her it must have been a stiff wind that distorted my words, and I most definitely do not want to be her husband.

Fake husband.

"It wouldn't be a real thing. Just, you know, on paper so you could get that douchebag off your case. After a year or whatever, we'll tear up the paper and go on with our lives. Your folks will see that you're perfectly capable of running your business without your ex, and after we've established that, we'll each go our merry ways."

"What do you get out of it?" She points a finger at my chest, but her expression is more confused than accusing. That makes two of us.

I look up at the sky as though I'm casting about, trying to come up with something. "Well, I…I guess maybe there's a way this benefits me too. Like, for example, my reputation for dating a lot of women has been getting in the way of business." I explain the recent problem with Soltero. "If I'm seen as tied down, I'll be free to wine and dine growers without anyone's husband looking twice."

"Seriously? People judge you like that?"

"Yeah. People judge."

She nods. "Yeah, I know they do." I wonder if she's referring to me or to herself, but she doesn't say more.

I nod as well. "We need to expand our distribution in order to keep our growth projections on track, and that means we need to produce more wine, so I can't be the problem child in the bunch."

I'm a terrible liar, and I feel disingenuous because my siblings basically sent me to this dinner with the idea of buttering Mallory up, even if she doesn't seem suspicious.

"You need to buy grapes." She nods, understanding where I'm going.

"Yes. But I don't want you to think I'm trying to manipulate you into something for my benefit." It's exactly what I'm doing. The problem is the more time I spend with her, the more I want any arrangement that binds us together. And it has nothing to do with grapes.

She dismisses the thought with a wave of her hand. "It's business. You'd be doing me a huge favor, and I'd want you to benefit from the arrangement."

The flirtatious connection that's been building disappears,

and I suddenly hate that I turned the conversation to business. But the fire in her eyes and her genuine smile make up for it.

"Really?" I ask.

"Really. This could work, Dash." For the first time tonight, I see the clouds clear from her expression. Without knowing what was bothering her, I had no way of making it happen before. I tried to entertain her with my stories, and her laughter seemed genuine, but it still hung there—that cloud.

Now I understand that she's been buckling under the weight of her asshole ex and his hold on her. And now…I have a chance to make that cloud disappear. I want to be the one who accomplishes that for her.

One dinner with this woman, and she fucking *has* me.

Leaning on my car, I scrub a hand down my face and try to calculate how much wine I had at dinner. We shared a bottle, and I didn't finish my second glass. If I come back after tonight with an inside track on Mallory's first harvest once she starts growing grapes, I'll look like a hero.

It all makes sense. She doesn't seem to have any problem with it, even if it feels like a shard of metal is wedged under my breastbone, trying to dig out my heart.

There's another reason that getting married appeals to me, one that I'm not willing to say out loud. It's been growing inside my head to the point of being a near shout: I'm sick and tired of my reputation as the local heartbreaker, the man-slut who can't ever seem to settle down. True, I've done my part to encourage the image over the years, but not lately. It's been over a year since I've hooked up with anyone, but all anyone seems to remember is the string of one-night stands that became a habit in my twenties.

I'm nearly thirty now, and it's possible that I'm broken. Maybe I don't have what it takes to appeal to a woman long-term. Or maybe I need a jump start on rewriting expectations. Being married to Mallory for a year could convince the folks around here that I'm a worthwhile investment too.

Maybe I'll even convince myself.

That's not something I'm even considering telling the woman who's contemplating giving me a shot at not one but two things that could change my life. I'll just stay quiet and let her think she's getting the better end of the deal, which is the only reason she's still here with me. I'd like to see the easy smile she's worn for the past ten minutes more permanently on her face.

"So…how're we going to do this so it looks legit? You heard Felix. People talk around here, and he'll start making noise if it seems like we're trying to pull a fast one." Mallory's eyes dance, and I'm tempted to pull her into my arms right now and show her exactly how legit I can make us look.

Instead, I lie. "We'll need to make sure people around here see that we're dating, but we'll have to be so comfortable with each other that they believe it's been going on a while."

"Yes. We should be so smitten that we seem oblivious to onlookers. It'll convince people we're in love and have been for a while, so they'll start to believe they must've known about it, even if they didn't."

"Gonna take some good acting on my part, but I think I can manage to convince folks I'm in love." I feel my dick twitch in my pants as I utter the word *love*, and it surprises me. I shouldn't be turned on by it, but I can't deny that I'm a little bit excited to fake being in love with her.

She swats my shoulder. "Glad you feel confident in your acting chops. Might be harder for me." She grins, and I can't tell if she's kidding. I hope so.

I duck my head close to her ear and whisper, "I was in the high school play. I have practice, you know." I hear the soft catch in her breath. Backing away, I run a finger down her cheek.

She shakes herself out of a semi-trance and squares her shoulders. It's on.

Gripping my bicep, she pulls me toward her and coos so

seductively it gives me goose bumps. "Yeah? Which play? What was your role?"

"I played Christian in *Cyrano de Bergerac*." I can barely get the words out because my dick is pressing hard against my zipper now.

She takes a step back and laughs. I inhale a needed breath.

"Seriously? Talk about typecasting. So you were the pretty-faced guy who needed poetry and one-liners from your romantic friend in order to woo Roxane?"

I swallow hard at the memory. "I auditioned for Cyrano himself, but…"

"Hard to play against type, I guess."

"Yeah, and like the walking hard-on I was back then, I fell hopelessly for my leading lady. Guess I couldn't tell the difference between acting and the real thing." I laugh, thinking back on my inexperience with women. "It took me months to get over her. Not that I ever told her or admitted it to my friends. Or anyone, really."

Her eyes flit to mine. "So this is the first you're letting that secret out in the world?"

I shrug. "Guess so. There you have it, Marshmallow, my soul bared before you. But don't worry. I've learned a few things since then. I know the difference between acting and reality now. I can totally play this role for you without falling in love, trust me."

Her expression clouds. A crease takes up residence between her eyes, and the corners of her mouth tip down. I want to erase all of it, but more than that, I want to understand why my high school theater role bothers her. Or maybe it has nothing to do with me. I want to understand that even more.

"You okay?"

She blinks the creases away and forces a smile. "Yeah. Fine. Of course I trust you not to fall in love. We're adults."

I don't know her well, but I know she hides something behind that smile. If nothing else, my inquisitive part intends to find out why she wears that mask. There is no reason our fake marriage can't be a learning experience.

"Guess we should go places together whenever we can so we're seen—we've already been together at the grocery store and Dark Horse. That works in our favor. How long do you think we'll need to act like we're falling in love before it's reasonable to get married?" she asks, all business, taking her phone out to consult her calendar.

I'm impressed at her matter-of-factness, even if a tiny part of my ego deflates at how easily she treats our fake marriage like a fake marriage.

Yeah, yeah, I just heard it.

"Are you serious? You're going to calendar it?"

Her gray eyes sparkle, but she's all business. "Yes. And you should too. Let's say I asked you out a couple of weeks ago."

I laugh. "You did."

She glares. "Yeah. Let's include the part about how you blew me off at first. Also believable because plenty of women around here think you're a pompous heartbreaker."

Her characterization stings a little, but I'm not above acknowledging my reputation. More than a few women probably don't have nice things to say about me.

"Fair enough," I concede. "But then we did go out, and the attraction surprised us both. You saw another side of me than what you thought you knew."

"Maybe you saw the same in me. It caught us both by surprise how we'd misjudged each other."

"And the physical chemistry was off the charts."

She laughs, and it softens her eyes. "Of course it was. Orgasms for days."

"That's how I roll." I smile, wanting her to believe it. "Then I'd say we started seeing each other on the down low to keep prying eyes away from our budding romance. My siblings knew, of course, but we swore them to secrecy. We were worried that other people's opinions would kill the intense feelings we couldn't ignore."

"Makes sense." Her voice is soft and sultry, her eyes wide and clear. "So that puts us at, what, a month or so into a whirlwind courtship? That tracks with getting so swept up in our feels that we got engaged quickly."

"If you say so. I have no experience in this area. I don't do relationships."

"Trust me, it happens. Maybe not to us, but it happens. So fast-forward to a week or two from now when we're at a big event, and we just can't keep our hands off each other despite the prying eyes."

My eyebrows bounce. "Oh, I think I'll be able to play that part quite convincingly."

Mallory rolls her eyes. "Yeah, I'll bet." She looks at the ceiling, calculating something. "It's perfect, actually. We have the gala for the new theater coming up next week. That'll be the night. You can do something alpha and possessive because you can't stand looking at me from across the room and not being able to touch me."

I almost laugh at her passionate description and the careful scrolling through dates on her phone. "Sure. I can be possessive."

Is it my imagination, or do her eyes heat at the thought of it? Well, game on, sister. If she wants an Oscar-worthy performance, she's going to get one.

"Okay, sounds like a plan. So we arrive separately, but then we're caught in a compromising position? Or you get possessive if another man gets too close?"

"You really like the idea of me being possessive."

"I do. No one's ever done that for me before."

"Fools, all of them. And where are they now?"

"Exactly. Certainly not at the gala with a possessive hand on my lower back."

The scenarios are getting me more excited than they should.

The wood in my pants will give me away in another minute, and she'll probably call the whole thing off.

I think about baseball instead. Boring baseball. A no-hitter on a brutally hot day when I'm miserable sitting on a plastic seat. That does the trick.

When I've calmed myself enough to look her in the eye, I find her studying me as though she's never seen me before. She has a faraway look I don't understand.

"You are not at all what I expected." It seems hard for her to admit it. She shakes her head as though she wishes it wasn't true.

Yeah, well, that makes two of us.

"Oh? Why's that?" I ask. She brought it up, so she gets to be the one to spill her guts first. I'm afraid that if I start talking, I'll inadvertently say something I'll regret, like telling her I can't stop staring at her.

Don't want to stop. Won't stop.

"You're a good guy, Dash. Let's just leave it at that."

I nod. But I don't agree.

CHAPTER 14

ash

Me: Have you checked your schedule yet?

Mallory: What?

Me: Dinner. When are you free for dinner?

Mallory: I'm sorry, who is this?

Me: Haha.

Me: ??

Me: You must have forgotten to respond. I get how that can happen. No harm, no foul.

Me: um, okay…

Mallory: Right? It sucks when that happens.

Me: Can I ever make this up to you?

Mallory: Diamonds wouldn't hurt. And sure,
dinner on Wednesday

"CHANGE OF PLANS," I say, walking into the lunchroom of the brown barn, where my siblings wait to start our meeting.

"Thanks for gracing us with your presence," Archer grumbles.

Normally, I'd take the hit for being late, but today, they can all work on Dash Time, which lags approximately thirty minutes behind normal time. I dare them to be annoyed with me after I tell them what I accomplished on my night out with Mallory.

I even take a moment to pour myself a cup of coffee and mix in some oat milk before taking a seat.

"Sure, take your time. Would you like one of us to cook you breakfast while you're getting settled?" Archer grumbles.

"Oh, cool it, Arch," PJ says. Since she got engaged to Archer's billionaire best friend, Colin Hathaway, she's had no problem putting him in his place. It's nice to see someone in the family call him on his bullshit moods. "What's the change in plans?"

Four pairs of eyes stare at me, and I meet each of them before beginning. "I worked something out with Mallory Rutherford. We should be set on grapes as soon as she plants her first harvest."

Jax grins like a canary-eating cat. "I'll bet you worked it out. Her favorite way of doing business."

"Look, just because you two crashed and burned three years ago doesn't mean she's not a good person."

"Mallory Rutherford, a good person?" he asks. "Okay, now I really know she has you bamboozled. The sex must've been off the charts."

"Would you cool it?" Beatrix smacks him across the shoulder. "You're happy now. Leave Mallory out of it. And let Dash talk, for heaven's sake."

Jax looks chastened. He leans back in his chair, head down. "Fine. Sorry. You know I'm just messing with you, right?"

I nod. "And you'd better change your tune about her because she's about to become a part of the family."

I let that concept land without explanation, just to enjoy the chaos in the room for a minute. There are a lot of "what the hell?" and "sorry, what?" comments thrown about.

Then I explain our arrangement and how it benefits us both. My siblings seem appeased by the explanation, but then the questions begin again.

"Are you really going to be okay being married to her, even if it's only temporary?" Beatrix asks. She can't sit still when she thinks, and she's already pacing circles around the room.

"I think it'll be fine," I say, realizing I haven't thought everything through. The fake engagement seemed harmless enough, but when we're married, we'll be living together. She and I ought to talk about how to pull that off without annoying each other or getting in each other's way.

Jax pins me with a stare, face a mask of seriousness. "All jokes aside, this is Mallory. She's out for herself, and I don't want you to lose sight of that. Just...don't let your guard down, okay?"

I wave a hand. "I'm a big boy." Besides, he sees what everyone else does in Mallory. I'm the one in the family who's a good judge of character. "I don't see red flags, so let's not assume the worst, okay? All for the good of the business."

I get some wary nods and a smile from PJ, who sits next to me. "I kind of love the idea, honestly."

"Yeah? Why's that?"

"Because I always thought you got a raw deal in terms of your reputation, and it's not fair. This will shut people up, and they need some shutting up."

I reach over and wrap an arm around PJ to hug her. "Thanks, PJ." The youngest boy and youngest girl need to stick together. We've always had a special bond.

As to the rest of my siblings, they'll just have to go along with it because Mallory and I are setting things in motion at the gala this weekend.

"As long as you're good with it, so am I," Beatrix says. My brothers nod in agreement.

"I am." At least, I think I am.

CHAPTER 15

*M*allory

Dash: Pick you up at seven

Me: I'll meet you there

Dash: Wouldn't a fiancé pick you up?

Me: Not tonight. You had to work late

Dash: I did?

Me: Yes. Making a little extra dough to buy me a present

Dash: Ah. Message received

I'M NERVOUS. I shouldn't be nervous because this is about the one-millionth fancy gala I've been to in my life, and I know how to do this. I know how to dress, work the room, smile at the appropriate people, and tug them along on the invisible string of hope.

Only tonight, I'm not going to hint at any of those things.

"At least the dress is gorgeous. The rest of you...kind of a mess," Mary confirms, standing next to me and assessing me in the full-length mirror. We're a mismatched pair, her wearing a pair of pale yellow overalls and red lipstick with her hair in a frizzy knot and me in a floor-length dress, bone-straight hair, and no makeup.

Rufus is splayed out on the floor, snoring like a bulldozer.

"Thanks, Mare. Not really the look I'm going for, though." She's right, however. The dress is perfect for tonight. Long, silky, black. It hugs every curve, and my four-inch stiletto heels make me look taller and slender.

Then there's the rest of me. Dark circles rim my eyes because I haven't slept in two days worrying about what will happen tonight with Dash. I'm not sure I'm a good enough actress to pretend I'm smitten with him. Or to convince myself that I'm not.

"It just feels like a lot. It's stressing me out."

"The lying part?

"Yes. I don't know if I can make it seem believable that we've been secretly falling for each other when I'm pretty sure I've forgotten how to do that."

Mary studies my dress in the mirror before hiking it up at the waist. "Are you sure this wouldn't look better with a belt?"

I laugh. "I'm sure."

"It needs something. It's too plain otherwise. Do you have jewelry or something? Or maybe it's your hair. Can we do something to it so it's not hanging down limp?"

Given that I went into St. Helena earlier for a blowout, I'm not thrilled with Mary's opinion of my hair, but now that I've been studying myself in the mirror for the past ten minutes, I have to admit she's right. Something is missing, and it's not just undereye concealer.

"You think I should curl it?"

"No, I think *I* should curl it." Mary tromps off toward my bedroom, where I hear her rustling around. She returns a moment later with my blow-dryer, a round brush, and a curling iron. "You have all these tools, yet you go to a salon for a blowout?" She tsks and walks right past me to the kitchen where she opens and slams cupboards.

I stand in my living room, the only place in my house with a full-length mirror, and contemplate biting my nails. The only thing that prevents me is the fresh coat of polish from my manicure earlier today.

A second later, I hear a staccato popping sound in my kitchen, followed by the slam of the microwave door. Mary appears with a bowl of popcorn and a bottle of beer. She hands the bowl to me.

"Here. This will keep your hands busy and won't ruin your appetite for tonight."

"Thanks. Where did you find popcorn here?" I try to recall buying it, and I'm pretty sure I never did.

"I brought my own. Never trust another person to have the right kind of snacks."

Gesturing to the beer in her hand, I assume it's part two of her plan to calm me down. "I don't want to be tipsy before I get there, but thanks."

She holds it close to her chest while she plugs in the curling iron. "Sorry, mate. This is for me. You need to keep your wits about you and remember why you're doing all this. For the sake of your future, the one you've been busting your arse for all these years going to business school."

"I know. You're right."

"Good. Now let me fix your hair and do your makeup. One benefit to growing up in a town where there's not much to do is my friends and I were great at makeovers. I'll have you looking so good that it'll make Dash's job easy. Everyone in the room will believe he's fallen for you."

I laugh at her confidence. "He's got some acting chops. He'll be able to pull it off either way. I'm just worried about keeping up my end."

Mary chuckles and shakes her head.

"What?"

"You really think you're going to *marry* Dashiell Corbett and not fall in love with him?"

"Come on, you've met him. He's not all that."

She bites her lower lip and shrugs. "I have seen him, and he's quite nice to look at. And his hot meter went up even more when he sent Felix off running scared."

"His hot meter?" I laugh, gathering all my makeup supplies in one hand and pulling a chair over so Mary can get to work. "I did enjoy that, I'll admit. But now that I'm getting to know him a little bit, the spell is broken. He's just a regular guy."

"So you're telling me you don't fancy him even just a little bit?" Mary picks up some undereye concealer and unscrews the cap. She squirts a little onto the back of her hand and uses a brush to dab it beneath my eyes before blending it. Presto, my dark circles are gone.

"He's fine. He's no different from any other man I've gone on a date with in hopes of laying some groundwork in the winery world for when I start cooking on all burners and relaunch Autumn Lake. It's just business."

Lies, lies, and, oh yes, even bigger lies. But maybe if I keep telling them to myself, I won't turn into one of his groupies. The last thing I need is to develop feelings for a guy who doesn't do relationships.

"Look down." Mary sweeps some powder across my eyelids. "If I wasn't already your friend, I'd really dislike you. Your skin is perfect. Not a blemish."

"Thanks. You grow up on a farm in California, you wear a lot of sunscreen."

"So you and I aren't that different in how we were raised, I'm discovering." She dips a brush into a pot of liquid eyeliner. "Close your eyes."

I obey, slightly worried Mary and her friend in the English countryside may have a different style of makeover than I'm looking for tonight. I hope she doesn't overdo it. I feel her dabbing little dots onto my lashes and then feel a breeze as she fans my face with her hands.

"You can open." She studies my face like I'm a work of art, stepping back and tilting her head before picking up another brush. She dabs liquid blush onto my cheeks, fans it with her fingers, then applies lipstick with a tiny brush. Another head tilt. Then a nod. She seems satisfied.

Before she lets me look, Mary gets to work with the curling iron, and moments later, I feel bouncy curls hit my shoulders as she releases them. I brace myself for the decent chance I'm going to have to scrub off half the makeup and straighten what I'm certain are ringlets worthy of a schoolgirl.

A few minutes later, Mary has finished her beer and my hair. She leads me over to the full-length mirror to see her handiwork.

I have to do a double take. The woman staring back at me in the mirror looks a thousand percent better than how I normally do when I try my own hand at makeup.

"Wow. You're really good at this."

Mary blushes but covers by going back to my kitchen for another beer. She returns a moment later, tapping it against her cheeks to cool them.

"Glad you like it. More subtle, yes? Keeps focus on your gorgeous eyes, and then we go for red on the lips. Boom. Dash won't know what hit him."

"Ha. I don't think that's the goal tonight."

"Now you're being absolutely ridiculous. It's always the goal." She picks up the liquid eyeliner and gives my eyes a smoky rim that will definitely get Dash's attention. Then she waves her hand like the fairy godmother she is and sends me on my way.

CHAPTER 16

ash

Mallory: Running late

Me: No prob

Mallory: Fashionably late

Me: What's the difference?

Mallory: The more nervous I get, the later I am

Me: Just come, honey. I'll calm your nerves

Mallory: Too sweet. Made me even more nervous

Me: Fuck off, jerk. Better?

Mallory: Be there in a sec!

"SHE WAS SUPPOSED to be here an hour ago." I put my phone away and loosen my tie because it feels like a vise. My dark suit feels stiff across my shoulders, and I look around the rustic indoor event space for signs I'm overdressed.

I know I'm properly attired. This isn't my first time at a fundraiser, and everyone who drives around in a pickup truck and muddy boots during the week has turned out in finery tonight. It would be weird for me not to dress up.

The room is half full even though it's thirty minutes past the starting time for the cocktail hour. Guess the other half of the town knows to come fashionably late. The guests mingle with stemless wineglasses in their hands and nibble on hors d'oeuvres passed around on serving trays.

If I've been to one of these events, I've been to a hundred. Always some sort of raw fish on some sort of crispy thing; always something overly cute like a shot glass filled with tomato soup and accompanied by a tiny triangle of grilled cheese.

I could eat fifty of these appetizers and still want to grab a burger by the end of the night.

Beatrix grabs us two glasses of cabernet from where they're lined up on the bar for guests. "She'll come. She lives for these things." Beatrix rolls her eyes, and I bristle at her opinion of Mallory, which seems influenced by my brother.

I told my siblings about our arrangement because they need to pretend they've known about us for a while. They were all pretty impressed with the potential business benefits, and they all assume I'm in it for the sex. I don't care enough to set them straight.

Unfortunately, my sister is like a bloodhound when it comes to uncovering secrets. It's her superpower. One look at me when I walked in tonight, and she knew something was up. She's been plastered to my side, trying to get to the bottom of it ever since.

"You did something different with your hair," she accuses.

"Did not."

"You smell…different. Like fresh soap instead of that sport-scented body spray you think women like."

"You're insane. I don't wear body spray."

"And you're…fidgety. Why do you keep checking the door? What's the big deal if Mallory arrives fashionably late? That's normal for her."

"You know why. We're supposed to be seen together, and I want it to go smoothly."

Even the strongest of people would find it hard not to cave under the questioning scrutiny of my sister, but I usually manage to send her chasing some new bit of gossip because I'm observant and I notice things.

Case in point: Lloyd Perkins stands alone at the bar, checking his phone every two minutes. He's hoping he'll hear his Reserve Cabernet has gotten a "best of" designation in *Wine Spectator* magazine.

Across the room, Sally Perkins, Lloyd's wife, holds court with a group of friends, laughing and trying to get her husband's attention because he's been so focused on work that she feels sidelined. Every minute or so, she glances in his direction, but she misses it each time his eyes roam toward her.

I point these things out to Beatrix, but she seems way more interested in why I keep eyeing the door to the place.

"I'm just looking around, being observant, like always."

Noticing things makes me good at my job, like finding the right employee for the right position, which is often completely different from what they think they want. I shouldn't be noticing everyone in the room right now, not when my sleuth of a sister clocks my every move.

"Being observant about Mallory, you mean." Her eyebrows go up so high they nearly hit her hairline. "You like her."

"No. I just want it to go well."

"You really like her. Tell me, or I'll corner her when she comes in and make things very uncomfortable for the two of you." She raises an eyebrow.

"Don't even think about it."

"Oh, it's happening, pal, unless you spill it right now. What's with you and Mallory?"

I glare at her. She glares back. I take a step away and turn my back. She comes around to the other side of me and gets in my space. Now I can't see the door, and I'm even more edgy, so I turn back around, too overwrought to fend her off.

"You should work for the government, Trix. Spies would be flipping and blurting secrets left and right."

Beatrix smiles. "Yeah? And what are yours?"

With a glass of wine already coursing through my bloodstream, I tell her that I may have felt a twinge of interest the few times we've been together. "And that's all."

She gives me a knowing smile, but I know I can trust my sister not to say a word to the rest of my family. She may know how to get information out of anyone, but she's discreet and trustworthy.

Ordinarily, I'd let it go. It's no one's business who I fuck or why, but in this case, I feel the need to be clear. "It's purely business for both of us. We're only keeping up the appearance that we're a couple. It stops as soon as we're out of the public eye."

Ironically, this plan and the time I've spent texting back and forth all week with Mallory have me twisted in knots. I expected the all-business Mallory once we made it clear we were co-conspirators, but instead, her texts have been flirty, teasing, and fun. If I'm not careful, I could fall for my own lies about us being a couple.

Relax, asshole. She has boundaries, even if you don't.

"Okay." She holds up her hands in protest. "Whatever you say."

"That's what I say," I bark. The anticipation has my skin crawling with nerves. I need Mallory to get here already so I can stop thinking about how all this will go down. The last time I remember feeling jittery like this was when I was in that damn play.

"Ugh, he's here." She tips her head at where Graham, our half brother, stands near the bar drinking red wine.

"Cleans up okay. At least he owns a suit," I say.

"I know it's not his fault that Dad screwed around on Mom, but it's still hard not to take my anger out on him. And I feel like he wants something from us."

"He wants family. He said that to me and PJ."

"Don't be a sucker, Dash. He's Kingston Corbett's son. He wants more than that."

We're both staring at him when he sees us. I give him a wave. He raises a hand in greeting and looks at my sister before turning back to the bar.

"I think he's aware you don't like him."

"Yeah. No welcome wagon here."

"Ironic because he is growing the exact grapes we need," I mention.

"No way. Nope." Beatrix shakes her head.

"I know. I get it."

Slugging down most of the wine my sister handed me, I feel it hit my nerves like a balm. I feel only slightly better, and I'm tempted to start on a third drink before Mallory even gets here.

It's a foreign feeling. I've never felt nervous about a woman before, and I tell myself it's because we're about to put on a show. A small flame of concern licks at me, but I ignore the voice telling me I'm nervous because this feels like more of a real date than our actual one.

I'm about to reach for another glass of wine when a swish of black fabric catches my eye. In an instant, my entire focus lands on the woman who just walked into the room. Her hair rolls down the front of her dress in shiny waves, and I can see her eyes sparkle from here. She doesn't see me, so I have a moment to drink her in without censoring my hungry gaze.

A second later, her eyes meet mine, and I school my expression, clenching my teeth and fixing my jaw as I move through the crowd toward her. I realize halfway to the door that I didn't say a word to my sister. Just left her hanging and disappeared on her.

At least she understands why.

I give myself a few more seconds to take her in before spending the rest of the night pretending I can't keep my hands off her.

Dark hair falling in loose waves around her face like she had it wound up in a bun until five minutes ago, and now it's wild and free.

Her eyes are dark, cheeks bright. Lips a deep cherry red.

And that dress. Holy shit. It's a plain swath of silk hanging from her shoulders by spaghetti straps, and the soft fabric hugs every curve. Her arms hang gracefully by her sides, and somehow, she manages to look utterly unfazed by the attention of every set of eyes in the room, and also like she owns the place.

I could just stand here staring, but I have a job to do, so I weave through the crowd and make my way to her in seconds.

"Hey." I extend a hand toward Mallory, and her graceful, manicured fingers land in my palm. Wrapping my hand around hers, I squeeze, hoping to reassure her if she's as nervous as I feel. Instead, a zing of electricity shoots from her palm to mine, and I almost drop her hand.

My eyes shoot to hers to ascertain whether she felt the same thing, but she gives no indication.

"Hi." Her voice is quiet and breathy as she leans in to kiss my cheek. Purely friendly. We'll play our parts and ramp up to something gossip-worthy later on, but this is just a cursory greeting. And I hope we'll be able to keep up the act we've planned.

Sure, but as her lips graze my cheek, she might as well be setting fire to my skin with a lit match.

Fuck me. Is she doing this on purpose?

I back away and lock eyes with hers, trying to discern whether she felt close to what I had just experienced. She gives me a closed-lipped smile and moves alongside me into the crowded room. She doesn't seem nervous, gliding along in heels that make her nearly as tall as me.

Mallory surveys the room, her sharp eyes missing nothing. I follow her gaze, noticing who's with whom, who seems to be with a date I've never seen before, where each of my siblings is, and whether anyone is looking at Mallory and me.

Curling her hand around my bicep, Mallory tips her head against my shoulder like she's happy to see me after too long an absence. Her hair sweeps past my nose, and I inhale the sweet scent of jasmine and some other flower I can't place. I don't really know my flowers, but we have jasmine all over Buttercup Hill, so that one's a gimme.

"Ready to make an entrance?" Mallory asks, taking us on a winding route through the room that ensures we pass by as many people as possible.

"Ready if you are." I'm vaguely aware of the people we pass noticing us together. I make a point of running my hand down Mallory's bare back and the silk of her dress, my hand lingering on her ass for just a moment before settling around her waist.

More than one person tries to be subtle while pointing out the fact that we're together.

"I'm ready for a cocktail, so that's where we're going first."

We make our way to the bar, and I grab two glasses of wine without asking Mallory whether she'd like red or white. She accepts the glass of red without comment and takes a large sip. It's the only evidence that she may be the least bit nervous about our act tonight.

I'm impressed at her calm under pressure.

"You're gorgeous. Like jaw-dropping, head-turning, I'm-the-luckiest-guy-in-the-room gorgeous." It's the truth, and I realize she's making it very easy to play my role.

"Aw, you're sweet." Her voice sounds as silky as her dress.

"I'm not being sweet. I'm being honest. You're the most stunning woman in the room, which makes me the luckiest man in the room." We're within earshot of everyone at the bar, and a few heads turn. A few people smile and pretend they're not surprised to see us together.

Mallory's eyelashes flutter, and a flush rises on her cheeks. I'm impressed that she can do that on cue.

Or maybe… For a second, I allow myself to imagine that she might feel a shred of something real. Just as quickly, I banish the thought.

Once we've clinked glasses and given the people near the bar something to gossip about, I steer Mallory to a quieter area of the room, keeping my hand on the small of her back.

"That was easy." She glances behind, and her hair flips over her shoulder, the glossy curls bouncing and tantalizing me with that jasmine scent. "By the end of tonight, everyone here will know we're dating."

"No." I lean in and whisper near her ear so there's no chance of misinterpretation. "After tonight, everyone here will know you're *mine*."

I feel her quiver beneath my hand on a shaky inhale.

Good.

She brings her glass to her lips. When they part, I want to run my tongue over her plump bottom lip, but instead, I watch as she takes an unsteady sip. I'm glad I've thrown her off her game. She deserves it after showing up looking like a goddess who takes my fucking breath away.

Being near her, my skin buzzes and I have to remind myself to breathe. I need to know she's not immune to me, and it has nothing to do with convincing other people we're a couple.

I run a hand down the smooth skin of her arm. "Now the

pressure's off. We can just enjoy the night and drink our drinks." I try for a carefree tone, but I'm lying through my teeth. I'm two drinks ahead of her, and it's done nothing to take off the pressure I feel to get everything right tonight.

When my hand reaches her wrist, I brush my fingertips against the soft skin where her pulse beats rapidly. Her head tips against my shoulder, but then she seems to recover her composure, shaking her head.

"Come this way," she says, moving gracefully ahead of me to greet an elderly winemaker whose property is adjacent to Autumn Lake. She kisses him on the cheek and puts a hand on the arm of his dark suit. "Gene, you know my fiancé, Dash Corbett?"

The older man smooths a hand over his full head of white hair and peeks at me over the reading glasses he's using to glance through the auction catalog. In his navy suit, he looks slightly bored, like he's been to a hundred of these events. This is why we need to get Buttercup Hill back on track. I don't want to be sweating it out in a suit thirty years from now because we need to make nice with everyone in town.

He extends his hand. "Gene Bradbury. From Bradbury Acres. Congratulations, Mallory. I didn't know."

"And I didn't know you were producing Shiraz. It's an incredible vintage," she says, putting a hand on his shoulder. This is the Mallory I know, able to work a room and make everyone in it feel special.

"It's already the talk of the town. It's a new bar for the rest of us," I say. He'll hear it ten more times tonight, partly because he makes good wine but also because this is a feel-good event designed to make everyone want to be generous and donate to the new theater.

"You're kind. I could say the same about your Cabs, but you already knew that. Buttercup is legendary. I knew your father back when we were both starting out. He here?"

I shake my head. "No, he doesn't come to these things anymore, now that he has all of us running the winery. He's enjoying his golden years."

"Smart man. Traveling?"

I nod because I'm not about to admit that my father has Alzheimer's when it's still not public knowledge, but it drives home the fact that my father isn't enjoying his golden years on an exotic trip.

Mallory chats with Gene for a few minutes more and I disappear into my head, thinking about my dad and wondering how he'd feel about me entering into a fake marriage in order to fix some of his mistakes. The man who found fault with all of my lazy teenage ways would probably chalk it up to one more irresponsible idea of mine.

When Gene moves off to talk to someone else, Mallory pins me with a stare. "What's wrong?"

"Nothing. Why?"

She continues to fix me with the steely gray of her eyes, and I take the opportunity to look at them. Even in the dim light of the event space, they're luminous, a blue-gray that makes me want to keep looking into their depths.

"You went quiet when Gene mentioned your dad. And it's not like him to miss an event like this when he's better at working the crowd than anyone. I haven't seen him for months. Is everything okay?"

I open my mouth and promptly shut it, unprepared to answer her question or even entertain the idea that she's someone I could confide in. A fake marriage is one thing. Sharing personal family secrets is entirely different.

"Everything's fine," I say with an edge in my voice. She hears it. Her eyes dart around, and she bites her bottom lip, deciding whether to press me or not. Finally, she nods.

"Okay."

"Okay. Thank you for leaving it alone."

She nods again. "Sure."

I look away, but I can feel her studying me. I know I should probably tell her about my dad's condition, but I'm not sure yet if I can trust her. Better to keep our most sensitive family secrets to myself for now.

Instead, I lead her farther from the crowd.

This is one of those moments we talked about, a quick instance when we slip away but stay in view of enough people to get them talking if they see us sneak a kiss. Or something more salacious.

Mallory looks at me expectantly because she sees the opportunity for what it is. Now it's on me to pull out my best acting chops. I kind of wish I'd taken my theater elective more seriously back in tenth grade, but it's bygones now.

"I brought you a present."

"Oh, aren't you sweet?"

I roll my eyes. "Yes. Sweet enough to follow instructions."

She laughs, and it sounds like bells. I want to clear everyone out of the room or stop them from talking so I can listen to this sound without distraction.

I take a small package from the breast pocket of my jacket and hand it to her. "Sorry, I didn't have time to wrap it."

Mallory turns it over in her hand, and the wrapper crinkles. So do the corners of her eyes when she smiles down at the Mallomar candy in her hand. And the tiny flecks of gold dance in her eyes when she looks up at me.

"It's perfect. Thank you." She wraps her arms around my neck and nuzzles my cheek. She's very good at playing this game. Too good. I need to keep my wits about me.

I encircle her waist with one hand and feel her relax into my hold. Sliding a knuckle beneath her chin, I tip her face up to angle toward mine.

She has the same determined look I saw at the bar that night, ready to do what's necessary to convince anyone looking that we're a couple madly in love.

Fine. I can do that too. I block out everyone else in the room, which is easy because I only want to look at her. Plump lips, a wave of heat in her steely eyes. What man would be crazy enough to be this close and not kiss her?

When my lips graze hers, I feel her tremble in my arms. She doesn't hesitate to kiss me back, angling her face to meet mine.

I don't need to pull out any acting chops to bring this home. It feels too good, and she's too perfect. So expert at this game that I forget for a moment that it's an act. I kiss her the way I've been wanting to since that night at the bar when I barely got a taste of her cherry-sweet lips.

Moving my hands into her hair, I'm oblivious now to anyone who might see us. I'm taking what I want right now, and it's not for anyone else's benefit. Except maybe hers…because the way she moans softly as I deepen the kiss can't be heard by anyone else.

Makes me wonder again if maybe, just maybe, she's feeling something for me. And as much as that kind of terrifies me because this is business, a bigger part of me wants her to feel it. I want her to feel what I can't deny I feel.

When we break the kiss, Mallory inhales a long, shaky breath that mirrors how I feel. She wipes her bottom lip with the back of one knuckle and looks up at me, a shy smile playing on her face. "That oughtta do it," she says.

"Yeah. Guess so."

I immediately shut down the shreds of feelings that threaten to derail this entire plan because there can be none.

Eyes on the prize, Dash.

I know very clearly what that prize is—all the cabernet grapes we'll ever need to ensure long-term growth at Buttercup Hill. That can be my only focus. Tiny thoughts about Mallory being an even bigger prize—one I'm starting to believe I want even more than I want what's good for our business—can never enter into the equation.

I know this, and yet…the more I play the role of a guy in love with the woman who's too good for him, the more I find myself starting to believe it.

It's not like I don't know the difference between acting and reality. Maybe the issue is that pretending to be smitten with Mallory Rutherford doesn't require any acting at all.

"If I knew it would feel like that to kiss you, I'd have said yes to a date four seconds after you texted me."

Mallory laughs. "Yeah? So you didn't respond because you thought kissing me would suck?"

"I didn't respond because I'm insane. And now I feel like the luckiest bastard in the room because now I have an excuse to kiss you whenever I want."

"Seems like Christian doesn't need Cyrano to feed him lines. He's a sweet talker all on his own."

I chuckle because I assume she's ribbing me, but the expression on her face says otherwise. Heat in her eyes. Chest heaving beneath that wisp of a dress.

And for the moment, I revel in that, taking in her beauty and believing the charade we've created. But only for a moment. Then I push the thoughts away for good.

CHAPTER 17

$\mathcal{M}$allory

ALL THE BIG fundraising events have live auctions, and it should come as no shock that the people around here like their wine. Everyone has a friend of a friend with access to a rare vintage from a collector who's willing to donate a bottle or two in exchange for a well-placed note of thanks in the auction catalog. One sits atop the black tablecloths on each high table scattered throughout the room.

This isn't a stuffy sit-down affair, but people like to crowd around the tables with drinks and appetizers. Some of the tables have stools around them, and Dash leads me to one where we can perch on seats. The table couldn't be closer to the center of the room if he took out a measuring tape.

"Let's keep up the act, keep being seen as a couple," I mutter.

Dash pulls my stool out and waits until I'm seated before dropping onto his own stool next to me.

"Very chivalrous." I'll never admit this to him, but I'm not hating spending the evening as his date. He's kind and attentive, and being by his side saves me from making useless chitchat with half the people in the room.

"Men should always pull out chairs for you."

I roll my eyes. "Don't feed me your canned lines, mister."

He reaches for my hand sitting limply on my lap and lifts it onto the table. Covering it with his own, he turns his chair to face me. "Let's get one thing clear. Fake relationship or not, nothing I say to you is a line."

The sudden seriousness of his words and tone catches me off guard. "I thought we were just playing our parts." Is he actually… offended by my presumption that this is an act, lines and all?

He nods. "Yeah, there's a hard line I won't cross. And lying falls squarely on the wrong side of that line. Men *should* pull out chairs for you. If they don't or they haven't in the past, it just makes them rude or stupid."

My mouth opens but no words come out. I still can't make sense of why he's so stuck on this point. But I like it. In fact, I'm sick to death of men lying to me to get what they want, so I decide to take him up on his promise not to do it.

"No lying. Got it. I appreciate that."

"Goes both ways, Marshmallow." The smile is back, and I feel a surge of relief even as I gulp at what he's telling me. I need to be honest too.

His dimpled grin is hard to resist. When he turns on the charm and hits me with his thousand-watt smile, I feel a little stir in my chest. I can see why women melt at his feet.

Even the ridiculous nickname is growing on me.

"Sure, Dash. No lying."

He nods and turns back toward the table. We've intentionally mingled with people other than his siblings. The more people outside our immediate circles who see us canoodling, the better; they already know we went on a date.

Keeping his hand on top of mine on the table, Dash leans in

and whispers, "My siblings think what we're doing is a little crazy, but they're playing along."

My eyes go wide because this is the first he's mentioned of telling his siblings. Of course I'd expect that he would, but it's all feeling very real and official. My heart is flitting around in my chest, and I feel flushed.

"What did they say when you told them we're engaged?" I choke out the whispered words because hearing that his family knows makes this all too real. And insane.

"They understand how it benefits us both. They're cool with it. Don't worry." Tell that to the butterflies swarming my chest at the reality of being engaged, fake or not, to the gorgeous man on my arm. Despite the rumors that have circulated for years, Dash doesn't strike me as a careless flirt who's only interested in himself.

If anything, he's gentlemanly and sweet. I never could have known this about him based on the rumors about his lady killing ways, but he's kind of a sweetheart underneath the pretty face and shoulders so broad they're practically tearing his suit.

I rest a hand on his shoulder, then let it slide down his bicep. I have to stop myself from sighing at the muscular curve of his arm, which makes me want to touch more of him.

"Ah, there's the happy couple." I bristle at Felix's raspy voice, which irritates me a little more each time I hear it.

"Nice to see you," I say politely, hoping he'll leave it at that and go away.

He nods. "You too. Always happy to see you." He twirls his finger around a tendril of my hair and tucks it behind my ear. It's too familiar, but that's Felix. Not good with boundaries.

"Get your goddamn hands off my wife." Dash's voice booms in a low, threatening growl. It's not loud enough for anyone to hear beyond our table, but it sends a chill down my spine.

A delicious, beautiful chill I'll feel for days. He's hotter than hot, and it's all I can do not to reach over and lick his neck.

Down, girl. Eat the Mallomar instead.

Felix removes his hand like he touched something hot. "Neanderthal," he mutters, walking away.

"Possessive like that?" Dash asks with a smirk.

"Yes. Exactly like that. Your high school thespian work is really paying off."

His smile dims just a bit, and I worry I've offended him somehow. But then PJ sweeps past Dash and gives him a playful pat on the head. "These seats taken?" She points at the two empties opposite us.

I see Dash start to protest, and PJ tugs at her blond updo with a smile. "Not for us, silly. But there's a reporter here from *Wine Style*, and I want her sitting right in the middle of all the action. Save the other seat, too, in case I nab another reporter." PJ handles press relations and social media for Buttercup Hill, and I know she's good at her job based on the great coverage the winery always gets after events. "Thanks for bailing us out with the offer of your harvest, by the way," she whispers.

I sit bolt upright. Dash mentioned needing grapes when we made our deal, but we never talked about me selling them.

"Hey, am I selling grapes to Buttercup Hill?" I try to keep my tone light.

"What?" Dash looks confused.

"PJ just mentioned it."

He waves a hand. "No, she's thinking of something else," Dash explains. "And she's also annoying."

"Spoken like an older brother."

Now that I watch PJ in action, I see that she curates exactly who she wants to have photographed and does nice things for magazine writers to ensure Buttercup stays on their minds. But I can't help wondering if all of his talk about honesty is just the way he plays his game. He knows how to sweet-talk people. I need to make sure I don't fall victim to it.

"These are all things I'll need to do when Autumn Lake rolls out its first new vintages," I say, taking mental notes. "I'll either need to hire someone like PJ or do it all myself. Kind of have a feeling I'll be doing it myself. At least at first."

I barely realize I'm talking out loud until Dash answers me.

"You can't do everything yourself. You'll burn out. But you'll cross that bridge…"

He's silenced by the tap on a microphone by the auctioneer who's just stepped to the front of the room. He's a tall, barrel-chested man, and with that comes a deep voice. He introduces himself and directs everyone to the auction catalogs on the tables and the numbered paddles we were all given when we entered.

"Who's ready to bid on some wine and do some good for the community?" his voice booms to a round of applause.

"You gonna bid on anything?" Dash asks, thumbing through the catalog and squinting at the vintages of wine offerings by the flickering candle on the table.

I shrug. "There are a couple in there I wouldn't mind drinking someday, but I probably shouldn't be spending big bucks on rare wines if I want to focus on growing a business."

"On the contrary. Bid, win, make a name for yourself here tonight. People will remember it when Autumn Lake's first vintage is ready for tasting. You'll be the one with the discerning taste in wine."

He may have a point. I look around the room and see that everyone has their eyes on the auctioneer, so I focus, taking a pen from my purse so I can mark items that catch my interest.

There's more than just wine here. I note a weekend for two at a posh spa I've never been to, but I need to stick to wine. That's what will get people's attention in this room. Dash is right.

"Let's open with a 1986 bottle of Lafite Rothschild." A hum reverberates through the room. This is a crowd who knows that vintage will go for well over two thousand dollars.

Dash looks at me, and I shake my head. "Too rich for my blood." He pulls my stool a little closer to his. To anyone bothering to look, we seem like a couple. Whispering to each other, little touches, leaning in. But most eyes are focused on the auctioneer who closes bidding on the Lafite Rothschild at twenty-seven hundred dollars.

Applause fills the room, and the bidder, Calliope Bruner, nods and smiles. Everyone knows who she is because her winery is in the middle of Silverado Trail, and she's a fixture at these events. But she plays her cards close to the vest, only associating with the small group at her table, and most of them don't live around here. I don't know anyone in this town who's actually friends with her. Kind of reminds me of me.

She sits with a group of women who surround her protectively. They remind me of the Pink Ladies from the musical *Grease*—one brunette, a blonde, and a redhead, all dressed similarly. The only thing missing is their pink satin jackets. I find myself wistfully thinking about how it would feel to have a crew of women like those, all of which seem ready to go to the mat against anyone who looks at their friend the wrong way.

My attention shifts back to the auction when the first bottle on my short list comes up for bidding. It's a 2010 Château Latour from France, and I was lucky enough to taste it once. I raise my paddle high, staring straight at the auctioneer. He notes my bid and asks for the next incremental raise. "I have three hundred; can I get four?"

Out of the corner of my eye, I see other paddles go up. "Five?" I boldly raise my paddle again, calculating how high I'm willing to bid for a single bottle of wine, but this is about more than something to drink.

I can feel the eyes of nearly everyone in the room land on me, and if anyone didn't notice that I'm with Dashiell Corbett, they're noticing now. So I give them a little something to look at, turning to Dash and smiling adoringly. He drapes an arm over my shoulders and leans in to kiss my cheek.

It's subtle, but it's enough to register on the radar of anyone paying the slightest bit of attention. We look like we're being discreet, yet we're so besotted with each other that we don't notice anyone else in the room.

I've never experienced that in a relationship before, but it feels nice to pretend. I can almost convince myself that I have those budding feelings for Dash. He's a convincing actor, and it hits me once again why women fall for him so easily. Then I remind myself that he loves and leaves them on the same night and feel glad that we're only pretending.

"Did you know the most expensive bottle of wine ever bought at auction went for over half a million?"

"Dollars?" I gasp. "No, I did not know that. Who'd spend that?"

He chuckles at how aghast I am. "Collectors. If more than one person wants something, someone's guaranteed to pay more than they should."

"I won't be doing that tonight." I raise my paddle again when the auctioneer asks for eight hundred dollars, but this is my ceiling. If anyone outbids me now, they can have it.

"We have nine hundred. Next bid, one thousand dollars." I exhale a small sigh of relief at not having to pay eight hundred dollars just for the sake of optics. Then I look around to see who else is still bidding.

I'm surprised to see that Trevor Stagwood is one of the bidders, and he's looking straight at me as though he's just proven his fortitude. He's asked me out a few times, and I've avoided committing to an actual date. I wonder now if this is his way of getting noticed.

I nod in Trevor's direction and turn my attention to another guy with his paddle raised. I don't recognize him, which is unusual for one of these events. Maybe he's new to the area or the friend of a friend.

"You know that guy?" I ask Dash, who has to swivel on his

stool to see the man. Dash bristles and turns back toward me, whispering, "I do know him. Long story."

"I'm not going anywhere."

The guy makes the winning bid at sixteen hundred dollars, and now I want to know whatever Dash can tell me about him. It's not just that we have the same taste in wine—lots of people like Château Latour—but I'm good with faces, and it surprises me that I don't recognize his.

Dash turns on his stool and leans in close. "That's Graham Garcia. My half brother." He lets the words land with the weight of a lead balloon, anticipating my goggle-eyed reaction.

"You have a half brother?" I've known the Corbett family for years, and this is the first time I've heard of a bonus sibling. Now I want to skip out of this room and hear everything.

Dash nods. "Only found out about him a few months back. It's…a whole thing." He looks back in the direction of where Graham sits amid a buzz of congratulations from the people around him, but then the auctioneer snags his attention when he starts up bidding on the spa weekend.

"Hang on. I want this." He readies his paddle, gripping the handle in his large hand.

"You do?" I'm puzzled because Dash doesn't strike me as a spa weekend kind of guy. Plus, if he and I are going to sell this relationship charade, he can't be whisking other women off for stolen weekends. I'm about to remind him of this when the bidding opens, and he raises his paddle in the air.

From then, it's a madhouse. Husbands egged on by wives, couples having anxious conversations about how high to bid. All of them desperate to secure the luxurious accommodations at a winery retreat with a two-year waiting list.

"I have four thousand. Do I have forty-two hundred?" A dozen paddles rise in the air. The auctioneer is ramping up the bidding at a breakneck pace, talking a mile a minute and reaching ten thousand dollars in under forty seconds. My head spins at the number of paddles rising and lowering.

The chatter in the room is also increasing as everyone gets excited about the funds raised and the audacity of how much people are willing to spend.

"Come on, it's for public theater. And that means shows like *Frozen*, *Wicked*, all the great productions your kids will beg you to see. Come on, do I have eleven thousand? It's for the kids." The auctioneer is good at his job, smiling as he increases the raise to five hundred at a time.

Through it all, Dash keeps raising his paddle. I look at him pointedly, trying to remind him that he can't reasonably use this fancy weekend anytime soon. Maybe he's already planning ahead for after our eventual divorce. It would make sense, I guess, since the waiting list is so long. So I sip my wine and let him do his thing.

He flashes a smile and rubs my bare shoulder. The heat of his fingers floods down my arm, and I lean closer to him, wanting more contact.

The bidding edges higher, but I'm distracted by how good Dash's hand feels on my skin. I'm even more distracted when I remind myself that I shouldn't be feeling things at all.

I join the applause when the gavel slams on the auction podium for the winner. Then I notice that everywhere I look in the room, I see eyes staring back at me. And Dash.

That's when I realize that Dash is the winner with a bid of fourteen thousand dollars for a single spa weekend. I'm about to ask him if he's gone 'round the bend when he stands up from his stool and quiets the din in the room.

"I'm super stoked to win and even more excited that my bid will go toward construction of the new theater." He holds his glass up, and people around the room mirror his movement, toasting him and applauding.

Someone yells, "Who're you taking?" and the crowd laughs. A

few more inquisitive souls join in a chorus of, "Yeah, who's the lucky girl?" I stiffen in my chair, not wanting to make this kind of a public declaration of anything. We're just supposed to be subtly giving people the impression we're an item, so no one—especially not Felix—questions that we're engaged.

There's no need for Dash to wave and clear his throat dramatically, but that's what he does. A hush falls over the room, save for the muttering of people wondering what he has planned as he continues to speak.

"Most of you probably know Mallory Rutherford...my fiancée." He waits for the appropriate titters and whispers among the crowd. "I'm normally not one for hotel spas, but maybe that was because I'd never met a woman before who made me want to break the bank for a chance to spend a weekend there with her."

He bends down and kisses me sweetly on the lips, the perfect expression of smitten endearment for a public place. "I'll take the room key, thank you very much."

Smiles and gentle applause validate the cuteness of Dash's soul-bearing speech, and when he sits back down next to me, I catch a smug grin on his face.

"Pleased with yourself?" I ask.

"You have no idea."

He turns back toward the table as the auctioneer proceeds to the next item as though he didn't just make a grand pronouncement in front of the entire room. He was only supposed to make us look legit as a couple, not give the entire town something to talk about on Monday at work.

"I can't decide whether I'm mad at you or not," I tell him. He's so damn sexy in his suit, and it confuses me. I want to be mad, but I also want to climb him like a tree.

"You're not." He takes a sip of wine and flips through the auction catalog nonchalantly. This is the Dash I've heard stories about. Cocky, charming, and convincing when he turns his attention toward you. It feels like a golden beam of sunlight shining on my face after a cold winter, and I can't help it—I like the way it feels.

I give myself exactly thirty seconds to bask in what it would be like to have a man say what Dash did and really mean it. I'd love to hear those words and know they were true.

Then my thirty seconds are up, and I return to reality.

Don't fall for the playboy. And definitely don't believe his flattering words. They're just talk designed to get a woman into bed.

And that's not happening tonight. No way, no how. Even if we've convinced everyone in the room that we're a couple, I know the truth. I may just need to feed myself daily reminders so I don't forget.

I look over at where Sue Clayton is still eyeing Dash like he's the one who got away. I never want to have that look on my face when it comes to a man. Especially not the one sitting next to me, making me feel things I have no business feeling. So I lock my heart down tight, smile back at Dash, and confirm. "You're right. I'm not mad at all. You were brilliant. Game on."

If anyone in the room had a question, it was answered with an ironclad defense able to withstand further scrutiny. Dash and I are getting married.

Which means people will expect us to have a wedding.

The thought sinks in my gut with a combination of relief and dread. We're really doing this. It's happening.

An hour later, as Dash walks me to my front door, I feel a new sense of dread. Now that it's just the two of us, with no one around to observe our "relationship," we've gone back to being acquaintances. Or maybe I guess we're friends. All the heat and flirtation I felt all night long disappeared as soon as we pulled out of the parking lot.

Dash was quiet on the drive back, and now, as I fish through my purse for my keys, he's quiet again. Stoic.

"Found 'em." I hold them up. "Thank you for a fun evening."

"I think we pulled it off, don't you?"

I nod emphatically. "Your spa weekend stunt was the clincher."

He smiles, but it's not his usual wide grin. It's a barely-there smile that may even be laced with sadness, but I don't know him well enough to tell.

Standing at my door, I feel the weight of so many dates when guys used this moment to go in for a first kiss. Every one of the others falls flat compared to the kisses I've shared with Dash. Even if they were just for show.

Is he going to kiss me now?

The air around us feels soupy, with the evening mist rolling off the mountains. It syncs with the unease in my gut. I want him to kiss me, but I don't *want* to want it.

"Okay, Mallomar. Sleep tight," he says softly, trailing a finger down my arm until it lands at my hand. He gives it a squeeze.

I open my mouth, thinking I'll concoct some excuse for him to stay. I could make coffee or…

He leans over and kisses my temple. I freeze, hoping his lips will stay on my skin, which craves more contact with him. He lingers for a moment longer, and I hear a low rumble in his throat. I inhale a shaky breath and turn to face him, our mouths only inches apart. The air between us hangs heavy. Dash's heavy-lidded eyes drop closed, but then he pulls away.

"Good night." The rasp of his voice sends goosebumps over my skin.

"Good night," I say. "Thanks again."

As I start to go inside, Dash calls after me. "Hey, you have any plans tomorrow?"

"No."

He nods. "I'll call you."

And there it is, this budding feeling I can't identify at first, and I sure as hell can't explain it.

Because it feels like excitement. And that's something I should never feel about a playboy who's about to do me a favor for the good of the business. Yeah. Tell that to my heart.

CHAPTER 18

ash

Mallory: How's your day going?

Me: I'm sorry, who is this?

Mallory: Your fiancée. You're eternally devoted to me, remember?

Me: I do.

Mallory: Save that for the wedding

Me: Right. I'm off to buy you diamonds, as instructed

Mallory: I love a fiancé who listens!

I WASN'T LYING about the diamonds.

I should be at the gym. That's what I'd normally be doing at noon on a Saturday.

After a late night with friends and a chance to sleep in for once in a week, I'd be sweating on the treadmill to warm up for three rounds of weights. Same thing nearly every day.

Instead, I'm flying up Highway 80 on my way back from a ring shop in San Francisco. I spent the morning with Owen, a buddy of mine who owns restaurants in Napa Valley and divides his time between there and a house in Hayes Valley.

Initially, he recommended a place in the jewelry district and even offered to bring his wife with him when he met me to look at stones. "Isla has better taste than me," he'd said when I called him last night in a panic. His wife is a renowned baker who supplies bread to the nicer of the two restaurants on the Buttercup Hill property, but she's one of those women who's good at everything, so I'm not surprised she knows something about diamonds too.

I secretly think it's her bread that helped Butter and Rosemary earn its Michelin star a couple of years back, but she's too modest to admit it. "I just make the sourdough starter and bake. It's where you take it from there that has everyone swooning," she always says.

Despite Isla's taste, I panicked. "Stones?" I'd asked Owen. "I thought I was buying a ring."

He explained to me that I needed to choose the stone and the setting, and then the jeweler would make the ring to my specifications.

"No, no, no. It doesn't need to be that complicated. I have no specifications."

"Well, maybe *she* does." I love how married guys make it sound like it's so obvious that every decision and question actually has one right answer, and it's whatever his wife says. He was once a dummy like me who didn't know such things, but now he relinquishes his choices like everyone else.

"I just need a ring," I said, at which point he told Isla not to bother coming with him. I could hear him explaining, "He's lost sight of reason. I'll handle it."

When we met at a different jewelry store, one that had rings with stones already in them, he peppered me with questions. "Who is she? How'd you meet? How're you planning to propose?"

I gave him the party line Mallory and I came up with involving our messy meet-cute in the pickle aisle, our attempts to keep our romance under wraps, and my admission to how nuts I am about her.

He smiled and nodded as though he understood how that could happen. I know he felt that way when he met Isla, and he's known me long enough that he sees beneath the facade other people around town think is the real Dashiell Corbett. "Glad you found someone good. You deserve it."

He's one of my oldest friends, so I debated coming clean with him and telling him it will be a marriage of convenience, but then I decided that the fewer the people who know, the better the odds of us pulling it off without anyone suspecting we're not really in love.

The trip to the jewelry store was relatively painless because I told myself over and over that it was simply a business transaction. Buy the ring, marry the girl, see Buttercup Hill live to do business for another decade. Big picture thinking.

I didn't tell Owen any of that, but on my drive back to Napa, it's all I can think about. I know I'm making the right decision by agreeing to marry Mallory for the good of our family business.

With two older brothers who are seriously type A, it's always been easier to take my place at the back of the line and let them do the heavy lifting on the financial and strategic end of Buttercup Hill. They're exactly like my father, and it only makes sense for them to make the big decisions.

At least it did…

I may be friendlier and more outgoing than them, making me

perfect for my job as the employee liaison. I'll talk to anyone, and it's easy to convince people to see things my way because I'm not an asshole about it. That's the thing neither of my brothers seems to understand. A good attitude and a genuine smile go a long way.

But it doesn't mean I'm not smart. It doesn't mean I can't be the one to save our business from financial ruin. And the idea of spearheading this nutty plan has me excited enough that I drove my ass to San Francisco at the crack of dawn to buy a ring.

And it has me driving straight to Mallory's doorstep to deliver it.

I exit the highway and begin the drive up the narrower road toward Napa. I pass several farmstands, and after the third "you pick it" sign, I pull off into a small dirt lot next to rows of corn and tomatoes. I browse among the freshly picked produce and flowers and select a few items I hope Mallory will like.

It occurs to me that I don't know so many things about her— her favorite flowers, how she likes her coffee, what kind of workout she does—but I'm actually excited to spend time finding out as we're pushed together in this little ruse.

I tell myself that it's just natural curiosity, that I'd be interested in getting to know anyone, that there's nothing special about the woman who's been on my mind all morning.

I'll keep telling myself all of those things until I believe them.

* * *

THIRTY MINUTES LATER, I'm knocking on Mallory's door, having no idea what she does on a Saturday. For all I know, she could be in some Pilates class or riding a horse.

I almost dart back to my truck and speed the hell off her property. I'm a bundle of nerves, which is ridiculous. This isn't a real proposal.

So why does it feel like a big fucking deal?

I should leave. Except that the front door is opening. Apparently, Mallory is home. She stands in front of me wearing a pale blue tank top that shows off bronzed skin that has no right to look that soft. My eyes trail down from her collarbones to the top's contours, making it clear she's not wearing a bra. Curves all day long.

Good day for me to show up unexpectedly.

Because instead of standing here imagining what her breasts might look like under a filmy swatch of cotton, I have a complete picture. Her perky nipples bite through the fabric, and I can't stop staring. Maybe I really am just a guy who ogles women for sport. At the moment, I'm an Olympic athlete at ogling, and I don't feel one bit apologetic about it.

Until she clears her throat.

My eyes shoot back to her face, which has a decidedly confused and perturbed expression. Her pretty mouth turns down in a frown, and she squints at me as though I'm too bright to handle.

"Hi." She crosses her arms over her chest like any sane person would when faced with a panting lapdog ready to lick her from head to toe.

"Hi." I'm safer to start with that than blurt out inappropriate things about how good her long, bare legs look in the cutoff denim shorts she's wearing.

"What are you doing here?" The confusion hasn't left her face, and I realize she has a legitimate right to look at me that way, given that I showed up at her doorstep unannounced in the middle of a weekend when we didn't plan to see each other.

"Right. That." I had the entire drive up from San Francisco to come up with some idea of what to say to her, and right now, none of those thoughts occupy my brain. I feel like an awkward preteen boy standing before the prom queen on a dare.

Sometimes, when I look at Mallory, I feel like the geeky freshman I never actually was, thanks mostly to a deep voice and muscles that developed early. Now, I have sympathy for every one of my pale, skinny friends who struck out with girls on the regular.

Mallory clears her throat, making me realize I'm staring at her without explanation.

"I, um, figured we should make it official."

Driving up here under a bluebird sky framed by wispy white clouds in the distance, I imagined what Cyrano would tell dopey Christian. I tried to come up with my own silver-tongued magic to get the girl.

But then I stopped myself, remembering I'm not a lovestruck suitor. I'm just a guy who made a deal he wants to honor. I pulled off the highway at a smoothie shop and ordered two strawberry-banana frozen drinks.

I thrust one of them toward Mallory, who reaches for it. "Thanks."

"Strawberry banana. Not sure you like that flavor." The sight of her has reduced me to a pimply middle schooler asking a girl to go steady.

"Who *doesn't* like that flavor?" She takes a sip, and her eyes drift shut. "Wow, that hits the spot after yoga."

The sun hits her face, and she looks like she should be modeling for a smoothie company or something. That's how perfect she looks, with her pink lips wrapped around the straw and her dark lashes grazing her cheeks each time she blinks.

I'm tempted to call it a day and leave. Smoothie success. But Mallory notices the loose bouquet of red and orange ranunculus I chose from the farm stand. I carried it under my arm from the car and put it down before she opened the door.

"Oh. I brought you these too. Do you have a favorite color of flower?"

Now she looks at me quizzically. "Is this some kind of get-to-know-you visit? Do you have a carload of props?"

"Nope, just these."

She juts a hip out to the side and puts a hand on it, studying me. "Do you have a favorite flower color?

"Whatever ones won't die the soonest are good in my book."

She chuckles. "That works too." She stares at me watching her. I need to salvage this before it becomes really awkward.

Before it becomes really, *really* awkward...

So I wrestle the ring box from my pocket and present it to her. Mallory's eyes go wide, and she drops her smoothie. I catch it before it hits the floor and squeeze the cup so hard that a squirt flies up through the straw and onto my shirt.

Now I have a big pink arch of strawberry banana on my chest, and Mallory laughs.

"Not what I was hoping for when I went out and bought a ring."

"Sorry. I'm just still processing that part. You...bought a ring? An engagement ring?"

"Um, yeah. Pretty sure you dropped a hundred hints about diamonds."

"I was...I was kidding!"

I dismiss the thought with a wave. "Come on, Marshmallow. A ring is important when two people are going to waltz around in front of a certain ex-husband and look convincing."

She laughs. "I am looking forward to the waltzing."

And because Mallory rarely does what I'm expecting, instead of taking the box from me, she takes a step backward and uses the large windowpane glass to check her reflection. She pulls her hair out of its topknot, shakes it out, and straightens her tank top. Throwing her shoulders back, she stands up taller.

"Okay, a little better. I'm ready. Let's hear it."

"Hear what?"

"Your proposal."

"Um..." All thoughts leave my mind simultaneously. I did spend a few miles of the drive thinking about what people say when they get engaged, but that was mainly because the ring box digging into my leg kept bringing my focus back to it.

I didn't think about what I'd say to Mallory because this isn't a real proposal.

Right?

The way she's standing here impatiently waiting for me to make good on whatever is supposed to accompany an engagement ring, I stammer some more and think about that damned Cyrano play again and try to remember any of the lines that could help me here. Unfortunately, I have a shit memory, and I'm on my own with only a jingle for a fast food hamburger chain running through my mind.

Time to get creative.

I drop to one knee and gaze upward, tracing the long, tanned leg to where it gives way to Mallory's curves and, finally, her gorgeous face.

Mallory doesn't react to my position. Maybe she thinks I dropped something or I need to tie my shoe. Maybe she's waiting for me to grab some other random get-to-know-you item and ask her more irrelevant questions.

"Mallomar, in the time I've gotten to know you a little bit, I have to say you've surprised me. You don't let people see the real you, but I like the glimpses I've caught. And I'm looking forward to getting to know you better. I know this is all a business deal for both of us, but you still deserve a real engagement. A story you can tell people about when they ask."

I gesture to the flowers and the smoothie as though they'd make any sort of a decent engagement story. But when I look back at her, she's motionless and focused on me.

Her mouth drops open, and her hand goes to her chest. "Dash, this is really sweet of you."

"You deserve a real proposal for our fake engagement." I stop myself when I hear how ridiculous it sounds. "I know that's probably weird…"

"It's not. Thank you." Her soft, kind voice emboldens me to finish what I came here to do.

Gesturing around us, I take in the rolling green acres of farmland, and a different kind of calm settles over me than I feel when I'm at Buttercup Hill. This place is all unmanicured, fertile green patches of plants. It isn't a business yet, just open land, the fresh scent of loamy soil, and a dozen types of plants and grasses. There's freedom in that and I like how it feels. Messy and untamed like Mallory, who doesn't suffer fools.

"You could do so much with this." I gesture around us. "Dry farmed vines, grazing patches for animals, a sustainable agriculture incubator, educational walking tours."

She smiles. "I love all of that. You have a good eye."

It screams potential, and for the first time, I feel proud to be helping Mallory do what she wants with it. I don't have much say at Buttercup Hill, but this…this feels like a fresh start."I don't just want to be another guy who admires you from afar. I want to be the guy who sits across the table from you at dinner and hears about the boring parts of your day. I want to be the first one to see you smile when you get good news. And I want to be the guy who helps you build this place into your dream."

My words take on a life of their own as I say them, but I mean every word.

That's why I stop talking. I realize I'm professing real feelings, or at least words that sound like real feelings, and that's not the point here.

I want to seal it all with a kiss. I want to do so much more, but none of that is part of our arrangement. We're not in public, and there's no public benefit to pulling her into my arms and kissing the hell out of her, despite what I might want to do.

When my gaze returns to her face, I notice her soft jaw and glassy eyes. I allow myself to think that maybe, possibly, this could be a real moment between us. She licks her lips like she's getting ready for the kind of kiss I'm aching to give her.

The moment hangs heavy between us. Nothing stops me from kissing her except the fear of future awkwardness if I'm wrong about how she feels. We have a wedding and a marriage ahead of us, and I don't want to ruin it because I can't keep my hands to myself.

So I swallow down my impulse and take the ring out of the box.

"It's not an engagement if you're not wearing my ring, so let's see if it fits."

She tentatively holds out her hand but snatches it back before I can slip the ring on. "Wait, aren't you forgetting something?"

"Am I?"

"You didn't actually ask me to marry you."

A smile pulls at my lips because I love that she wants the whole proposal, not just the ring or a few canned lines.

"Mallory Rutherford, I want you until the end of days. Will you do me the honor of being my wife?"

She starts nodding before I get all the words out. "Yes. Yes, I will, Dashiell Corbett."

I slide the ring onto her finger and feel like I've conquered something huge. Maybe my own fears. I don't know why I'm filled with deep feelings over a ring. It's a wonder how this tiny piece of jewelry carries so much weight and how wars are fought and won over women who possess a fraction of the beauty of the one standing before me.

Mallory holds the ring up to the light, inspecting the flawless solitaire, emerald cut diamond. I spent more than I needed to, but I didn't want anyone to doubt my intentions or question my sincerity. Especially her.

"For the record, you got it right," Mallory says, her eyes never leaving the ring as she picks up the flowers and tugs one red bloom from the bunch.

"You like red flowers," I confirm, feeling lucky the bright batch that caught my eye happens to be what she likes.

"I don't just mean the flowers." She holds up the ring and lets the sun catch its facets so it sparkles. "You got everything right."

Hearing her words does something to me, hits me deep, and I want to kiss her.

I take a step closer, then another. Gently reaching for the flowers, I pull them from her hand and put them on the porch swing. Her eyes follow my movements as I put a hand on her hip and guide her closer to me.

She doesn't resist when I slide the other hand into her hair and run my fingers through the silky strands before cupping her cheek. There's fire in her eyes as they meet mine, and her lips part. I suppress a groan when the tip of her tongue slips out and licks her bottom lip.

The air crackles between us, swollen with electricity that sparks my desire even more. I hesitate a second longer to enjoy the anticipation before I sink into her lips and take what I don't want to resist anymore. Her eyes drift shut and I hear a quiet intake of breath.

I hesitate a second too long.

A truck barrels up the driveway and skids into a dusty spot next to mine. Mallory's eyes shoot open and my head whips around to identify the intruder. Mary swings open the door to her truck and emerges with a white pastry bag.

"Biscuits are on me today." Fucking cheerful, irritating Brit.

Mallory takes a step back and my hands drop from her body. Mary makes her way to us and Mallory walks past me to greet her and show her the ring.

"Nice work," Mary tells me. "You do fake engagements right."

Mallory's apologetic smile tells me she regrets the interruption, but Mary's words are what ring in my ears. *Fake engagement.*

I may have let the ring and the moment sweep me up and make me believe we really are an engaged couple in love.

But she's not that woman. She's my business partner.

So I can't be that guy.

ash

Me: Hi

Mallory: Hi

Me: Hope the biscuits were good

Mallory: You should've stuck around to find out

Me: You should've insisted

Mallory: You should've insisted I insist

"WHOA, REALLY?" Archer's incredulous voice booms from twenty paces away, as soon as he recognizes me jogging toward him on the path around the lake.

"Yes," I mutter, fully aware that at seven in the morning, this is not on-brand for me. As Archer draws closer, breathing in the easy way runners do, I get ready for all his mocking, but he surprises me.

"Good on you." He high fives me as he runs past, never breaking stride. I suppose I should be grateful that we're moving in opposite directions, which makes conversation impossible. Because I have no good explanation for what I'm doing.

After Mary disrupted us, Mallory and I seemed to have an unspoken understanding that we needed a cooling off period. I didn't hear from her all day, and even though I was itching to show up on her doorstep to finish what we started, I fought the impulse all fucking day long.

That led me to a latenight workout, which ended with me in the shower, fisting my dick and thinking about Mallory. Which led to a restless night of sleep and useless energy with nowhere to burn it.

Hence the early morning jogging and persistent thoughts about what Mallory meant when she texted that I should have stuck around.

To eat cookies? To finish what we almost started?

I round the lake at Buttercup Hill and feel a glimmer of understanding of why Archer likes to run out here each day. It's peaceful when the only sounds are birds and insects. It's the quiet before the shitstorm that's our daily effort to save our family business from what always seems like the edge of a cliff.

The thoughts bring me back to Autumn Lake which has nothing but potential ahead and the freedom to unfold. I wonder if my grandfather felt that sense of potential when he started Buttercup Hill. I imagine so. It makes me all the more motivated to help Mallory's vision come to life.

It makes me more motivated to go back to her house. But not just for biscuits.

 allory

"Oh, I'm going to kill him, I really am," I mutter, marching to my front door. I can't believe Felix has the gall to show up here again after I told him to leave me alone the other night.

The guy is persistent, I'll give him that, but that's all I'm willing to give him.

I shouldn't even open the door, but that will all but guarantee he comes back again with some new plan to get me to let him back into my life and into my plans for Buttercup Hill.

"Not happening," I say, whipping open the door.

I've been meaning to install a peephole or get a camera or whatever, but it's pretty safe here, and we have a full staff of strapping men working the farm a hundred yards away. I always feel comfortable opening my door.

Dash's brow creases in confusion, and the corners of his mouth tug down into a frown. "Sorry?"

Oh. It's not Felix. I need to calm down.

Now I have Taylor Swift lyrics running through my head as I size Dash up. Judging from his navy blue track pants and the beads of sweat on his brow, he jogged here. He wears a tight workout tee that rolls over the contours of his chest and abs like it's enjoying committing the shape of his body to memory.

Oh wait, that's me.

Rufus saunters past me, gives Dash a cursory sniff, and disappears around the corner of the house.

"I thought you were someone else." I cross my arms over my chest defensively out of habit. The last few times someone came to my door haven't gone well.

He quirks an eyebrow, and a smirk forms on his lips. "I can only imagine."

If he's insinuating that I may have a long line of ex-husbands or even suitors calling on me, I want to set him straight. I haven't spent the past several years busting my hide to take business classes for people to continue seeing me as a tease who'll do anything to get what I want.

"I was referring to my ex."

"I assumed as much." He crosses his arms, but it doesn't look menacing when he does it. It looks hot. His backward baseball cap makes him look younger than his thirty years, and his muscles all look pumped from whatever he just did. He smells like a mixture of clean sweat and a foresty body wash or deodorant.

No one smells good after a workout. No one except this man, apparently.

I wish I hadn't noticed, but he's making it nearly impossible at this distance.

Some people go to the gym or go for a run and look like a sweaty mess. Hair askew, clothes wet in awkward places, faces too flushed. Not Dash.

His biceps flex under the short sleeves of his shirt, roped forearms folded across his chest. The sun kisses his cheekbones and highlights the sharp line of his clean-shaven jaw. Blue eyes dance mischievously. He's dangerously handsome, and I can't get a full inhale of air into my lungs without my pounding heart tripping me up.

He should always walk around like this. I almost tell him as much, but then I regain some shred of my senses.

But man…was he this smoking hot when helping me up from a puddle of pickle juice?

Or is it just that damn baseball cap and the rippling chest muscles?

I need to regain control of the situation, so I lean against my doorjamb and pin him with a stare. He glances down at the cutoffs I'm wearing, and from the way he swallows hard, I think he likes what he sees.

I shift my weight into one hip, leaving the other leg extended out in front of me. I watch Dash's eyes scan the length of my leg slowly before raking up the rest of my body. He doesn't stop until his eyes reach my face and land on my lips.

I pull my bottom lip through my teeth, and he stares, swallowing hard once more.

Balance of power restored.

"What brings you here?" I ask.

Dash looks at me blankly for a moment as though I'm not speaking words he understands. Like one tanned leg is enough to scramble the thoughts in his brain so thoroughly that he's forgotten why he came.

Blinking a couple of times, he regains control.

"Why'd you ask me out?"

Oh. That.

I wasn't expecting him to show up here, and I really wasn't expecting to have to answer that question, so I defer.

"Wasn't it obvious? I wanted a date."

He shakes his head and takes a step backward as though I'm slightly toxic. "No. That's not it."

"What makes you so sure? You don't even know me."

"I think I know you a little bit. Why'd you ask? Of all the guys in town, why'd you pick the one with a reputation for being a flirt."

"I don't even really remember. It was a spur-of-the-moment thing."

"Bullshit. Tell me." He keeps asking, and I get the feeling he doesn't plan on leaving my porch until he gets an answer. Unlike Felix, whose persistence riles me up, something makes me want to give Dash what he wants.

Only I can't.

I don't want to tell him the real reason I asked him out. Now that I've gotten to know him, there's no way I'll tell him.

Besides, having him standing here is giving me a whole other reason that will sound equally plausible. Or at least that's what my lady boner is telling me.

"I wanted a date. A night of meaningless hookup fun. Thought you might be good for the job."

He knows I don't see him that way now, so it surprises me when his face falls as though he was really hoping I'd say something else.

A wave of regret washes over me. I didn't mean to hurt him. Is that what just happened?

"Really?" He looks skeptical, as though he can intuit the real reason. I know he can't, but still. How does this guy keep leaving me off-balance?

"Yes. Really."

"And now? Is that still what you want?" He winces a little at the question like he doesn't want to ask it, but he needs to know.

I start to answer, but the words won't leave my mouth. So I just nod.

I do want it, but not for those reasons.

Sure, it's been two years since I've been with a man. Two long years. For most of that time, I've been fine. Haven't missed the complications of a relationship. Definitely haven't missed Felix or the type of guys who get possessive and try to run my life for me.

I don't just want a man. I want *him*.

I want the conclusion to all those kisses that left me aching to dissolve into Dash's body and lose myself in his capable hands. The more I get to know him, the more I want all of that to come with real emotions on his part, but I know I can't ask for that, so I'll take the physical part if that's what he's offering.

"I do want it." I grab his shirt and pull him toward me. "You?"

"I'm sweaty," he protests, yet he's here.

"I don't care."

"What if I care?"

"There's a shower upstairs." I point, and his pupils dilate. The blue of his eyes intensifies.

"Careful, Mellow Yellow. I might take that to mean you want us to shower together."

"Maybe I do," I say boldly, even if I'm unsure what I mean. The words fall from my mouth as though my rational brain has come unhinged from my basic thoughts—he's here, and I want him.

Dash takes a step closer to me. Ordinarily, this would feel like nothing, a meaningless adjustment in proximity. Instead, it feels like everything.

Just moving a couple of inches closer, Dash has the effect of a force field, and I'm drawn to him like he's a hot, sexy magnet. I step forward and meet his gaze, challenging him to make another move.

We stand only inches apart, and I feel a hum of vibration throughout my body. Dash's pulse thrums beneath the taut skin of his neck, and I want to lick him right there, taste the salt and sweat. I watch his hand move slowly toward me until he cups my chin. His touch feels hot against my skin, and ripples of heat rush down my neck, dead-ending at my core.

This is lust, pure and simple, and I'm here for it.

His thumb rubs circles beneath my chin, and I suck in a breath. It seems impossible for such a small movement to elicit such a strong feeling, but there it is.

Dash tips my face up slightly so it's aligned perfectly with his. I have one more chance to stare into the stormy blue of his eyes before he's too close for me to focus, and my eyes drift shut.

Then his lips are on mine with all the heat and intensity of my daydreams. This isn't soft or tender. We're not in love. This is feral, hot, and driven by need.

I want him, and now that he's here on my doorstep, I can't let him leave without seeing this through to the end.

Dash kisses me like he's on a mission to save himself before the end of the world, and I'm his only hope.

He feels like mine.

His tongue sweeps across my bottom lip before he nips at it. Gently at first, teasing. Then he bites down harder, and a jolt of heat races straight to my core. I move closer to him, pressing against his leg because I suddenly need some kind of friction. I need everything all at once, and we've only been kissing for ten seconds.

Our lips stay locked to each other as I take several steps backward, walking us in through my front door. Dash kicks it with his foot, and it slams behind him. Now that we're inside, away from the bright sun, the mood changes.

Dash pulls me harder against him, our bodies melting into one another while our tongues tangle, and Dash runs his hands through my hair. There are almost too many senses firing at once for me to untangle them, so I don't even try. What's the point of listing the ingredients in a chocolate soufflé when it tastes so damn good?

"Upstairs?" I pant against his mouth.

He doesn't need to be told twice. Dash nods, and we fumble up the narrow staircase from my entryway to the large loft where

I have my bedroom and a small office. We're kissing and touching and looking down so we don't trip, eventually making our way to the top step.

It's lighter again up here, and Dash stops to glance up. "Wow, cool."

"Yeah. Skylights."

We sound like cave people. Our brain cells are too busy calculating how to kiss some more and get each other's clothes out of the way.

Arms wrapped around me, Dash walks me backward until my legs hit the bed. He holds me close, and I blink up at him, wondering what he's thinking about me, my bedroom, and this crazy idea of hooking up. "Do you make your bed every day?"

He smiles or, rather, smirks while his eyes drift around the room, taking in a mismatched set of furniture—a tall dresser painted antique white, two bedside tables in raw oak, a giant fluffy comforter on the bed, and yellow throw pillows on a green upholstered bench at the foot of the bed.

It always strikes me as amusing when people say things without self-editing. I do it all the time, and it feels comforting to have Dash do it now. It softens his hot guy facade. I'm sure he doesn't care a bit about whether I make my bed, but the thought entered his head, and instead of resuming kissing his way down my body, he asked the question.

"I don't always. In fact, about two days a week."

He's still smirking. "So...did you just have a feeling you'd bring someone up here to see it today?"

"Nope. Just lucky, I guess."

I'm not sure what he's getting at. Does he really think I make my bed on weekends because I think a guy may end up in it?

"I do feel lucky." His voice comes at me like the growl of a cheetah, and I have no problem being his next meal.

"Yeah?"

He nods and licks his lips. Then he pushes me backward, and

I topple onto the bed with Dash on top of me. He holds himself above me, and I reach up to run my hands over his muscled arms.

"Don't move a muscle. Just let me make you feel good."

"Seriously?"

Bending to kiss me again, Dash sweeps his tongue along the slit of my mouth until I open for him. His tongue melts against mine and answers my question ten times over. Moving down my body, Dash pushes my shirt up, exposing the skin of my stomach. The cool air in my house gives me goose bumps. Oh wait, no… that would be Dash doing that with his tongue.

"Yes," he growls.

Holy moly. A girl doesn't need to be told twice to lay still.

I'm pretty certain Dash has a magic tongue. Everywhere he touches me, my skin flames up like he's igniting kerosene with a lighter. I shudder as he reaches his hands up, pushing my shirt higher until it hits my chin, and I wriggle free of the annoying, unnecessary fabric.

Then, ahh. Dash's tongue circles one nipple while his hand plays with the other one. My breath leaves me in a shaky exhale, and I reach for something, anything, to grip. When my hands land on Dash's back, I sink my fingers into his muscular form until he lifts his face to mine with a sparkle in his eyes.

Shaking his head, he reminds me, "That's not laying still."

"But I need to touch something. And you're the something."

Placing each of my hands back on the bed, he ruffles up some of the covers and shoves handfuls of the feathery down into my fists. Then he resumes his ravaging of each breast until I moan.

I feel weirdly jealous of all the women who've gotten this treatment before me and also grateful because they've clearly made it possible for Dash to be as talented as he is today. I decide to focus on that part. No reason to get all in my head about other women when I've asked to be another in the long string of them.

Sliding my pants slowly down my legs, he runs his fingers along the skin of my thighs. I slip out of the sweatpants and lay beneath him, naked except for a flimsy lace thong, not at all uncomfortable with him seeing new parts of me.

I'm nervous because I want and don't want this at the same time. Or let me rephrase. My body wants this, and it won't shut up about it. That much is clear. It's like a bell ringing in my head telling me it's long past time for me to have a good time with a man.

That other part of me…the part that doesn't want it…that's the romantic part. It's the woman who screams silently, telling me I should hold out for real romance and the kind of relationships with the type of men I know don't exist. It's easy to quiet that voice because I have the weight of experience on my side. In all the years I dated, I never met anyone who came close to satisfying what I wanted—intense chemistry and deep understanding. It was always only one or the other. Or a bit of both. Or neither.

I know better than to keep holding out for something I won't find. I'm mature enough now to focus on my goals for Autumn Lake like an adult.

Yet…doesn't mean I can't have a little fun.

This is Dashiell Corbett. He has a reputation for hookups, and I have every reason to trust the legend that precedes him. But maybe, just maybe, this is something more. That idea is enough to push me forward.

Dash lowers himself to the floor, and I tilt my head to see him kiss his way along one leg, which he places on the bed, bent at the knee. He does the same with the other leg. And then his tongue lands right at my center, hot and wet against the shred of fabric that separates him from where I want him to be.

I gasp at how good it feels, even through the fabric of my thong. "I was hoping you'd be wet for me," he says, that same smirk-smile still on his face. "But you outdid my expectations."

"It's just a small piece of fabric," I tease.

"Still soaked." He pulls the fabric away and sucks my clit into his mouth. I gasp as he circles me with his tongue before sliding the thong down my legs and putting it into his pocket. "And now it's mine."

I don't have time to protest because his tongue is on me, sweeping up my center and delving inside. I can't stop the moan that leaves my lips each time his tongue goes back for another pass, circling against my flesh and teasing my clit.

Oh. My. God. I finally stop thinking about how Dash got this good at what he's doing because I'm lost in it. I'm panting. I'm moaning. I'm flying.

There's no limit to how high he seems like he can take me with his mouth on my most sensitive parts, so I keep flying higher. Higher. Until I'm cresting the top of a peak I've never visited before.

The cascade of tiny bursts of light and heat continues, and I ride out the orgasm until I'm not sure whether I'm here or in the middle of a fever dream. The only thing that gives me a clue is the sight of Dash stripping off his running clothes and standing in front of the bed with an erection that makes me salivate.

"Okay, Mallomar, now you can move," he says, giving his stiff length a few pumps in his fist. I sit up and greedily replace his fist with my own, circling the head and running my hand down his beautiful hard length.

He exhales through gritted teeth and lowers himself onto me as I continue to work him, running my hand up and down his shaft. "Fuck," he bites out, moving my hand and interlacing our fingers.

I feel drunk on the weight of his body on mine. It's been a long time since I've been with any man, let alone one who elicited so much pleasure.

He circles my entrance, teasing me with tiny previews of how he'll feel inside until I'm writhing beneath him and moving to position myself better. But he's toying with me, making me want him more and not giving me what my body craves.

He's also kissing me, which feels so good—just not good

enough. He knows exactly what he's doing to me. I'm breathless and desperate for another orgasm like the one he just gave me. It's a drug, and he's pretending he doesn't know how badly I want it.

"I need you inside," I pant, more exasperated than seductive.

He laughs. "Am I frustrating you?"

"Yes." I hate to admit it because I know it's what he wants, but it feels like the only way to get what *I* want.

"Sorry, not sorry?"

He kisses me again and moves so the tip of his erection is just inside me before pulling away.

"You are killing me…" I groan.

"And it feels so good to lose control to someone else. Admit it," he whispers. I hear a condom wrapper tear open and don't have the wherewithal to figure out where he got it.

Just as I'm about to agree and disagree at the same time, he pushes inside me fully, and I lose all sense of time and place. Every pleasure center in my body flashes to life at the same time, and I cry out because it's all I can do. It's all anyone can do when she's with a man who feels this good. He's bigger and thicker than any man I've been with, like I've been waiting my whole life for something I didn't know existed.

I want him to stay inside me forever, and that's insane. It's certainly not something I'm going to tell him even though I'm pretty sure he already knows from the way he's staring at me.

He looks like he's seeing something incredible, eyes wide and amazed—or maybe just scared because I probably look like I feel. Like I never want to let him go.

It's crazy and it's incredible and it's scary as hell because I absolutely need to let him go just as soon as we're done here because that was the deal.

So I do what any responsible, man-hangry woman would do in my situation, which is to let Dashiell Corbett work his magic tongue and hands—and goddammit, his amazing cock—on me until I'm screaming his name at the top of my lungs as well as things about god and other nonsense because he's giving me the most incredible orgasm I've had in my life.

And from the way he's cursing and panting my name, he feels exactly the same way.

Which is why I'm totally screwed. Literally and figuratively.

ash

MAYBE I SHOULD BE STRESSED out. Ordinarily, sex makes things complicated. It's why I stopped hooking up with women and stopped dating at all, for that matter.

The questions about where things are going and the fear I'll hurt someone because I don't have deep emotional feelings that accompany sex…those are all good reasons to keep my dick in my pants and say good night with a kiss.

Oddly, I don't feel any of those concerns here.

It's been six days since Mallory and I had the best sex of my life, and I can't get her out of my head. Thankfully, we agreed that we can be real friends who are fake-engaged and have white-hot sex when we want to—which is pretty much all the time.

Nothing complicated about that. Fight me if you disagree.

We're walking through the fallow fields at Autumn Lake and imagining vineyards as far as the eye can see. "I can ask Archer, but I think cabernet grapes would do best on this side. They're hearty, and this soil is perfect, so you can pretty much take your pick."

"No, I was thinking about planting cab on this side too." She smiles. "Brilliant minds."

"I still can't believe your parents have been sitting on all this land, knowing its value to the winemakers around here and just…"

"Growing weeds? Yeah, they're unreliable wanderers," Mallory says, walking past several sheep that graze on a combination of grass, weeds, and wildflowers.

I'm struck by how different Autumn Lake is from Buttercup Hill. Our property is manicured and planned from end to end. After he inherited the business from our grandfather, our dad devised a master plan for every inch of the space. I wasn't even born when he started developing the expanded acreage into our cabernet vineyard.

All I remember is growing up running among the vines and eating the sweet grapes until my hands and face were stained purple. Part of that was probably due to my general cluelessness, but I also got used to a huge number of trucks and workers on the property all the time. Something was always happening somewhere. Progress all the time.

By the time I reached high school, Buttercup Hill looked much the way it does today, with a café, a high-end restaurant, and inn on the property, with the old barn serving as a sort of headquarters. Now it's the one place every guest wants to see. Display cases in the lobby show older iterations of wine labels and a photo history of the property.

Eventually, our dad began building houses on the perimeter of the property, and now each of us lives on-site. Looking at the vast fields surrounding us, I can picture it developed with vineyards and buildings because that's all I know.

"Why unreliable?" I ask, swiping a bright orange California poppy from where it spikes up from the surrounding grass.

Mallory wears low work boots, a green flannel shirt over a tee, and jeans. She couldn't look more natural walking among the fields here. It's easy to picture her the way I remember my dad as he strode around with me in tow, pointing out where he planned to start the food garden and assessing the sunlight and soil to decide where the grapes would grow best.

"They don't have a great sense of time. They leave when they find an interesting opportunity, and it doesn't matter what's happening around them. It's why they never did much with this property. Running it requires actually being here to make decisions about it. Even if they had a staff of people doing it for them, they'd need to have a plan. They're not planners."

"Maybe there's something reliable about that. Unreliability can be its own little paradigm."

She turns toward me, shielding her eyes from the sun over my shoulder. "You're a philosopher now?"

I move so I'm blocking the sun from her face and lower her hand, intertwining our fingers.

"Would it bother you if I was?" I can't resist and kiss the tip of her nose.

"No, but I want you to understand what it was like here all these years. It wasn't all cute and sweet with sheep running around. It was disorganized and barely functional with sheep running around."

I look at our surroundings. They're not manicured like Buttercup Hill but don't look disastrous. "How do you see this place five years from now?"

I don't know what I expected—a vague idea of a few vineyards and flowers? But Mallory's eyes blaze with a fire I haven't seen yet. She spins in a circle, taking in the entirety of the place, or at least what she can see of it from here.

"I have drawings. Want to see them?"

"Yes. But first, let's finish talking about your family. Does it bother you that they wandered unreliably?"

She laughs. "I mean, kind of." She extends her arms in both directions. "Look at the opportunity they had right here to do something really cool. And they were more interested in farming potatoes in little Irish country towns than taking advantage of the potential here."

"Maybe some people are better at farming other people's land. 'Potential' can be a daunting concept."

"Not to me."

"I can tell."

She shakes her head. "Literally been waiting my whole life to do something with this place."

"Almost your birthday. You've waited long enough." I squeeze her hand. "Let's go see your plans."

* * *

I DON'T KNOW why it surprises me that Mallory has mapped out the entirety of Autumn Lake down to the square inch. It's exactly what my father did, and it makes sense when planning something of the magnitude of two hundred acres.

"Why do you look so shocked?" Mallory eyes me warily.

Rubbing my chin, I try to find the right words. "It's just a lot of work. When did you have time to do all this? Are you an architect in addition to getting a business degree?"

She smiles. "I hired someone to do the actual plans, but we worked together for the past year on it."

I bend closer to take in the smaller details. Most of the space is mapped as vineyards, which makes sense because Mallory wants to sell grapes. But there's also an expanded wine-making operation, two new houses and a café.

"These are houses." I point at the buildings on the set of plans.

"Yes."

"Who's going to live in them?" I ask.

"Seasonal workers if they need a place to live. I want to be sure people who work here can afford to live in the area. It's getting more expensive, and it's hard."

It makes me think about Graham living with his mom on the outskirts of town. Housing was affordable then, but Mallory is right. There's no way seasonal workers could afford to live there now.

I love that she's thinking about her employees' well-being before she's even hired them. I consider our own employees and realize I don't even know where half of them live.

"What?" she asks, creases clouding her brow.

"I'm such an asshole. I should know where our employees live since I was the one who hired them. For all I know, they're commuting from two counties away."

Scrubbing a hand over my face, I feel my last bit of self-worth slip away. I'm not even good at my job. I'm just a pretty boy who thinks he understands people. But how can I when I don't ask them basic questions?

Mallory pulls my hand away. "Hey. Don't do that to yourself. You're not an asshole."

I cock an eyebrow at her.

"Okay, not because of that. And not even for the reasons you think." She moves closer and leans against me, but I'm stiff and unwelcoming. It takes me a moment with her this close before I feel my frustration slip away enough for me to wrap an arm around her.

"What reasons do I think?"

She twists in my arms to see my face when she speaks. "You think you're not smart enough. You think you're just a pretty face who was handed the job no one else wanted because you're a flirt and that's handy when it comes to hiring people."

I swallow hard because I feel myself readying the long list of reasons I don't deserve any of what I've been given in life. It comes so easily to rattle off the worst of my traits. But she doesn't give me a chance.

"You think that all anyone sees when they look at you is a guy who's perfect for a good time and useless when it comes to anything real." She looks deep into my eyes, and I watch the tiny flecks of gold dance in hers.

"Well, I'm here to tell you, Dashiell Corbett, that they couldn't be more wrong, so get those ideas out of your head. There's so much more to you. That's how I see it." She smiles. "And we've already established that I'm the most brilliant woman in the world, so…"

Even if I can't wipe away a decade of negative opinions of myself with her sweet words, they warm me nonetheless, mainly because they're *her* words. Because she's quickly becoming the only person whose opinion matters to me.

allory

IN THE WEEKS after our engagement, I get busy. My parents return from their trip to Europe, and I give them two days to get over their jet lag before inviting them to my house for dinner. The timing of their trip away works perfectly to explain how they didn't know about my new relationship. That, and the fact that I don't tell them everything.

"I just can't wait to meet him," my mother says through bleary eyes and a yawn when she spots the engagement ring on my finger as I drive them back from the airport.

"You already know him," my dad chimes in. "It's Dash Corbett. You've known him since he was a kid."

"I knew him, but I didn't really *know* him," my mother explains. "Isn't it funny how you can think you get what someone's about, and then they up and surprise you? Who'd have known the offspring of Kingston Corbett would have romance in his blood? That's all I'm saying."

"Forgive your mother. She's still on French time," my dad grumbles with his eyes half-closed in the back seat.

But I know what my mom means. I didn't really know Dash either, and the things I'm learning continue to surprise me. His proposal, for one thing. It's had my heart reeling for a week.

Even though I know he was making stuff up on the spot because I forced him to come up with a proposal, his words burrowed deep into my heart where they most definitely don't belong.

I spend the morning of our dinner shuffling through recipes and gathering the ingredients from the farmers' market and Sunshine Foods, where I steer clear of the pickle display.

Then I drive everything back to my house, stopping at a dessert place in town to get some strawberry tarts. When I pull in front of my house, I'm surprised to see Dash leaning against the side of his car, waiting for me.

His sunglasses reflect the midday sun and with his hair brushed back and the muscles of his chest and abs visible through the fabric of a navy tee, he looks like a magazine ad for a car. Or sunglasses. Or anything else he feels like selling.

I'd buy.

He turns when he hears my car rumble up the drive and cups his hand over his eyes to see me in the sun when I hop out.

"Hey." He says it like it's obvious why he's here, but he seems to like showing up unannounced.

"Hi. What's up?"

He shrugs. Maybe he's not sure. "You said your folks were coming for dinner. Thought you might need help cooking."

"You cook?"

His golden retriever smile fades. If he had a tail, it would have stopped wagging. I need to stop sounding so skeptical of him when he's already made it clear he's not what I think.

"Sorry. I need to stop doing that."

"What?"

"Underestimating you."

A sliver of the smile returns, but it's so much better than the broad, happy look he wears most of the time. This little sliver is earned, and I want to make an effort to gain more of them.

He leans toward where I'm holding a grocery bag against my hip. "So…what are we cooking?"

I start for my front door, but Dash is already wresting the bag from my grip and slipping it under his arm like it weighs no more than a pound. His shoulders flex, and I'm not above enjoying the view.

"Spaghetti puttanseca with goat cheese, a garden salad, and a chocolate tart."

Dash spins around. "Chocolate tart?"

I bat my eyes innocently. "Yes, why? Do you know someone who likes chocolate tarts?"

He pulls me into his arms and kisses me. Like almost every kiss, this one gets hot fast, and Dash nearly drops the bag of groceries as our tongues swirl against one another.

"Damn," he says when we break the kiss. "Never gets old."

"Nope."

It scares me a little bit how good it feels to kiss him because this arrangement is fake and I can't get too attached to him. But it's better than anything I've ever experienced with a man. More and more, being with Dash doesn't feel like an act. It feels like we're dating.

We start unloading the groceries in my kitchen, where Dash moves a fruit bowl off my center island. I open the blinds wider to let in the afternoon sun, which casts warm light on all the pale green-painted cabinets and kisses Dash's face. I can't blame the sun for wanting to do that.

Dash shuffles around my kitchen, taking out spices and various pots and pans as though he's cooked here a million times. Together, we work harmoniously without recipes, pinching and dashing our way to a dinner that sizzles on the stove an hour later when my parents arrive.

"Dashiell Corbett," my mom says, shaking out her blond bob and grasping both of Dash's hands in hers. "Haven't seen you since you were a kid. When Mallory told me about the two of you…I was just delighted. Dad's checking the engine on the car. He heard a noise…"

"I can go take a look," Dash offers.

"That would be wonderful." She kisses Dash on both cheeks. "How the Europeans do it," she explains, gesturing for me to follow her into the kitchen. She carries a brown paper bag, which she sets on my center island. "Sourdough. You can serve it with dinner or have it tomorrow. It's from a little farm in Healdsburg."

"Thanks."

She tips her head toward mine conspiratorially and speaks quietly. "You two look happy."

"We are," I assure her. "Which was why I was so upset you insisted on giving Felix so much control."

"Oh, well dear, he's family."

"He's *not* family. But Dash will be. So you can send Felix packing."

The light coming through my kitchen window makes my mom look like she has a halo of sunny frizz, but the angle makes it hard to see her expression. I move to the other side of the island, and she turns to face me.

She's frowning. "I think it's wise not to make any rash moves."

"Like what?" What could qualify as a rash move for a woman who putters around after sheep all day?

"Felix isn't going anywhere, and he's capable of running things here. If and when you're actually married again, we can revisit the situation."

"If and when?" I couldn't have heard her right.

"I'm just saying, long engagement, a lot could happen. It's good to have options."

I wipe a hand over my face because there's no talking sense into my mother. She can "if and when" my ass because I'm going to make sure our wedding happens sooner rather than later.

Dash and I have a date on the calendar, but there's no reason we can't move things up. His family owns the premiere wedding venue in the entire town.

My mother won't know what hit her. In the meantime, the discussion is over, and I walk back out make sure Dash isn't underneath my parents' car, only to find them walking into the house together.

My dad, whose beard has gone gray, tips his fedora at us and pats Dash on the back. "Glad we got that solved, Mr. Rutherford," Dash says. I have to turn away to hide my smile at his boyish politeness.

"Nonsense. Henry, please."

"Henry." They stand two feet apart, both clearly nervous.

"Good to see you, Mallory." My dad kisses my cheek. "Makes us happy to know our daughter has a partner watching her back."

"Well, I'm watching more than that," Dash says with a wink. I expect my parents to choke on the implication, but nothing can dim their smiles. "Let me pour us some wine."

My dad holds up a bottle he brought. "Show me to the corkscrew. I'll do it."

Before Dash leads him to the drawer of kitchen tools, I pull on his shirt and drag him closer to me. "They love you!" I whisper, and I'm treated to both cheek dimples and a kiss on the temple. "Oh, and we're gonna need to push up the wedding date."

He tilts his head. "Yeah?"

"Yeah. I'll explain later."

"Okay. Plan for world domination. Activated," he replies before attending to the wine opening task.

Activated, indeed.

ash

"WE DON'T NEED to go to the carnival if you don't want to," Mallory says, handing me a piece of buttered toast. She invited me over for breakfast before our plans to hit up the annual carnival at the high school. It's a local tradition.

I flip the toast upside down and take a bite, letting the buttery side melt on my tongue. If the toast is this delicious, I can't wait to dig into whatever else she's cooking.

"I want to go. With *you*." I want to be sure she knows I'm not in it for the Whack-a-Mole game.

"Okay." She casts me a sideways glance, maybe searching for meaning behind my emphatic reply. I reach for her chin and guide her face to meet mine so I can kiss her. It's a better explanation than any words I have. When I pull away, her eyes have that dreamy, dazed look I love.

"Okay," she concedes.

End of discussion.

When I arrived a half hour ago, the scent of melted butter hit my nose as soon as I opened the door to my truck. I practically sprinted to her front door, only to find it cracked open. I knocked even though the door seemed like an invitation to enter, but Mallory didn't answer.

I walked through her front entryway to her kitchen and saw why. In a beam of sunlight that looked like a movie pro had choreographed it, Mallory swayed to a Taylor Swift ballad I recognized because it had been playing at the Dark Horse on the night Mallory and I revealed we're "engaged."

Holding the spatula up like a microphone, Mallory sang along to lyrics about a guy who sounded like a big mistake one summer. I wonder if it's a coincidence that the same song is playing from that first night. Maybe it's a personal favorite of hers.

She intermittently stirs a pan of eggs and stops to sing into the spatula, her back facing me. It's fucking adorable, and I'm torn between letting her know I'm here and staring at her for as long as I can without her knowing.

From what she's singing, she keeps returning to the guy even though she knows it's a mistake all summer.

I wouldn't be the first person in the world to do that. I've had my share of picking the wrong person.

Mallory bops along to the song and shakes her ass, which looks goddamn amazing in a pair of white denim cutoffs, and now I feel like a creeper staring at her without her realizing it.

"Hey."

She doesn't hear me. She's singing too loudly, swiveling her hips and stirring the eggs. It doesn't matter that her voice is a little off-key—I'm here for all of it. Between the smell of toast and buttery eggs and the sight of her dancing in front of me, it feels like Christmas morning, and I'm not sure which gift I want to open first.

I take a step closer and tap her on the shoulder. She practically jumps out of her skin, whirling around and holding up the spatula like a weapon. Her eyes shine bright in fierceness and a tiny bit of fear.

"Oh. It's you." She lowers the spatula.

"Who did you think it was?"

"I don't know. It could be anyone. I left the door open."

I can't help but chuckle. "And you did that even though it would freak you out if a stranger showed up here?"

"Well, yeah. I didn't want to miss your knock."

Grinning, I point at her spatula. "Excellent choice of weapon, by the way. I'm glad you didn't use it on me."

I'm actually lying. Spatula play might be fun.

She turns back to the stove, stirs the eggs one more time, and turns off the heat. Continuing to bustle about, she opens the refrigerator and takes out two jars of jam, then grabs silverware from a drawer.

"You should get a peephole, by the way. Not smart to open your door if you don't know who's out there."

"I hope you're hungry. I made a lot of food." Mallory gestures around the kitchen. If I hadn't been staring at her dancing, I'd have noticed a bowl of berries, some kind of sliced berry loaf, a stack of toasted sourdough, and what looks like a green salad.

"Salad for breakfast?"

"I know it's not for everyone, but I like a little greenery with all the butter and carbs."

"Suits me. I'm grateful you invited me over."

She stops moving and tips her head up to assess me, almost like she doesn't believe I'm being genuine. "Grateful? Actually grateful?"

"Absolutely. Breakfast is my favorite meal, and I rarely eat it. I usually run late in the mornings because I stay up too late and have to grab coffee and a muffin on the go."

She nods, seeming satisfied with my explanation. "Well, we have that in common."

"You skip breakfast?"

"No!" Her eyes go wide as though the idea is blasphemy. "It's my favorite meal. Why would I skip my favorite meal?"

It seems obvious, but… "For the reasons I just said. If you're running late…"

"If I want to do something, I make sure there's time to do it."

Putting my hands up in surrender, I don't plan to argue with her. Not when the food is hot, and my stomach is ready to digest itself. "Words to live by. I'll try to do better."

She stares at me. "Really?"

"Yes. Why would I say it if I didn't mean it?"

"To placate me. And because you're hungry."

With the various smells assaulting my senses, it's hard to take time out to keep talking, but this feels important. "Mallomar, I'm a guy. I'm pretty much always hungry, and I will always be grateful to you if you feel like cooking. But I will never lie to you in an attempt to placate you. Never. Got it?"

She doesn't move for a second, and I worry that she doesn't believe me. Then slowly, she starts to nod, and the tiniest smile creeps across her face. "Okay, no lying. Sometimes it takes me a while to let an idea sink in. But I like it."

As much as I'm dying to understand why it's a new concept, I've waited about as long as I'm capable of when the food looks and smells this good. Topic for another time.

Meanwhile, Mallory brings various plates of food to her kitchen table, which has two place settings complete with paisley cloth napkins. I grab the remaining bowls and plates and join her at the table.

Mallory pours us each a cup of coffee and I notice a creamer and sugar bowl in the middle of the table. I wonder if she eats like this every day.

When the first sip of coffee hits my tongue, I groan, all my tastebuds firing at once.

"Good, right?" Mallory says, sipping from her cup.

So good.

* * *

THE CARNIVAL IS a candy-colored assortment of rides moving in orbit like a Rube Goldberg experiment. Small yellow carts fly down the one long roller coaster rail that encircles the grassy space at Oak Tree Vineyards, which puts on the carnival every year.

Word has gotten out over time, and now the "small, local beanbag toss," as Oak Tree still bills it, has nearly outgrown its space. They've added a Ferris wheel, a swinging pirate ship, bumper cars, and several spinning rides that Mallory rejects outright.

"Nope. No rides. Not looking to lose my breakfast and get dizzy, thank you very much," she says, steering me away from a ride that has swings flying out like octopus arms as the middle of the ride spins at a healthy speed.

"Not even one?" I don't intend to push her, but I do love anything that whirls me around at top speed.

She stops walking and faces me squarely. "Thank you, no. You're welcome to go without me."

"Offer rejected. I don't want to go without you." As the words come out, I'm aware of their potential double meaning. Mallory waits as though she expects me to explain that I'm only referring to the carnival ride, but I have no intention of modifying what I just said.

I watch her throat work as she swallows and blinks up at me. I stare her down, daring her to question my meaning.

"Let's go this way," she mutters, clearing her throat.

On a long exhale, she grabs my hand and starts walking me toward the game booths, as though that was our destination all along. Eyeing the roller coaster, I promise myself I won't leave

180

today without getting Mallory onto one of the rides, even if it's just the merry-go-round.

I'm all for game booths, so she'll get no complaints from me.

The first one that catches her interest is the basketball pop-a-shot game. From her little cross-body purse, she unfurls the long strip of tickets I bought when we walked in. We have enough to play this game for eight hours straight if she wants. I wasn't about to put limits on our carnival fun by being stingy with the tickets.

"You a baller?" I ask, smirking because she most definitely is.

Mallory points at herself. "Tall. Made me a natural go-to for the coaches at my school. I wasn't great, but I'd give it a try."

"Care to make it interesting?" I pull out my own tickets, which I've neatly folded into groups of four.

"What do you have in mind?"

We get in line behind a dad and his son, who bounces on his toes with excitement, his blond hair practically white in the sun.

Eyeing the setup, which consists of a basketball hoop mounted over a vinyl slide to return the balls back after each shot, I have a feeling I can take her, even if she did play as a kid. I have two brothers so I have some game.

"Little bet? Loser has to wear one of those hats around for the rest of the day?" I point at a row of prizes, all ridiculous hats. There are foam top hats with spinning pinwheels sticking out, baseball hats with monster faces, felt fuzzy hats in crazy patterns and colors.

"Ha. Get ready to walk around in a purple furry cowboy hat, buddy."

It's the closest thing to an endearment she's used for me, and it surprises me how much I like it, even if I know a buddy is only a friend.

"Confident. I like it."

"You'll like it less when you lose."

"I changed my mind. Not confident. Cocky! Get ready to parade around the place in a baseball hat with a donkey face, Mellow."

She laughs and shakes her head. "That may be the first and last time anyone's ever called me that."

When it's our turn to take shots at the side-by-side hoops, I can see why. The buzzer sounds, and she approaches it like it's her job.

A few seconds in, she's already made two shots while I stand there gawking at her like a schoolboy who finds himself standing next to the prom queen. She ably shoots with both hands and then bends to scoop up the other ball and take the next shot. It's poetry.

I'm already losing the bet, but I can't take my eyes off her finesse.

Each shot banks neatly off the backboard and sinks through the hoop. No net.

One or two of them miss, but she leans forward and scoops them up, eyes on the net, ready to take the next shot. I'm willing to believe she hasn't played basketball in years, but there's no way she's new at this game.

"You didn't tell me you're a ringer at pop-a-shot."

"You didn't ask. We used to visit a cousin in Sebastopol when I was a kid, and the only thing to do at the time was go to the arcade. This was my game."

Talking doesn't throw her off her game, but I realize ten seconds have elapsed on the timer, and I'm still standing motionless with the ball in my hands, taking in her grace and beauty next to me. Finally, she stops, ball in hand, and turns to me. "You trying to give me an advantage? I don't want it. Take your shot."

The words land on me with multiple levels of meaning. True, there's no way I can beat her at this game unless she starts missing an awful lot of baskets, but I hear what she says, and it gives me a new mission.

I want to win this woman over. I'm taking my shot.

Palming the two basketballs because I have big hands, I toss one toward the hoop, and as soon as it swishes through the net, I launch the next one. By then, the first ball has rolled back to me, and I toss it up with one hand. Again and again.

Little bells sound each time a ball makes it through the hoop, and between the two of us, we're conducting our own little bell orchestra. A group of spectators has gathered to watch our grudge match, a few rooting out loud, mostly for Mallory.

"You've got a fan club," I observe.

I'm not trying to throw her off by making her skip a beat. Or maybe I am.

The timer keeps ticking. We're forty seconds in, and Mallory is two points ahead of me. She looks at my score for the first time, and her brows crease. She hates to lose.

Well, too bad. I hate it more.

A couple of my shots miss, and my adrenaline shoots through the roof. Five more seconds on the clock, and we're tied. She sees it too.

We both fire off shots like crazy, frantically frustrated as the balls take too long to roll down the plastic and make our way back for the next shot. The bells chime in quick succession, and I can't keep track of who's making which shot and who's ahead.

I toss my ball up, and it sweeps through the net. Next one too. I glance at Mallory's score. She's one point behind me, and the timer is ticking down to the last two seconds. I put up one more shot, which misses. I'm distracted. But when I reach down to grab a ball, it's not there.

Next to me, Mallory tosses up a final shot, a buzzer-beater that brings her score to one ahead of me, just as my other ball returns to my waiting hand and I toss it toward the hoop. It slides through easily, but the buzzer has already sounded, so I don't get the point.

"Winner!" she yells, pumping her fist in the air.

"Cheater!" I point at where three balls now sit beneath her hoop. "You swiped my ball."

"Is it cheating to see an opportunity and take it?"

"If it prevents me from scoring the winning basket, it does."

Browsing the display of silly hats, Mallory shakes her head. "What makes you think you would have scored?"

I laugh. "Oh, I always score when I want to."

She rolls her eyes, but she can't stop her smile. "I know. I just really wanted to win, and I couldn't get the balls in my hands fast enough."

I can't help smirking at that. "Good to know you like balls in your hands."

She buries her face in her hands, and I pull her in, wrapping my arms around her like I've wanted to do since she sank the first shot. Peeling her hands from her face, I look down at her flushed cheeks and plush lips.

"Let's get you a hat." I boop her nose and get ready for her to yell at me for doing it, but she shakes her head and laughs.

"Fine. Do your damage. I can take it."

"Oh, I plan on it."

I rub my hands together as though I'm hatching an evil scheme, but really, there's no bad choice in the hat department. They're all crazy, and she'd look goddamn adorable in any of them. I make her try on a big red-and-white-striped hat made of foam, but it makes her taller than me. Then I point at a baseball hat with a dragon tail sticking out of the back and an open mouth in the front.

It's nutty, but I decide I can do better with a bright blue beanie that looks like a foam airplane landed on top of it. When Mallory puts it on, the wings stick out on both sides, and the big grin on the face of the airplane makes me smile right back.

"This is it," I say.

"You sure?" Mallory looks in the mirror, tilting her head from side to side. As she does it, tiny lights on the airplane light up.

"Oh my god, there are motion-sensitive lights. I actually kind of love it!"

She grins beneath that ridiculous fucking hat, and it hits me that I could fall in love with this woman.

Yeah. Except…I already have.

CHAPTER 24

*M*allory

AGREEING to wear this ridiculous hat should be enough of a victory for Dash, but somehow I let him convince me to go on one ride.

All the spinny things are out, so I agree to the Ferris wheel because it seems benign. Or rather, Dash shames me into it after I lobby for the bumper cars. "Bumper cars aren't a ride," he says definitively.

"I'd be riding in a tiny car. That makes it a ride," I insist.

"No, you'd be driving in a small parking lot. You need to leave the ground for it to be a ride."

"I've never heard that definition. What makes you the expert on what is or isn't a ride?"

"Trust me, Marshmallow, I know what constitutes a ride. For one thing, it needs to be fun, and it should make your heart do a flip at some point. There should be a tiny bit of fear involved."

I almost tell him that being with him today has already made

186

my heart flip over itself several times, but he doesn't need to know that. It's been happening since the day we finally lost control and had all the amazing sex. And now, even though I'm mostly bathing in the afterglow of what I'm sure half the ladies in the county have experienced, I'm still all tingly inside.

When Dash grabs my hand as we walk through the carnival and try a few other games, I'm aware that no one seems to be looking twice at us. Our engagement is already old news. So is the idea of a couple holding hands while they walk around a public space.

So why do I suddenly feel his hand against mine like it's leaving a heat seal on my skin? I can barely concentrate on anything except how my hand feels in his, and I find myself wanting his hands on more parts of me.

"I think you should kiss me." All in the name of public displays of affection. I stop and stand in front of Dash so he either has to kiss me or move around me. He makes the right choice.

"Don't have to ask me twice, hon."

I feel a secret little thrill at the endearment. It's meaningless, and he probably doesn't even know he said it. For all I know, he'd say it to his sisters. But I don't care. It has meaning to me.

"I like when you call me that." Maybe I shouldn't have said it. Maybe he'll think it's weird. I promised him honesty, though, so he might as well know.

"What? Honey?"

"Or the abbreviated version you just did. It's sweet."

It surprises me when he squeezes my hand, almost as though he's doubling down on the affection. "*You're* sweet."

He brings my hand to his lips and kisses it. Like we're a couple. Not the kind of fake couple we've been pretending to be. Somehow, today I feel like a real couple.

It's the sex, obviously. It's confusing me, and I need to get a grip before I catch feelings that have no business in our arrangement. And yet...we are keeping up appearances, after all. No harm in going along with it. If I let myself get swept up today, I'll just talk myself down later on.

It's fine. It will all be fine.

Meanwhile, Dash is steering me toward the bigger rides. The area with the kiddie rides felt comforting. I figure I could handle a merry-go-round or a rocking horse, but that's not where we are now. The roller coaster towers overhead, and I fear that's Dash's idea of fun.

"You're not serious with this." I point at where the yellow cart whizzes by overhead, filled with screaming teenagers with their hands in the air. "I am not going on that."

"You made that clear. How about a compromise?" He points at the Ferris wheel off to the right. It's huge and light with neon stripes on the spokes, but I have to admit that it doesn't seem to be moving very quickly. "Even old ladies can handle the Ferris wheel."

His smirk is back, complete with a dazzling dimple in his cheek. I want to punch him for comparing me to the elderly, but I'm also a tiny bit curious about the ride. Not that I'll give him the satisfaction of admitting it.

"Old ladies, eh?"

"Wait, here's where you turn out to have spent time working at the circus as a child or something. And now you're going to climb the outer rungs of the damn thing to prove a point." He stares up at the giant wheel, which has just stopped to let off passengers from one of its buckets.

"Nope. Never been on one. Not gonna climb it. No way."

"But you'll go?"

"I'll go."

He squeezes my hand again, and a ripple of warmth courses over my skin. I like making him happy.

Dash leads us through the turnstiles, and we hand over our tickets. A few minutes later, a couple wearing actual prom king and prom queen sashes exits the ride, and we climb into the open cart. The attendant shuts the door and latches it. A second later, we're rising into the air.

Dash keeps his hand on top of mine on the bench between us, watching my face as we glide higher. I don't freak out. I'm not sure who's more surprised about it.

"You good?" He has the worried look of a dad about to take his hand off a toddler bike and hopes his kid doesn't fall.

"I'm good." I gaze out over Napa Valley and let out a long exhale. "More than good. It's pretty awesome up here."

We're shielded from the midafternoon sun blazing relentlessly behind us in our little red bubble. The light casts a giant Ferris wheel shadow on the field beyond the carnival, and I watch it move as we do.

Settling his arm around my shoulders, Dash leans against the bench behind us. "You've really never been in one of these?"

"Never. I always thought it would go speeding into the sky and then drop in some sort of gravity plunge."

Dash chuckles. "How is that possible? When you watch a Ferris wheel spin, it's just doing gentle circles. There's never any plunge."

I shrug. "Don't know what to tell you. I guess I just pictured it that way in my mind and never bothered to look up."

"Ha. Sounds like the way a lot of people form opinions. Few of them are true. Not that it matters once people latch onto a thing."

He looks out over Napa, where rolling hills of green are peppered with neat rows of grapevines. At this time of year, grapes hang beneath the upper tufts of leaves, but we can't see them from here.

"You speaking from experience?" I ask, putting my hand on his knee.

His lips tip up, but I don't get a full smile. He looks more thoughtful than happy despite the view.

"Maybe. Probably."

I wait, but he doesn't say anything more. We're about a quarter of the way up, so the entire carnival spreads out below us, and even more greenery is visible in the distance. The wheel stops so people can exit and enter below. We move again and stop again.

Dash still hasn't said a word, but I wait for one more stop before prodding him.

"Care to elaborate?"

He turns toward me again, and his lips are on mine before my brain has time to catch up. I realize he has no intention of elaborating. And a moment after that, I forget why I asked.

As the Ferris wheel sweeps us higher, I forget about the view. Dash's lips roam across my cheek and down to my jaw, where he nips at the skin and soothes it with his tongue.

My entire body sighs against him as I find his lips again. And then his tongue. Searching. Swirling. Melting against each other until I'm shifting to get closer. To find more points of contact between us.

"Wait," Dash says against my lips. "I have an idea. Stay right there."

I start to explain that there's not exactly a lot of room to go anywhere else, but then I realize what Dash has in mind as he moves to the floor of the small vessel that's almost reached the top of the wheel.

There isn't a lot of space in our round bubble of a Ferris wheel car, so he seems to change his mind, placing his large hands on my hips and shifting me to one end of the bench.

My eyes go wide partly because he's managed to cram himself into the space at my feet, but mainly because of the cocky grin he gives me as he gently moves my knees apart.

"This is your idea?"

He nods and licks his lips. "To make up for the hat."

"I kinda like the hat," I say, slouching down and sighing as Dash starts kissing the inside of my thigh. "But I like this more."

Dash runs his hands up the sensitive skin of my inner thighs, and I stop talking. His breath is hot against my skin. His tongue even hotter.

His hands continue moving until they reach the apex of my thighs. I suck in a breath when he grazes my center with a finger, swiping gently back and forth until I can't see straight.

"When I saw you in this dress this morning, all I could think about was how much I wanted to kiss you here." He plants a row of kisses up my inner thigh. I sigh again. "And here." His lips land where his finger was a moment ago, and I gasp.

"God, Dash. Yes."

Sliding my panties to the side, he runs his tongue straight up my center in one long stroke, and I'm pretty sure our Ferris wheel has morphed into a roller coaster. I'm dizzy, moaning, feeling…every swirl of his tongue, every inch of his hot mouth, the edges of his teeth when he nips at my clit. Then he sucks hard. And I see stars.

The magic of the Ferris wheel reaching the top, looking out over beautiful vineyard views, feeling the warm air on a sunny afternoon, and then this… Dash with his tongue between my legs, taking me higher than any Ferris wheel ever could.

I want the feeling to last. I want the moment to stretch into minutes and hours. When Dash slides a finger inside me and keeps working circles with his tongue, I can't hold myself back.

"Fuck, honey, you taste so good," Dash murmurs.

That does it. Every pleasure center in my body fires at once, and the stars in my eyes turn to comets and whizzing meteors. I'm lost in space, found by Dash, and out of control.

I'm caught between closing my eyes to the best orgasm of my life and peeking to make sure we haven't reached the bottom. As much as we want engagement cred, I don't want the Ferris wheel operator to catch us like this. But we're nowhere near the bottom.

I pull Dash up and press my lips to his. Wrapping my arms

around his neck, I pull him close and open my mouth to taste myself on his tongue.

We spend the rest of our Ferris wheel time like this, locked in a forever kiss that only stops when we reach the bottom and the attendant asks, "Do y'all want to go around again?"

Dash barely breaks the kiss to answer. He yanks a handful of tickets from his pocket and shoves them in the guy's hand, along with a twenty-dollar tip.

We ascend once more, the Ferris wheel sweeping us into the sky. "Just one more round," Dash says. I assume he means once more around the Ferris wheel. But then he drops to his knees again, and I see he has other ideas. Better ideas.

* * *

IT'S GOTTEN WINDY, a late summer breeze that does little to disperse the stagnant heat of the day, but I'll take it. The dog days of summer hit hard around here, and a wind strong enough to flutter the leaves feels great.

I'll have to consider weather forecasts and the meaning of coastal winds once Autumn Lake is growing grapes, and I momentarily feel overwhelmed by the long lists of tasks I'll have very soon. I can't let worries shadow all the new business opportunities for Autumn Lake, but the nerves are real. The wine-growing community is small. People will know if I screw this up, and it can't happen.

Dash's reassuring hand on my waist grounds me and settles my thoughts. For now.

Somehow, we've spent nearly six hours at the carnival, way longer than I intended when I suggested the activity. It's been so much fun.

We've played most of the games, but we've only competed head-to-head in the basketball pop-a-shot…eleven more times.

We're at a dead heat, tied at six each, and I haven't cheated since that first game.

At one point, Dash wrapped his arm around my shoulders and pulled me in for a kiss right in the middle of the game, but that cost both of us valuable seconds, so I couldn't accuse him of distracting me for an advantage.

We've leveled up our prizes—except for the hat, which I will keep until the end of time—so by now, Dash is saddled with a human-sized stuffed bear, which he carries tucked under one arm like the third wheel on our date.

I've come to this event every year since it began back when I was in middle school, and I've never enjoyed it as much as I have today. The games are pretty much the same. The rides have only improved a bit.

That leaves me with the unescapable conclusion that I'm currently zooming around on a cloud because of the company.

"This way." Dash taps the brim of my hat and pulls me down a row of games, some of which we've already played. We were in a dead heat at Whack-a-Mole until he won, but then I beat him at a game squirting water to inflate small balloons. "Let's check these out."

We've already checked out everything, but I'm not complaining if he wants to stay at the carnival.

"Competitive, are we? You looking to regain your dignity by beating me at something?" I tease, elbowing him in the ribs.

"We're not going head-to-head on this one." He leads me past several game booths and stops at one we skipped the first time around. It's a simple ring toss, but he cautioned me earlier that it's harder than it looks.

"I thought you said this one was sneaky, designed so the rings bounce." Indeed, the rows of milk bottles mostly have rings lodged between bottlenecks rather than encircling them.

Dash nods but seems intent on trying. He hands the last of his tickets to a guy in blue-striped pants and a matching jacket and waits for him to retrieve a stack of rings. "Good luck," he says, presenting Dash with five rings.

"Okay, it just takes a bit of finesse," he says quietly as though giving himself instructions. The sign over the game says he only needs to ring one of the bottles to get a prize, which tells me it's designed to be difficult.

Dash holds the ring like a Frisbee and lets it sail free. The first one goes sailing over the bottlenecks and banks off one before settling into the crack between two bottles. Same result on the second try.

"It's supposed to be hard," I say encouragingly, feeling in my purse for more tickets in case Dash wants to keep going after this round. From what I know of him, he doesn't like to lose, so I doubt he'll walk away without a victory.

"Yeah."

The third ring hits the mark, landing cleanly around a bottle. The fourth misses.

I hadn't realized I was holding my breath. Exhaling, I look at the sign, reassuring myself that one ring wins a prize.

"One more," Dash mumbles, eyes focused on the field of bottles, which feel like they're taunting us. He seems to be taking this so much more seriously than all the others, where we laughed and talked smack as we squared off against each other. It's like he has a personal vendetta against the man in the striped suit. Or these three dozen bottles.

I want to ask why he's so intent on winning at this particular game, but I don't dare disrupt his concentration.

With a final skillful toss, Dash rings a final bottle, bringing his score to two. He stands up straight and looks at the row of prizes hanging at the back of the booth. I'm more interested in why he chose this game for some kind of personal showdown, so I don't focus on his conversation with the booth operator, who goes to the back with a hook and takes a prize down.

But then Dash turns and holds his prize out to me. It's a Rosie the Riveter lunchbox.

At first, I'm baffled. It seems like an odd choice for a guy who doesn't need to bring lunch to work since there are two restaurants at Buttercup Hill and a catering staff.

"It's symbolic. For my badass future wife who plans to grow an empire. I don't want you skipping lunch."

The breath leaves my lungs. I feel dizzy at the thought of this man caring enough to win me a lunchbox. And not just any lunchbox—one with the baddest badass of all emblazoned on the front.

My heart, which was already so full after spending the day here with Dash, now pushes its very boundaries in my chest. So much so that I put a hand against my sternum as though I can keep it from bursting.

"Dash...wow. That's so incredibly thoughtful." I feel tiny pinpricks of tears at the corners of my eyes, which is silly because it's just a nice gesture. I shouldn't be getting so emotional about it, but I can't help it. "Seriously, thank you."

I stand on my toes to reach his lips. It's a kiss that has nothing to prove except how much I like him. Unlike all the ones for show, this one feels like it's just for us.

Best kiss of my life.

hree Weeks Later

MALLORY

Beatrix had to scramble to pull off a wedding in record time, but she said she likes a challenge.

"I can't believe you're really going through with this," Mary stage whispers from a chair next to me, where she sits in a peach-colored bridesmaid dress and black cowboy boots.

It's my own fault. I specified that the bridesmaids should wear light colors, but I didn't say anything about shoes. I, Mallory Rutherford, forgot to specify shoes. Falling for my fake fiancé has made me go soft.

"Excuse me, I believe it was your idea."

She snorts. "Sure, it was an idea. I have lots of ideas, very few of them good. But look at you, you ran with it." Then her squinty smirk turns to a real smile, and she kisses my cheek. "Are you nervous?"

"No," I insist.

"Yes," I admit a second later.

I shouldn't be nervous about a fake wedding.

In fact, I should be excited. This is the closest I'm likely to get to a real wedding, and at least I'm going through the motions with a gorgeous guy who treats me better than all the men I've dated in the past. I might as well enjoy it.

Sipping from a champagne flute that PJ deposited silently before slipping away to have her makeup done, I choose not to dwell on the irony of my life. I mean, sure, Dash has been acting like the model fiancé, defending my honor, attending to my every sexual need, and listening to me describe my hopes and dreams and taking them seriously. He's exactly the kind of man I would actually consider marrying, and the sham of a wedding we're about to enact couldn't have less to do with reality.

"Up or down?" A voice disrupts my thoughts.

"Sorry?" I meet the eyes of my hair stylist in the mirror.

"She was asking whether I think you should wear your hair up," Beatrix says as the stylist piles my blown-dry hair on top of my head.

It's early afternoon as I sit in the bridal suite at the Inn at Buttercup Hill, where Dash insisted we spend our honeymoon night later on. He also insisted I use the suite all day to get ready.

Beatrix took over from there, ordering in platters of finger foods and a bar cart filled with drinks, everything from sparkling water and orange juice to wine and champagne. My college bestie has been having her nails done with PJ and my mom on one side of the room while Beatrix hangs with me and confers with the stylist like I'm not even here.

"Well, don't bother asking me. Not like I have an opinion." I don't mean to sound snarky, but Beatrix herself admitted she sometimes gets carried away and forgets she's the event planner, not the bride. And I know how it feels to be a woman in her thirties in a small town where some of the love matches seem to have been forged at the swing sets in preschool. If she wants to live vicariously as a bride through the events she plans, I'm certainly not about to stop her.

"Sorry. She's asking both of us what we think, but I guess I answered first."

I'm just nervous about getting fake-married, and I shouldn't be taking it out on the nearest person, but that's what's happening. The neckline of my long, silk sheath dress cuts low, and I suddenly worry that it's too sexy for a wedding dress, even though it is, in fact, a wedding dress.

"You don't need to apologize. Sorry if I'm being a bitch."

Beatrix laughs. "You're not. You're being a bride." She leans in and whispers so the stylist can't hear. "And doing a good job of faking it." Straightening up, she meets my eyes in the mirror and winks.

I give her a closed-lipped smile that masks how I feel, which is uncomfortable in this too-sexy virginal dress and a little unsure I'm doing the right thing by marrying Dash for the good of my future business dreams. But I'll just smile my way through it. I'm good at that.

If Beatrix and I had stayed better friends since high school—and if she wasn't related to the man I'm fake-marrying—I'd admit that I can be bitchy without being a bride. I might even admit that I have confounding feelings for my groom and ask her what to do about them. But I'm not sure how Beatrix feels about her brother doing me this favor even though he's assured me his siblings are supportive. So I say nothing. Better that she thinks we're marching forward in this charade for the good of our family businesses and keep things simple.

The stylist continues piling my hair on top of my head and uses a few bobby pins to keep it there. Then she pulls down some long tendrils around my face. I take in the image in the mirror. On one hand, I look like so many brides I've seen in so many social media feeds. It's like she's given me the insta-bride updo that assures I'll look the part.

I should love it. Add a little tiara and I'll look like a little girl's dream of a perfect bride. But this fake wedding has been so far away from perfect bride territory that I just can't do it.

"I think I prefer it down," I tell them. "Is that very un-bridey?"

The stylist stops fussing with my hair and lets it fall down my back. As the picture-perfect bride image falls away, I instantly feel more like myself.

"It should be however you want," she says, arranging my hair over my shoulders and plugging in her curling iron. "I think we could add some soft waves. What do you think?"

"Soft waves sound good."

Beatrix nods.

I sip my champagne and hope it will calm my nerves.

Almost like she can read my thoughts, Beatrix meets my eyes in the mirror. "It's still nerve-wracking, isn't it?"

I watch my brow crease in the mirror and unconsciously bite my lip, nodding.

"Hey, how about a bathroom break?" Beatrix asks me, standing up and gesturing with a tilt of her head before I agree.

The stylist doesn't have to be told twice. "I'll get some coffee. We have plenty of time," she says, dismissing me. It's like both of them see something I don't, but as soon as I stand from the chair and start following Beatrix out of the suite's main room, a cold sweat breaks out across the back of my neck.

"Yeah, it is nerve-wracking," I mutter, not fully understanding why I can stand in front of a room full of men and present my business ideas, but the idea of wearing a frilly dress for a few hours and acting like a bride has me flustered.

Beatrix opens the door to the bridal suite and walks into the hallway, and even though there's a perfectly good bathroom in the suite, I blindly follow her lead. She walks quickly, and I need to gather my wedding dress and hold it against my hips so it doesn't drag on the floor. I'm still barefoot, and the dress is hemmed for my three-inch heels. The last thing I need is to trip.

As soon as we're away from the bridal suite, I relax slightly. Too many people in that room. Too much anticipation of the big wedding.

Beatrix bypasses the public restroom in the hallway and ushers me outside through a glass door leading to a private patio. I haven't spent much time at Buttercup Hill, so I follow her to wherever she plans to take me.

She stops and points at a pair of chaise lounges under a giant orange umbrella, so I drop onto a soft white towel atop one of the chaises. She takes the one next to me, but not before sweeping my dress off the ground and gathering it around my ankles to keep it clean.

"See, if I were a real bride, I'd know to do that," I mumble, air leaving my lungs as I give in to how ill-prepared I am for my role. "I thought on the day of the wedding, some sort of bride sixth sense would kick in, and I'd be able to run on instinct. Guess not."

I don't plan to sound so defeatist, but the words took up residence someplace in my chest about an hour ago, and apparently, they took their first opportunity to escape. I sneak a look at Beatrix, expecting to see disappointment in her eyes. After all, she should expect a better performance from me when I've spent years convincing everyone in town that all I've ever wanted was a husband.

So it surprises me when she reaches over and pats the back of my hand. She meets my eyes, and I don't see disappointment. If anything, it seems like she understands how I feel, which is impressive since I'm still grappling with it myself.

"Let it out." Without removing her hand, she leans back on her chaise and closes her eyes. Warm afternoon sun kisses her skin, and I feel tempted to crank the umbrella above my head shut. Eyes still closed, Beatrix points at the lever. "Don't."

"Don't what?"

"Your makeup looks perfect. Stay in the shade so you don't sweat it off, for heaven's sake."

"Are you a mind reader?"

Beatrix shrugs and lets out a laugh. "I'm an event planner. Kind of the same thing. I also double as a therapist, punching bag, and general idea person for anything that has nothing to do with event planning."

"In other words, you're like a professional friend?"

She opens her eyes and swivels her legs around so she's sitting on the lounge facing me. "Yup. If you need one."

Some people collect friends like treasured mementos. They tuck them into their friendship bank regardless of whether they shared an apartment for two years or met on an airplane and talked for only an hour.

New friends enter the collection like seashells pocketed on vacation or ticket stubs from a favorite event. And there they stay, a link to some meaningful time or event in the past. A roadmap to new treasures in the future. Why would anyone squander that potential?

I can't answer that because I do the opposite. Friends correspond to the moment in my life when we were thrown together, and generally, I leave it at that. I assume it's what the other person wants. The only ones who've chased me have been men, and they want sex, not friendship.

So Beatrix confuses me with what sounds like an offer of friendship at the very moment when I could use one. At least, I think that's what she's doing.

"I—I think I always need one." It's way too confessional for a moment between future fake sisters-in-law on a couple of chaise lounges. The champagne must have gone to my head.

"You do."

"Sorry?"

"We all need a good friend. Doesn't have to be a best friend, but yeah. You should always have someone to lean on. Talk to."

I open my mouth and close it again. I want to tell her that she's right and wrong at the same time. I'd love to have that kind of person in my life, sure. Who wouldn't? And it's worked out fine.

"I have…people."

"People?"

"You know, people who work for me and all that. I have conversations. It's all good."

Beatrix bursts out laughing. "You're funny. I really wish we'd stayed friends because I always really liked you."

I'm glad she can only see me from the side because my eyes are probably as wide as saucers. "You did?"

"Don't sound so surprised."

I shake my head and think back to high school. I try to remember what Beatrix was like and why I assumed she didn't like me all that much.

The high school Beatrix was similar to the woman sitting next to me now. Self-assured, beautiful, smart. She was all the things I aspired to be, but back then, I didn't know how to be any of those things.

I wonder how differently my life would have turned out if I'd stopped walking with my head down to avoid what I felt sure were judgmental looks from my female peers. Maybe I'd have a crew of women as friends now. Maybe I'd have gone to business school a long time ago instead of letting other people's perceptions dictate my path.

"Sorry. I guess I'm just nervous about the wedding."

"No worries. That's why I herded you out of that room full of cackling bridesmaids. I had a feeling your head was about to explode."

I exhale a long breath. "Was it obvious?"

She tilts her head from side to side in that way that says it was obvious to everyone except me. "It's normal bride behavior. Trust me, I've seen about a thousand of them, and you're no worse than anyone else."

"And I'm not even a real bride. What's my excuse for nerves?"

"From where I sit, you have even more of an excuse."

From an unseen pocket, Beatrix produces a package of Reece's Peanut Butter Cups and tears open the package. Without asking whether I want one or worrying about what it will do to my makeup, she hands me one.

I bite into it gratefully and realize it's the first thing I've eaten all day. "Maybe it's just low blood sugar. Even the hint of this on my tongue feels mood-changing."

"It's why I carry them around on wedding days."

"I appreciate it."

Beatrix lets me chomp through the peanut butter cup before handing me the second one. She fishes a napkin from another pocket and waits until I've devoured the second cup to hand it over.

"Thanks." I dab at my mouth.

"So you're good going through with this, the marriage?"

"Yes. It'll accomplish what we both need and we have clear parameters for ending it once my ex is out of the picture." It's the party line, what I've been telling myself from the get-go.

"That's not what I'm asking. I mean, are you really okay with it being fake? What if you want to date or what if you meet someone and fall in love? What if you fall in love with Dash?"

I'm not expecting such a pointed question, so it takes me a moment to figure out how to respond.

"It's not forever." I don't know why saying it out loud makes me more sad than relieved. Beatrix meets my eyes. "And as for the love part, it's fine." My voice breaks on the last word, and I fight back the tears that want to spring forth.

Makeup. Can't mess up makeup.

"Does he know?" she asks gently, putting a hand on my shoulder.

My heart sinks because if it's obvious to her, it's probably obvious to other people. Just not Dash because he doesn't feel the same way. I shake my head.

"You should tell him."

"Why? It will only make things awkward. My temporary feelings aren't important. I need to focus on the big picture, stay focused on business."

"It's all important." She gets up from her chair and extends her hand to me. I take it and she pulls me up, careful to keep my dress from touching the ground. I take over from her and hold the hem up as we walk back to the bridal suite.

It's all important.

Her words echo in my ears.

ash

THE ENTIRE BRIDAL party has taken their places around me at the altar—my two brothers, my sisters, Lucas, my best man, and Mallory's maid of honor. My dad sits in the front row under the shade of an umbrella and stares straight at me with a bemused smile on his face, but I sense that he has no idea where he is.

His nurse told me he'd take a sedative before the ceremony to ensure that he stays calm and relaxed. She says he sometimes confuses reality with what he watches on TV, and for once, I'm sort of glad that's the case.

But this isn't the time to retreat into my head and worry about anything except getting through the day so we can ensure that Felix Sutton takes a hike and doesn't come back. I know that's Mallory's only concern, and it's the only way I'll ensure that Buttercup Hill has a future.

I just need to keep reminding myself of why I'm here. It's

business. It's my chance to do something for my family when it's most needed.

Keep telling yourself that lie, buddy. Maybe you'll believe it.

When the music changes and it's time for Mallory to walk down the aisle, my heart beats a little bit faster. Every time we've talked about our wedding, it's been with a wry wink and acknowledgment that it's all just a game designed to hoodwink her ex, and we might as well have fun in the process.

"We might as well enjoy ourselves," she said when we first agreed we could handle being fake fiancés with benefits.

Now, it doesn't feel like a game. It suddenly feels very real when Mallory appears at the back of the garden with her parents. She's a vision pulled out of a mythical story. A simple long dress that slinks over her body and emphasizes the gorgeous curve of her breasts and hips while being wholly appropriate for a wedding day. It couldn't be better suited to her, and it sends a pang of guilt through my chest that I'm not here as a real groom. She deserves that.

As she moves down the aisle toward me, beaming and looking every bit like the bride I'll never be lucky enough to have for my own, my thoughts snap back to the present. Today, she's mine. She's marrying me.

Even if it's just for show, I might as well enjoy myself, right?

Mallory's hair falls in loose waves over her shoulders, and her eyelashes frame those sultry eyes that swallow me whole every time I look deep into them. Pink cheeks. Cherry lips.

My cheeks ache, and I realize it's because I've been smiling at her so hard since she began walking toward me.

I can't help reaching out and running a finger down her cheek and watch her eyes soften when I touch her skin. I'll never get tired of that reaction, even if someday she realizes she's doing it. I hope she never realizes.

Mallory's parents each kiss her on the cheek and step back to take their seats in the front row. She turns her face up to mine and smiles.

At that moment, I'm so fucking gone for her that it's pointless to tell myself otherwise.

Our minister clears his throat and begins the ceremony.

It's surreal. In all the years I wondered if I'd ever meet a woman I'd love so much that she'd lead me to this moment, I never expected to be standing here like this—faking a wedding in front of half the people I know.

And never in my wildest imagination did I imagine marrying a woman who seemed so perfect for me—someone who barely knew me but looked at me under shooting stars and saw me better than I saw myself.

The minister's words blur into the background as I sneak sideways glances at my bride. I want to remember this moment because I may never get another one that feels quite this good.

"We might as well enjoy ourselves."

Yeah. I'm going to enjoy the hell out of her today and all night long.

When it's time for my vows, I reach for Mallory's hand and cup it in mine. Her fingers are warm and delicate in my hand, and I immediately feel steadied by the contact.

The piece of paper in my pocket is wrinkled and crinkly, but I hold it in my clammy hand and read the words I wrote without bothering to censor myself. They sounded like good vows, the kind of thing someone worthy of Mallory would say to her.

I didn't overthink. I just wrote.

Looking at her face, I feel my nerves disappear. Pink cheeks. Bright eyes. I see every bit of beauty I've loved looking at over the past couple of months. I also see beneath it to a person who's stronger than most people I know and fiercely loyal to her family, even as they've misunderstood her ambitions and intentions. I see a woman I respect and love spending time with, and I feel confident that being married to her for a year will be one of the easier things I've ever done.

The minister speaks, and a few people recite poetry. There may even be a butterfly release, but I'm not paying attention to any of that. I can't stop staring at the most stunningly gorgeous woman I've ever seen.

She has me so gobsmacked that I'm worried I won't be able to form words when it's time to recite my vows. The minister points at me, and even though he sounds like he's speaking in a fishbowl, I realize he's telling me it's my turn to talk. I turn to Mallory and take her hand in mine.

"Mallory, you are the light of my life. It's true today, and it's been true since the day we met, although I could have done without the pickle bath. But that's just proof that even when the world seems imperfect, there's something magical if you know where to look. With you, I never see darkness. I never worry about falling.

"I want to see the sun shine on your face in the morning, and I want to kiss you in the moonlight at night. I want to be there when the seasons change, and when I have good news, you're the first person I want to tell.

"My world is better because I met you. I feel lucky to be your partner in sickness and in health for the rest of my life. And I feel lucky that after today, you will forever be my wife."

My voice catches on the last two words, and the minister jokes about me being nervous about commitment, but that's not what's happening here. It hits me when I say the words that I really do want Mallory to be my wife.

When I meet Mallory's gaze, I see her blinking rapidly as if to push back tears. I mentally pat myself on the back for doing a convincing enough job of saying my vows that she seems moved. No, wait. The tears are just for show.

Probably.

She knows how to sell this moment, and she's doing a fine job of it, so fine that I almost forget it's not real. Maybe that's because I really am falling for this woman who I'm about to wed and spend every day with, even if it tears at my very last shred of iron will.

I take a shaky breath and try to steady myself. I need to get a grip if I'm falling for the playacting we're doing up here. She's my wife in name only. And only for one year. I'd do well to remember that.

My knees buckle, and, for a second, I worry I'll be the subject of future stories about the groom who face planted after saying his wedding vows.

I regain my standing and swallow hard.

Mallory squeezes my hand and begins reciting her vows, voice clear and soft at the same time. I don't care if anyone else can hear her words because I want them for myself.

"In my business school program, they taught us to research, run through all the possibilities, and come up with the best course of action. But I didn't need to do any of that with you. I just had to spend an hour with you to know that marrying you was the right and best choice. I knew it in my bones when we met. I felt something that day in the grocery store that was unlike anything I'd ever experienced. It was the kind of magic I didn't believe in, but I knew it was real like I knew my own name.

"This is the easiest decision I've ever made, and I know it will make me happy for the rest of my life. Because I love you."

My heart jumps into my throat. People say "I love you" all the time with varying degrees of seriousness—they say I love you to a friend who needs an extra bit of support or to a coworker for bringing a cup of coffee when they're dragging. I'm under no delusion that the words have deep meaning just because someone says them.

But this is a new level.

Those three words sound so damn good winding their way

from Mallory's lips to my ears that I want to hear them again. And again. *Fuck.*

Even if she doesn't mean them, even if she's just doing what's expected at her wedding, her words hit me like a wrecking ball.

It's my heart that's getting destroyed. Because I love this woman for real, and I have no business telling her any time except for right now at our fake wedding...much less feeling like they're the truest thing I could say.

"I love you. Truly," I tell her. She smiles and squeezes my hand.

We exchange rings.

The minister says, "It is my honor to pronounce you husband and wife."

And I kiss the hell out of my wife until our guests whistle and applaud, and I don't regret it one bit. Not one fucking bit.

allory

"We're planning to take our honeymoon in a few months when we have time to do it right," Dash says to a college friend who asks.

"So much going on right now for both of us at work. We're gonna honeymoon in a few months," I tell my parents' friends, a nice couple who've lived in Calistoga longer than I've been alive.

He and I have been saying versions of the same thing all night long. No one seems to think it's strange that we're not hopping on a plane to some tropical honeymoon destination in the morning, so we keep spouting the party line. And dancing.

So much dancing.

I had no idea how fun it would be to dance with my new husband until Dash spun me around on the dance floor and dipped me at the end of each song. I can't get enough. Of him.

"Is it wrong to say I'm having the best time of my life at my fake wedding with my fake husband?" I ask as Dash pulls me into his arms for a slow ballad. I admit I'm fishing, wanting him to tell me that it's not all fake, that some of what we feel for each other is real.

"It's not wrong. This is an amazing night."

"It is." I want to say more. I want to tell him that I can't imagine dancing with anyone else or loving it this much. But I can't.

Our guests clap and give us room in the center of the dance floor, but after a few seconds, he's all I see.

Or rather, all I can hear are Dash's wedding vows. They play over and over again in my mind and it takes all my where-withal not to ask him if he meant any of them. Of course he didn't.

He may like me as a person, and our sex is off the charts, but he was very clear from the get-go about where he stands on rela-tionships. I would be asking for a very uncomfortable thirteen months ahead if I brought up the idea of our fake relationship turning real.

So instead, I let my eyes drift shut and concentrate on Dash's large, reassuring hand on the small of my back. And I dream about an hour from now when we can leave our fake wedding and have very real sex in the honeymoon suite.

* * *

"You have outdone yourself, husband." I sigh in an orgasmic haze. I'm pretty sure my hair is tangled like a bird's nest with strands plastered to my face. My cheeks feel hot, and I'm lazy and pliant.

Dash's quiet chuckle tells me I look just like I feel. "Back atcha, wife."

My cheek rests on Dash's chest, and our bodies are bathed in sweat. "I sort of want to shower, but I can't move."

"If you can't move, you can't walk to the shower." Dash's voice sounds like maple syrup, and my ears are just as happy as the rest of my body.

"True."

"I'd offer to carry you, but I thought you liked me sweaty." He nudges me under the chin and shifts me so his lips can fall to mine. They're salty and sweet at the same time, and I can't imagine ever getting enough.

The bridal suite has treated us well. After the wedding, we came back to a champagne and fruit plate, which we devoured after our first round of sex. Or maybe it was after our third.

"I do," I mumble against his mouth, which travels along my cheek to my temple, where he plants a soft kiss. "But I may not be quite as desirable when I'm a sweaty mess."

He shifts again and pulls back just enough to focus on me. Our faces are a few inches apart and we lay side by side. I wrap my leg over his hip, and his hand comes to my hip. It's like we can't be with each other without touching each other.

"Why do you do that?"

"Do what?" I'm still in a hazy, dreamy, post-sex fugue, so I'm really not understanding his question.

"Denigrate yourself. Suggest that you could possibly be unde-sirable when the very idea is an impossibility. You, my dear, are very, very desirable in so many ways."

"You just like fucking me." I don't want him confused about the reason.

"You just did it again." He looks confused and maybe even a little upset. And now I'm confused because I'm not sure what I'm doing that bothers him so much.

It seems important to keep the lines of communication clear now that we've included sex in our fake relationship. I want to make sure he knows that I know that he doesn't have to pretend to catch feelings too. We can just be honest.

"What?"

"I don't *just* like fucking you."

I tilt my head because all evidence points to the contrary.

He shakes his head. "Of course I love fucking you. I really love fucking you, but that's not what I mean. You said it like the only reason I find you desirable is because of this." He points at the space between us, but I get his drift.

"I love doing all manner of things with you, with and without clothing, if I'm not being clear enough. And I don't like you thinking that I'm only telling you I find you inexplicably desirable because I like fucking you. I find you incredibly desirable. Full stop."

I feel chastened like a kid in school, but I'm not about to argue when he's saying such nice things. So I say nothing and we lay side by side for a while longer in silence. I start to reach for his abs because they're too beautiful not to touch, but he intercepts my hand and holds it against his chest instead.

"You don't believe me," he says, fixing me with those hypnotic blue eyes.

"I believe you."

"You don't. In your heart of hearts, you still think I'm under the spell of a good orgasm or I'm just paying lip service because I'm being nice. But you don't truly believe that I desire the hell out of you."

I'm ready to sling back some sort of rebuttal when it occurs to me that he's right. There's no point in arguing because he's one hundred percent correct.

I squeeze my eyes shut because it's almost painful to feel this seen and at this proximity. I don't like such close scrutiny, especially when I can't control what he sees.

"Fine. You're right."

I don't open my eyes and wait for Dash to change the subject or get up for a glass of water. Or maybe the apocalypse will happen right here and now, and I'll be saved from having to finish this conversation.

But I don't feel the bed move, and it seems that Dash has stayed exactly where he is.

The apocalypse is a giant disappointment as well.

"Mallory." The use of my actual name surprises me. I open my eyes to find Dash's peering at me with concern.

I put my hands over my eyes instead.He gently lifts them away.

"What?"

"You know what. Talk to me. Why do you think I'm just blowing smoke up your ass?"

I take in a deep lungful of air and exhale slowly.

"I guess…in my experience…people tell me what they think I want to hear, even if it's not true."

"I'm not like that." The firm set of his jaw leaves no room for argument.

"Okay." I can't take the intensity of his eyes, so I look away.

He turns my chin to face his. "No, not okay. I need you to believe me. We've gotten ourselves in deep with each other with our plans to get married, get your business started, and now we've thrown sex into the mix."

At my attempt to protest, he taps a finger against my lips. "And I am very, very happy about that, so don't get any ideas about eliminating it." He removes his finger and I stay quiet. "I'd like to get to know you better. If I say you can believe me, it means that you can. If I have to keep reminding you until it sinks in, I will."

"Okay." It shouldn't be so hard for me to accept his honesty, but I guess I still carry lingering fears that people like Felix tell me. "Thank you." He nods, and I sense that he's waiting for me to say more. "You can trust me too. If I say something, it will be the truth."

He gives me a side-eye as though he's not sure. "Yeah?"

"Yes. I promise."

"Okay, good."

Dash's body relaxes, and he pulls me into him again. I mull what he just said and try to figure out why it makes me feel slightly uncomfortable. It's not so much the idea of being honest with each other that is a problem. It's more the idea of acknowledging that it means he'll know things about me, things I might tell him because I've just vowed to be honest with him.

I'm not sure I'm ready to do that with another person.

Maybe it won't come up.

"I like this," Dash says, kissing my temple, and I assume he means the way we're lying here in a sweaty heap after an orgasm that seemed like it lasted thirty minutes. It feels good here, curled against his chest with Dash's strong arms encircling me.

"Me too." I nuzzle into him a little more and feel his grip tighten. I don't dare tell him how much I like it because it scares me to think about it. When I'm in his arms, I don't ever want him to let me go.

Our inhale and exhale synchronize, and we breathe like one connected being. It feels like we're more than the sum of our parts.

"What were you like in high school?" Dash asks, rolling onto his back, putting his hands behind his head, and looking impossibly sexy doing so. His abs flex as he rearranges himself, shoving a pillow behind his head.

He was built to exist in this exact scene, post-coital on crisp sheets with morning sun highlighting every curve of his chest and abs. I almost can't look at him with a straight face because he's such a perfect physical specimen that it must be some kind of cosmic joke. But I look anyway because I can.

Maybe that's why I don't answer his question. I'm distracted and very content.

Then I notice his head tilt and his lips press together expectantly. I realize he actually expects an answer.

"Are you really asking me about fifteen years ago?" My gaze

returns to his abs until I feel his index finger brush beneath my chin, tilting my face to look at him.

"I am."

"Why?"

"Because I want to know."

I scrunch my face and shake my head, dismissing this ridiculousness. "I was…normal. You know. It was high school."

"That's a terrible answer."

"Sorry. It was a terrible question."

"Why?" The corner of his mouth rises in amusement.

I shrug. "No one particularly likes high school, do they?"

He rolls off the bed and strides to the bathroom to refill the water glass from my bedside table. I watch his tight, athletic ass retreat toward the open door of the bathroom, grateful that we didn't pull the shades last night. Every detail of Dash's back and legs glows under the warm morning light. He's like a walking Michelangelo sculpture.

When he comes back with the water, I get an even better view. All sculpted abs, broad shoulders, and large dick.

I don't realize I'm gawking in his direction until he looks very pointedly at me. I lower my eyes and feel the creep of heat across my face.

He drops back onto the bed next to me, and I hear his low chuckle. "You can look. God knows I can't stop staring at you every chance I get."

This makes me blush even more furiously, which is why I end up answering a question I didn't plan on discussing.

"So… tell me about the high school version of you. What was she like?"

"You knew me then. I'm sure you remember."

"I remember you as a hot senior that every sad little freshman like me looked at like the goddess you were. I didn't know you. I wouldn't have had the gall to say I knew you."

I roll my eyes but feel my face blaze, no doubt turning the shade of a roasted beet. "I was just a regular senior."

"But you were friends with my sister, right? Did you hang out at our house?"

"I didn't have a lot of female friends," I admit, telling myself it's safe to admit this without worrying he'll judge me for being antisocial. He had sisters. I'm sure he remembers girl drama.

"Not even Beatrix? Seems like she was friends with everyone."

"Not me." I press my lips together as though the truth is in danger of slipping out if I don't hold it back physically. I shrug. "Like I said, I wasn't friends with a lot of girls."

He turns to face me while still holding me in his arms. Moonlight streams in through the open window so I can see his features clearly. The aquiline nose, the soft eyes with sinfully long lashes, the strong cut of his jaw. A few days' worth of stubble rakes his chin, but it can't stop his dimple from popping when he smiles.

"Talk to me, Mallory. I want to know you better."

My heart twists in my chest because I want him to know me, and that's new territory after spending most of my life trying to keep people away. And it still shocks me that he's the one who's bringing these feelings out, tempting me to share more details about my life. He's making me feel like it feeds my soul to get closer to a person rather than protecting myself by pushing away.

The guy who doesn't commit is making me want to commit. To him.

It's a frightening thought, but like all other thoughts regarding Dash, I decide to let it ride. No point in analyzing it to death when my feelings are lust-fueled. That's all this is. I'm lying in a gorgeous man's arms, basking in the afterglow of incredible sex. Who wouldn't feel an overwhelming sense of contentment? Who wouldn't feel like everything's right with the world?

Who is too much of a chickenshit to be honest with herself?

A problem for another day.

"What do you want to know? I was just a normal high schooler. You had two sisters and plenty of girls in your own grade. I was like them. I just didn't happen to be friends with them."

"Why not?"

I feel like it should be obvious to anyone who remembered me back then, especially since he described me exactly the way most guys viewed me. Dash looks at me and waits patiently, his steady eyes threatening to bore into my soul.

Might as well lay it out for him. He wants to know me better? Fine. It'll explain a few things about my life now as well.

"Guys paid attention to me because I hit puberty early, had the big boobs and long legs when half the other girls were running around in braces and awkward bodies. I got a reputation for being fast even though I didn't hook up with anyone until I started dating my boyfriend junior year. Girls in my grade believed the rumors, didn't trust me, thought I was trying to steal their boyfriends."

It all comes out in one long breath like I'm eager to get rid of the words.

Dash listens without his expression changing, except at the end. He winces when I describe how other girls saw me.

"I bet Beatrix didn't think that." He shrugs. "But what do I know about girls? Maybe she was worse than any of them."

"It didn't matter. Even if there was a chance of us becoming closer friends, I wasn't interested. I didn't trust any of the girls in my class after enough of them said things behind my back that couldn't have been farther from the truth."

"I'm sorry," he says.

It's kind, but I don't want him to feel sorry for me.

"I played my part in it. Especially after high school. I just let people think what they wanted to and eventually figured out how to make it work to my advantage."

His brows quirk upward, and his eyes take on a new level of sparkle. "What do you mean."

I bite my lip, unsure whether I want to let him in on what I've started to think of as my superpower.

Turning to assess what Dash seems to think of me after what I've confessed, I see only sympathy in his eyes. And curiosity. Not judgment.

"Sometimes…it's useful to flirt and let men think that if they discuss business with me or let me ask some questions, they'll get something out of it—sexually."

"And you give them nothing."

Again, no judgment.

I shake my head.

Dash nods. "Fucking brilliant. I wish I could flirt my way to business success."

I want to tell him that he damn near has. That I wouldn't be here right now posing as his fake wife if he wasn't so good at what *he* does. Only in his case, he's not a tease. He's just a really good-looking guy who happens to be offering something I need.

"So there you have it. High school was pretty forgettable, if you can imagine. But I guess it got me where I am today, so I can't really complain."

I feel finished with the conversation, but I can see the wheels turning in Dash's head. He has more questions I don't feel like answering, not after I just feel like I exposed my poker hand and don't have another ace in the hole.

So I turn the tables. "How about you? Tell me about high school Dash."

His eyes float upward as though he can see a video playback on the ceiling. I'm tempted to look there as well, but it's too much fun to look at his face instead. He nods and smiles.

"Like I said, I had a good time."

I watch as he tries to suppress a bigger smile and roll my eyes. "Of course you did. What were you, captain of the football team, dating the head cheerleader. And all her friends? At the same time?" I watch as his guilty smile tells me I'm spot-on.

"I had a good time," he says quietly, which makes me laugh.

"Yeah, I can imagine."

"It was high school."

"And from what I heard, many years long after that." I'm saying what we both know to be true. At least, I think so.

I expect him to smile and laugh along with me since we're in agreement about his shenanigans. It's public knowledge around this town, and we've both lived here since high school. No secrets anywhere.

Instead, his smile fades and his eyes lose some of their sparkle. It's like the bright midday sun foiled by a fast-moving cloud. Maybe it will clear just as quickly as it came. I wait. The sun doesn't return.

"Everything okay?" Sitting up now, I swivel to look at him more squarely.

He nods.

"Liar."

"Takes one to know one."

"Oh, now we're really back in high school. Or more like grade school."

I get only a shrug. It sets me back because Dash is ordinarily so light-hearted and this mood or whatever this is feels different. Like he's just closed himself off to me.

"Dash, what's going on? Did I say something wrong?"

He stares up at the ceiling, contemplative.

"I guess old reputations die hard." He shakes his head. "Fuck it. Maybe there's no point in trying to change public perception. Not like it matters what other people think."

Dash shifts, pulling himself up into a sitting position and shoving a couple more pillows between his back and the head-board of the bed. He puts his arms behind his head again and looks at the ceiling instead of meeting my gaze like he normally does.

"It matters if you care."

Another shrug. He's shutting down in front of me, and I start to fear that those storm clouds may not blow away. "I care if what they think isn't true."

"Are you saying you haven't dated a lot of women?"

"Can we not do this?" He turns away or tries to, but I move so I'm still in his sightline. His lips twist into a grimace, but he grudgingly meets my eyes.

"We could...*not* do this." I debate letting him off the hook because this seems to pain him, but I'm curious now. And he did promise to be honest with me, so I'm going to take him up on it. "But you said you want to know me better. I'd like to know you too."

He says nothing, and I get the feeling he's finished talking. But because I clearly don't know Dash Corbett yet, he does the opposite of what I expect.

"It's true and false, the thing about my dating life." He opens his mouth but seems to think better of what he was about to say next. "I do date a lot, but it's because I'm a social guy. I like going out, and women seem willing. But I don't hook up anymore, mainly because it leaves me feeling empty, and it can get complicated. So I just date a woman once or twice and move on. Cleaner. Easier. More fun. I'm not the man-slut you think I am."

"I didn't..." I start to protest that he's wrong about my impression of him, but I can't lie. I absolutely thought he was a man-slut. It's part of why I approached him for a date in the first place. Had a feeling he wouldn't say no. "Okay, maybe I did have that idea about you. People talk and I didn't know any better. I'm sorry."

"It's okay. Not your fault. How would you know?" He slides down lower so he's halfway between sitting and reclining. His body looks more comfortable. Unburdened.

It takes me a minute before I realize what he's just inadvertently told me, but when it hits me, I sit up straighter. Blinking as my brain churns through new information, I finally lock eyes with Dash.

He nods, the sparkle returning to his eyes, which mesmerize me anew with their clarity.

"But you slept with me." I feel the need to say the words out loud even though we both know it.

"I did."

"Just because I asked?" I say the words slowly because I need to be sure of what he's telling me even without telling me explicitly. I need the subtitles. And the voiceover. And the footnotes. Dumb it down for me!

Finally, the icy facade cracks. "No, not just because you asked. I'm here with you because I don't want to be anywhere else. And I'm sleeping with you because I can't resist you. I can't stop. Don't want to stop."

He lets those new words mingle with the sudden thickness of the air around us. My body buzzes with electricity I feel across every inch of my skin.

The air leaves my lungs in a whoosh.

"Oh."

"Oh?"

I nod. Then I swivel around, throw myself on top of him, and fuse my lips to his. I don't have the words to tell him I can't stop either, so I show him another way.

I kiss his beautiful face and let my tongue slide down his neck while my hands take stock of every inch of his chest and abs.

And then I slide lower, where I already feel him rock hard beneath me. I've been wanting his cock in my mouth for weeks now, and I feel like I've just been given permission to take everything I want from him.

From the way he groans with pleasure, he's onboard. "God, honey…"

I tease him a little bit, running my tongue over the length of him before taking him fully into my mouth. He's large and thick and I love the feel and taste of him.

I love how he groans each time I take him a little deeper and swirl my tongue against him. I love how he runs his hands through my hair and grips it in handfuls as he gets closer. I love making him lose control as he bites out a curse and calls my name. My real name. "Fuck, Mallory. It's so damned good."

And I love resting my face on his chest after he kisses me beyond reason and makes me come with his long fingers and tongue.

I want to fall asleep right here with my arm over his stomach and his hands encircling me.

"I love you, Mallory."

He says it so quietly, almost like a quiet breath of words, that I'm not sure I heard him right. He didn't just tell me he loves me. No. If he really meant to say those words and have them mean what they mean, he'd have made a bigger deal of saying them.

He wouldn't just…exhale them. Maybe I didn't even hear what I think I did. Or maybe he tossed the phrase at me, offhand, like I've done with friends. "Love ya, babe." Only, I don't really have friends like that, friends who I really love.

And don't say things like that to people unless I really love them. So far, those people only really include my parents and my dog. And it's not the same, not the same at all.

Did he really just say he loves me?

Okay, great. Now I'm not going to sleep at all. I replay the last few seconds over in my mind and decide that either I misheard him or he said the words so casually that I shouldn't read anything into them. If he meant to tell me he loves me—that he's fallen in love with me—surely, he'd say it in a more direct way. He'd declare it like people do in the movies or in books.

He'd make a thing of it and I'd get weepy and tell him I love him too and he'd respond with how he's been in love with me since he first saw me and worried I'd never feel the same way about him, so he waited. And I'd say I worried he just wanted to be my friend.

And now I'm in the middle of an unwritten Jane Austen novel of my own making and I most definitely won't be falling asleep because I need to keep writing and see how it ends.

Next to me, Dash moves to wrap himself around me, curling me into his chest, which I can feel rising and falling against my back with each breath. In moments, my own breathing seems to synchronize with his, and now we're like one being, lifted to life by the air in our lungs, inhaling to bring ourselves flush against each other. Exhaling to bring ourselves even closer.

I start to get restless in Dash's arms, struggling to turn my head to see his face. I need to see his face to understand whether he meant anything by his words.

"Shh," he breathes against my ear, pulling me closer and wrapping an arm around me. Cupping one breast possessively, he dares me to flinch. I don't. It feels too good.

"Dash," I whisper in one last-ditch attempt to have a conversation.

"Go to sleep."

His voice sounds half sleepy, so I tell myself to stop thinking. That only semi-works, so I allow myself to get comfortable in Dash's arms and lie in bed, listening to his soft snoring. Meanwhile, I let my brain wander.

The first place it goes is down Love Alley, a place I've been avoiding successfully since our wedding out of sheer protectiveness. I don't want my heart to get any ideas.

And now, apparently, all protective layers have been stripped away, and my heart is beating out of my chest, chock-full of ideas. All of them revolve around how I feel about Dash, my husband, the man who seems to understand me better than anyone else

I've ever known—I've been trying to resist wanting more, but my resistance is slipping.

The longer I lie here awake, the less I can deny that I am, in fact, in love with Dashiell Corbett.

Oh, for heaven's sake, how did I allow this to happen?

And because I am writing the dialogue for both sides of my debating brain, I provide an answer. I fell in love with him because he's everything I'd want in a real husband. And he's kinder to me than I am to myself.

It's then that the other side of my brain chimes in with a solution—I need to create some distance and let my feelings ratchet down. It's the only way I'll make it through a year of marriage without losing my damn mind or falling so hard in love that there will be no reeling myself back from the abyss.

And there is an abyss. Big and deep and a long way down to the bottom. I know because I experienced it when I told the one man I ever felt that strongly for that I loved him. As soon as I said it to Felix, he grew distant. Cold. Disinterested. The chase was over, he told me.

He still wanted to get married because he considered me some sort of prize, and I went along with it anyway because I hoped I'd be able to win him back somehow. It never happened. I never made him love me because he wasn't capable of it.

So I stuck with him for a while because I'm not a quitter. I stayed in a loveless marriage that felt more like a business transaction than any millisecond of the deal Dash and I struck. It makes me all the more determined to keep Felix out of my life now, but it also makes me scared to death to feel what I do for Dash.

I need to talk myself out of it. I should be able to do that, no problem. Mind over matter.

Dash's leg falls over mine and he tucks me against him a little tighter. I feel my whole body give in to the feeling of being an extension of his. Like we belong together.

It's enough to make my muscles relax and my heart unclench. I feel myself calm and begin to drift off to sleep.

Mind over matter can happen in the morning.

ash

I SPENT much of the night lying awake, hearing the radio silence in the room after telling Mallory I love her. I didn't necessarily think she'd tell me she felt the same way, but I guess I'd hoped after she said it during the wedding ceremony.

A part of me believed her when she said it. She looked into my eyes and teared up. Is she really that good of an actress? By the end of a long night of mulling it over next to the most beautiful woman I've ever seen, I managed to talk myself down. It doesn't have to be today.

I really do believe our relationship is turning into something more than an arrangement, and I'll take it one day at a time. Hopefully, I'll win her over.

That or maybe she does just see me as the fuckboy she can have fun with while planning world domination.

I slip out of bed without waking Mallory, glancing back at her milky white skin against the crisp sheets and the way her dark hair dances across the pillowcase. No idea how I got so damned lucky.

In the little kitchenette of the honeymoon suite, I make a pot of coffee and debate ordering room service from the restaurant at Buttercup Hill or going to a diner in sweats. Both sound appealing.

"Hey, husband," her sleepy voice coos in my ear as she wraps her arms around my neck.

"Morning, wife." I kiss her nose.

"I still can't believe we did it. We're married."

Her enthusiasm makes me smile. I need to knock off all my overthinking and just enjoy what we have. It's good. More than good.

But then she finishes her thought. "Now I can get Felix out of my life for good. Thank God that's over."

Not a word about last night, no whispered morning-after sweet nothings or lingering romance of a wedding and wedding night where she really outdid herself with her performance. Good to know where I stand on her priority list.

I turn away and busy myself with the coffee in case the look on my face betrays me because fucking Felix was certainly not the first person who comes to mind right now.

I'm still stuck on Mallory's wedding vows, the feeling of her in my arms while we danced, the night we spent tangled up in each other. But that was last night, and now it's morning. I guess it's time to join the real world.

"By the way, I know we said we'd live together, but no pressure. This is for the sake of thoroughness. Wouldn't want to give Felix any reason to come sniffing, claiming this whole thing's a farce, but you should stay at your own house whenever. You know…"

It's passive-aggressive, I know. I don't claim to be one hundred percent mature. But I can't bring myself to tell her I love her again and suffer the awkward silence, so I'm following her lead. If her first thought is about her ex, I'll go there too, even if I'm hoping she corrects my misperception.

She doesn't. "Oh. Okay, great. Sounds good."

It does? Jesus, I really need to get my head straight.

"Yeah, I guess you're good to go now. Evil plan for world domination, check."

She laughs and comes behind me, encircling me with her arms. The feel of her pressed against me makes me think I'm overreacting. It's true that our marriage is a business deal, but that doesn't have to change what still feels like it could be a real relationship. For the first time in my life, I'm clear that I want one. With her.

"I was debating between room service and going to that diner in Calistoga. Do you know it?"

"Mmm, I like both ideas, but one of them lets us stay in bed for as long as we want…" I turn in her arms and find her smiling up at me. Dark long lashes, fresh face scrubbed of makeup, pink lips I want to bite. No chance I can resist her.

"Done. I'll text an order to Sweet Butter. Eggs, pancakes, croissants, quiche, muffins, fruit platter."

"Hmm, I guess maybe eggs?"

"It wasn't a question, Mellow Yellow. I'm ordering all of it."

She takes my hand and leads me back to the bedroom. "In that case, let me work up an appetite."

She seems happy. On the surface nothing seems different, other than the gold band on my finger and the fact that now we're legally married. I decide to let her comment about Felix and last night's uncomfortable silence ride for the time being. For now, I just want to take my wife back to bed and let my mouth roam every part of her body.

I want to focus on the present, where life seems very, very good. I'll worry about tomorrow after that.

allory

BIRTHDAYS WERE NEVER a big deal in my house growing up. Shocker.

My parents were out of town half the time for my birthday and almost all the time for theirs. "It's just another day," my mother always said. Yet she usually celebrated her birthday in some far-flung locale, even if she was doing something as ordinary as shearing sheep. In Ireland.

Complicated pair, my parents.

It was left to me and my friends to make a big deal about my birthday if I wanted a big deal to be made. Did I mention that I didn't have all that many friends?

So it surprises me—no, it shocks me—when I wake up on my birthday to find half the sunflowers in California in my room.

They're in tall vases along one wall beneath the open window, which lets in a whiff of lavender from the planters outside.

They're in round bowls on my bedside tables, where a

steaming cup of coffee with almond milk beckons me to grab it before brushing my teeth.

And they're wrapped in a fat red bow, held in front of Dash's otherwise-naked body as he plays a version of a birthday song by the Beatles on his phone.

There is no better way to wake up on a birthday. No better way to wake up ever.

My heart surges with so much love for Dash that I almost tell him, and it takes all my self-restraint not to blurt out everything I feel. But I don't because that's not part of our deal. If I have a year with him, I want it to be as good as possible, and I can't ruin it by creating awkward tension with feelings I promised not to have.

"You are amazing," I tell him instead. He rewards me with dimples and a broad smile, which somehow brings even more light to the room than the sun managed to do. And it's the freakin' sun.

"Happy birthday, honey."

I don't think I'll ever get enough of him, and it scares the life out of me, but that's a problem for another day. Right now, I'm grateful for the man who approaches the bed and hands me the giant bunch of flowers, leaving me with the perfect view of the rest of him. Happy birthday indeed.

"C'mere." I reach for his hand and pull him toward me on the bed. He rolls on top of me, holding himself up on his elbows. It's the perfect distance to gaze at his beautiful face. "Thank you. This is the perfect birthday."

He laughs. "It's only been five minutes. I have lots of other things planned. Don't count me out yet."

"Dash, I would never count you out."

He dips his head to kiss me, and even though I'm self-conscious about having morning breath, I let him. He makes me feel better about myself, even in the morning when I haven't brushed my teeth. That has to be some kind of superpower, and I love him for it.

There it is again, that feeling I'm not supposed to have. Well, I can't help feeling what I feel any more than I can stop the sun from rising in the east. And there it is, right outside my window.

As Dash kisses his way down my body, I decide I'll just sit with the blooming fullness in my chest and enjoy it. The feeling is just for me, just for today. Tomorrow, I'll talk sense back into my brain and get a grip. But today is my birthday, and for the first time in my life, I'm celebrating by being in love. Even if the guy doesn't know.

* * *

THE MOVING truck pulls away after depositing sixteen boxes in my entryway. I stand on the driveway watching the ribbon of dust rise into the air as the truck's tires grind against the gravel and seal my fate.

Dash lives here. With me. We're married.

And I'm in love with my fake husband.

Of course, the movers bear no responsibility for any of that, but I can't help feeling like they're leaving me to my fate as I stand here alone.

Dash is still at work, but we've given each other keys to our respective homes. We're going to spend time in both of them, so I'll be moving some things to his house as well. *But no pressure. This is for the sake of thoroughness. Wouldn't want to give Felix any reason to come sniffing, claiming this whole thing's a farce,* Dash said the day after our wedding.

It still stings a little to remember it, but I need to keep those words present in my mind so I remember where I stand with him. All the silly feelings I had before the wedding were one-sided. I was getting swept away in the lie. I'd do well to remember that and set my mind straight now.

Or at least tomorrow. Today is my birthday, and I plan to

enjoy the day and maybe plot a little world domination when Dash gets home.

Almost on cue, another rumble of a truck comes from Dash's blue pickup, which is festooned with easily a dozen mylar Happy Birthday balloons rising into the air. He pulls right up to where I'm standing and flings open the door to his truck, revealing a round, white-frosted cake sitting on his lap.

"Oh wow, you drove with that on your lap?" I lean over the cake to kiss him.

"Yup, and didn't get any on my shirt." He looks down at his shirt to be sure.

"Impressive."

"No, you're impressive. Happy birthday, Marshmallow. Or, should I say, happy birthday to the new owner of Autumn Lake?"

"I like Marshmallow."

"I do too. In fact, I love her."

My heart fills to where it feels like it's spilling over.

He kisses me slowly. Deeply. It tells me everything about how he feels, and I want to kick myself for doubting that what I felt between us was real.

"Now, let's go celebrate your birthday." He walks us inside and up to my room, leaving the cake on a table in the entryway. The balloons stay outside for now.

As Dash wraps me in his arms and lays me down on the bed, I can't help thinking I want my future to include him. I love him, and I want to tell him, but I can't. I just can't.

CHAPTER 30

allory

IT TURNS out that some of Dash's birthday plans for me are practical. Extremely practical, in fact.

By four in the afternoon, I'm dressed nicely, pumped up on coffee, and headed to see my family's lawyer, who has the papers drawn up for me to sign. Dash knows me well enough to understand that I don't want to wait a day longer than necessary to take ownership of Autumn Lake. It's one more quality in him that makes my heart feel full.

My parents, being my parents, are working on a farm in Georgia for two weeks, learning how to farm cotton.

Not that we'll ever do that here. In Napa Valley. Where people grow grapes.

In the days since Dash and I talked about what seems to motivate them, I don't resent their peripatetic choices as much as I once did. They may not be the best at parenting, but they do seem to contribute to the world in other valuable ways.

Maybe they're just meant to raise crops and sheep instead of people.

We can't control how our strengths play out in the world. I'm just grateful they decided to try their hand at parenting a person so that I could be born. If nothing else, they gave me my own chance to figure out how to contribute to the world.

It feels good to let the anger and resentment slide away and think about the future. And standing here in my lawyer's office looking at the deed to Autumn Lake, I feel like everything I've been working for is in reach.

"Here we go," Harold Cotton, our family lawyer says, laying a fat file folder on the mahogany desk in his office. Harold has been a friend of my parents for as long as I can remember, but I haven't seen him in a while.

His hair has thinned and turned whiter, and his cheeks sag beneath his chin. He wears a pair of wire-rimmed readers low on his nose and smiles at me like a parent. Looking at how he's aged reminds me that my parents aren't young either. Maybe it will be a relief to them when I take control of things. I hope so.

"This is the deed to the property and all of the stipulations for taking ownership of Autumn Lake."

I don't know why I'm nervous. Actually, I do. Until I sign the papers and see the deed in my own name, I'm going to be afraid Felix will pull a fast one. I pray my parents didn't sign anything that obligates me to keep him around.

He opens the folder and holds up a document. "This one's the important one."

I nod. "Right. The one that says I need to be married in order to inherit." I hold up my ring finger. "Done and done."

He cocks his head and studies the page in front of him. When he looks up, the crease in his brow has deepened. "These are the terms of your inheritance, yes."

It occurs to me that maybe Felix's name is in the paperwork someplace, so I need to set him straight. "I used to be married to someone else. Felix Sutton. But his name shouldn't be anywhere in these documents. He's not my husband anymore."

Holding the papers closer to his face, he reads them again. His finger slides across the lines of the page and his lips move, but I can't make out what he's saying. My pulse starts racing as I worry that something isn't right. I have my marriage certificate in my purse just in case I need to provide it as proof, but I'm getting a sinking feeling in my gut.

Harold puts the papers down and takes his glasses off. "Okay, I just wanted to be sure."

"Be sure of what?"

"The partnership clause."

The last time I heard that word was when Felix told me my parents had saddled me with his irritating presence.

"And?" My voice shakes, and I cough to cover it.

"Felix Sutton is to be your partner in operating the vineyard for two full years, and as such, he's due half the gross proceeds of Autumn Lake."

He lets that sink in, and my stomach bottoms out. Half the gross profits means I won't make a dime for two years after I factor in expenses. Felix is such a snake in the grass. Only a snake would ask for gross proceeds instead of net. He has me over a barrel, and I hate him all over again.

Harold holds up a finger. "If you do not require his services, you need to buy him out by bequeathing your entire first harvest as an operating entity to Mr. Sutton."

"Bequeathing?" Suddenly, Felix is Julius Caesar?

But still, that gives me an out. If I have to give him every grape on the future vines at Autumn Lake, I'd do it to be rid of him. It would mean I'd have to wait a year to sell to the Corbett family, but hopefully, I can make Dash understand that.

Will he understand? He's already sacrificed so much to be my husband.

"And the fact that I have a new husband doesn't change any of that? I thought I just needed to be married in order to remove Felix from the equation." Maybe there's still room to salvage this.

He shakes his head. "I'm not sure where you got the impression that marriage was a prerequisite for inheriting."

Wait, what?

"My mom said I needed to be married."

He looks again at the documents. "I don't see anything here that says so. Nor do I recall discussing it with either of your parents."

He has to be mistaken. The whole reason my parents agreed to keep Felix around in a supervisory capacity was that they didn't want me taking on the job of running the property alone. All that crap about needing a partner. My mother told me explicitly that I needed to be married.

Didn't she?

I rewind the phone conversation I had with her when she explained why she'd made the deal with Felix. Then again when she came for dinner. I'm certain that she kept emphasizing marriage, but did she actually tell me it was part of the written agreement? And if it isn't...do Dash and I need to stay married?

Harold Cotton begins reading the terms of the inheritance out loud, but I barely hear him. My head spins, considering the implications of what I've just learned.

I don't need to be married.

Yet...I am married to a man I love. And after today, I'll no longer be in need of his services. It should make me happy to be free of Felix and unencumbered by a man in general.

Instead, it just makes me sad.

* * *

I DON'T GO HOME RIGHT AWAY. Instead, I call Mary, and she meets me at the Dark Horse. I make up an excuse about forgetting that she wanted to take me out for my birthday, and Dash tells me to go have a good time. He's exhausted and will try to stay up, but I tell him not to worry if he nods off.

He's been working his tail off forging new relationships with growers and trying to staff Buttercup Hill back up to capacity. Now that people feel secure that he's not flirting with their wives, the number of meetings has tripled. It still bugs me that people are so small-minded, but it's a small town, and everyone's in everyone else's business, so I shouldn't be surprised.

Mary pulls into the parking lot just as I slam the door to my Jeep. I wait for her, and we walk in together.

A few minutes later, with two dark beers on our table, I can no longer contain myself and blurt out the news. "I don't have to be married to inherit Autumn Lake."

She takes a long draw from her beer and nods at the information. "So that's a good thing, yes?"

I tell her the rest. "Bloody Felix," she grumbles. "But that's just money. You'll be done with him in a year and moving on to do as you please."

I want to nod. I want to hold up my glass and toast hers. I want to be the emancipated, strong female I've always believed myself to be.

Instead, I feel the pinpricks of tears at the corners of my eyes because I want all those things, but I also want Dash. "Dammit, I'm crying over a man. After Felix, I swore I'd never do that ever again."

Letting out a long exhale, I glance around the bar to see who's here to see me lose my shit. Fortunately, other than a couple of guys in motorcycle jackets with their backs to us at the bar, the only other people in the place are a large table with middle-aged couples who look like they've had a very long day on the wine trail. Yup, they're sloshed and not paying a whit of attention to me and my tears.

"I already scanned the place. You're good," Mary says, taking another sip. Half her beer is gone, and she signals the bartender for two refills even though I haven't touched mine.

She picks up my beer and hands it to me. "Here. Drink some of this. Then we'll talk this through."

"Happy birthday to me," I mutter. Mary clinks my glass as I'm slugging down a long drink.

A moment later, two new beers are placed wordlessly on the table by the bartender, who only makes eye contact with Mary, who nods. It's like they're speaking some private pub language I don't understand.

"Okay, let's start from the beginning," Mary says after finishing her first beer and sliding the glass away. "First, happy birthday. I hope this year brings you everything you want. Which brings me to the next part. You inherited Autumn Lake. Congratu-fucking-lations. Let's not lose sight of that."

I nod. "You're right. It's a good day, no matter what else happens."

"Yes, and as to the third thing, yeah, you're gone for the guy, that's clear. And from what I can see, he feels the same way, so maybe you don't have anything to worry about."

"No, it's an agreement. We're playing a role."

"Him telling you he loves you doesn't sound like role-playing to me."

Here come those tears again. Dammit, I have no control over myself at all, and it pisses me off.

I shake my head. "I know. I think he might actually mean it."

"Might?"

"Fine. He does."

"And what about you?"

"I love him so much, Mare. But what if the same thing happens again? What if I tell him how I feel, and it takes away the magic? What if he's just in it for the chase? Or the wine grapes?"

"What if he isn't? What if he's there for all the right reasons, and *you're* the problem?" she asks quietly.

The jukebox starts playing "Wildest Dreams," and I just sit there and listen to the lyrics. I don't just want Dash to remember me after he leaves. I don't want him to leave at all.

The bartender drops off a basket of soft pretzels and mustard, the snack I didn't know I needed in my life.

"Listen, you can't know what's what until you talk to Dash. He should be part of this conversation."

"But what if he's relieved we don't need to keep up with our charade? What if he wants to divorce me tomorrow?" I take a choppy breath and wipe a new set of tears from my eyes with the back of my sleeve. "Dammit, why am I crying?"

"Because you love the bloke. And if you tell him how you feel, you just might get everything you never knew you wanted. But you have to tell him."

I nod. She's right. I know she's right.

I'll tell him tonight, but for now, I'll sit with my friend on my birthday and drink some beer for courage. We can call a cab tonight and pick up our cars in the morning.

And a couple of hours later, after a couple more beers and a lot more pretzels, I creep into my house, fully intending to tell Dash everything.

I find him fast asleep with a book on his chest, and I don't have the heart to wake him. We'll talk in the morning.

ash

I WAKE up in the middle of the night to the smell of smoke. At first, I think it's barbecue smoke and marvel at how the shifting winds could carry smells from our restaurant clear across the property.

A second later, I come to my senses. The clock reads four in the morning, and our restaurant isn't open. No reason for anyone to be cooking anything.

And now that I'm starting to pay attention, the smoky smell doesn't smell like a barbecue as much as it smells like a fire. That gets me out of bed in a flash.

After the Napa fires a few years ago, all of us exist on high alert to the potential of it happening again. In hours, miles and miles of vineyards burned to the ground. Fire officials said that in the valley where Napa exists between two mountain ranges, the fire created its own weather.

It blocked out the sun and created enough wind to burn a football field's length in mere seconds.

"Mallory." I nudge her where she's sleeping on the other half of my pillow. Her hair is splayed out behind her like a sunburst in the pale moonlight that creeps through a crack in the blinds. Ordinarily, I'd take a moment like this to gaze at her and thank the universe for my good fortune.

Tonight, I need a different kind of good fortune. She rolls to the side and blinks her eyes open. "What's up?"

"You smell that?" I'm out of bed and peering out the window where I don't see anything that looks unusual. Just the deep periwinkle sky to the east. But that doesn't mean much.

Cranking open my window, I'm assaulted with a much stronger smell. There's no question it's coming from a fire. Only issue is how close it is and whether it's under control.

"Yes." Mallory jumps out of bed and pulls last night's sweater over her head. A second later, she shrugs on a pair of my sweatpants from my laundry pile. She hands a second pair to me. "We should hear sirens."

As if on cue, the lonely wail of an emergency vehicle's siren sounds in the distance. It's reassuring, but I need more information about how close it is and where it's headed. The night's winds aren't helping.

I start texting my siblings and my dad's nurse as we head for the front door. As soon as we're outside, I feel like I've been slugged in the gut. In the distance, a good-sized plume of smoke rises into the sky. I don't see flames, but judging from where the smoke is, the fire seems close.

It's hard to tell how close because our land is so flat. It's deceptive to see something in the distance. It could be a few dozen acres away or a few miles away.

The sirens get louder, joined by a few more. Good that they're on the move, but I hope it's not a sign of how big the fire is.

"We should stay put until we know where it is and how it's moving. I remember that from the big fire," Mallory says.

We're both instantly on alert, all sleepiness gone. I put an arm around her shoulders and pull her close, protectively. "Hey, sorry I fell asleep before you got home." She stiffens in my hold, and I assume it's out of fear of the fire.

"Oh. It's fine."

"I want to hear. Everything good with the lawyer?"

"Um, yeah." She wrestles out of my grip and lets out a long breath. "All fine."

I want to ask if she's okay, but my phone starts pinging as my siblings respond.

Beatrix: I heard it's centered near the grove

She's talking about a wooded area that abuts the corner of our property.

Archer: I heard that too from a buddy at dispatch

Jax: Moving toward our property?

Archer: Winds are blowing away from us, but it could shift

Beatrix: Fire trucks pulled onto the fire road behind us

She's the only one who can see that part of Buttercup Hill from where she lives. I read all the texts to Mallory as they come in.

"Wait, how close is that grove to your property line?"

"It's right up against it. Part of the grove is actually on our property."

"Jesus. What do we do? Do we evacuate?" Mallory looks in the direction of the smoke, which still seems far away.

"Not if the wind is still headed that way. I think we just sit tight for right now."

The plume of smoke is growing as we watch it. "If it shifts, it'll move fast."

"Maybe it's still small, and they can put it out quickly."

I hate not knowing. My phone starts blowing up with texts again, each sibling reporting what they can glean from neighbors.

PJ: I just heard from Graham.

Archer: Fuck him. What's he want?

Archer will never forgive our dad for having a kid he never told us about, and I'm pretty sure he plans to take his anger out on Graham for good measure.

PJ: Fire's burning his property. He's telling us to
evacuate to be safe

Jax: Guess that's decent of him

So far, PJ and I have the best relationship with our half brother of any of our siblings because we met him first and became the unofficial liaisons between us all. I fire off a text to him.

Me: Hey. You okay?

Dots bounce on my phone immediately.

Graham: Yeah. Fire was burning through my
vines when I left.

Me: Where are you now?

Graham: Driving

Me: Driving where?

Graham: Around. Not sure where to go

I don't think twice before responding.

> Me: Come here. Not that it's the safest if the
> wind shifts, but at least we can figure shit out
> together

The dots appear again. Then they disappear. Again, it seems like he's typing. Then nothing.

> Me: Quit deliberating. Just come

> Graham: Fine

Five minutes later, Graham's green truck rattles up the drive. He looks shell-shocked as he walks over to us. His dark hair sticks out in all different directions like he was having a terrible night's sleep long before his property went up in flames.

I still have very mixed feelings about having a half brother, but the dude is clearly in a bad way.

"You okay?" I ask. I feel like offering him a stiff drink, though it's the last thing anyone needs in the middle of the night when a shifting wind could send flames off in a new direction despite the best efforts of the fire crew.

Slowly, he shakes his head. "I hope I never see anything like that again."

"What does it look like?" Mallory asks.

"Just...fire. Everywhere I looked. Burning down the vines like a spreading ball of flames. Then there was so much smoke I couldn't even see that, but I could hear it. I don't think I'll ever unhear the crackling sound of plants dying."

"How close were you?" I ask, shivering at the image he's painting.

"Close." He points across the drive to where a stand of oak trees shades the path between the main road on the property and my front door. It's a hundred feet, max. "Here to there. Initially, I tried to fight it with a hose, but I've lived here long enough to know that's how people die trying to save a house. I heard the sirens heading my way, so I got the hell out before the winds shifted."

"Graham, I'm so sorry," Mallory says, reaching for his hands. I watch her interact with him, just pure concern like one human should have for another human who may have lost his home in a fire.

I can't say that all my frustrations about Graham's very existence evaporate on the breeze. It's not that easy. I'm still plenty pissed at my dad, and it's hard to like a guy who appeared out of nowhere with a gift that put Buttercup Hill into turmoil.

On the other hand, it's not his fucking fault that our dad chose to knock up his mom. It's also not our fault that he was raised by a single mother and could never tell anyone he was related to the great Kingston Corbett.

There, standing on my driveway with a guy I barely know, I decide that maybe I can mend fences a little bit. Maybe that's more important than holding on to a grudge I did nothing to create. My siblings may have other ideas, but I feel good about where I stand.

"I'm sorry too," I say, extending my hand. It's not the first time we've shaken hands, but it feels different. Graham looks at my outstretched palm as though he knows something is different too.

He takes my hand in a strong grip and looks me in the eye when he does it. I meet his gaze, the same blue eyes staring back at me as I see when I look at my siblings. Only in his eyes, there's a different kind of ruggedness and a little bit of pain. I don't know where it comes from yet, but I decide I want to find out.

Mallory watches this silent interchange between two dudes with her lips pressed together to suppress a smile.

My phone pings with another text from Beatrix, who lives closest to the area where Buttercup Hill abuts Graham's property.

> Beatrix: Fire trucks at my house. Set up a
> perimeter to keep the fire from moving closer
> to BH

A barrage of texts from our siblings fire off at once. Smiling emoji and thumbs.

"Sounds like they're controlling it from this direction," I say, knowing that's little comfort to Graham.

He nods. "Yeah. Makes sense. They'll want to contain it, keep it away from your vineyards." He exhales and snaps his lips shut. I feel like he's not saying something.

"D'you think they won't try to save yours?" I ask. It's no secret that Graham is the new owner in the neighborhood, and folks do tend to take care of their own. But I doubt that extends to letting a fire ravage a person's property when there's a chance of saving it.

He crosses his arms and says nothing. Then he rolls his eyes. "I dunno. Guess I wouldn't be shocked if they worked a little slower than usual, is all."

I shake my head. "Fuck that. Better not be the case."

Graham's phone rings with what sounds like a mariachi celebration, and he shoves his hand deep into the pocket of his jeans to retrieve it. "Yeah," he says into it, stepping away from us to take the call. I watch him pace in circles on the driveway as he finishes the conversation.

A minute later, he shoves the phone back into his pocket and walks back over to us. "They've contained it. Still some hot spots, and the winds could pick up, so we're not in the clear, but it's something."

I look at Mallory, not wanting to ask Graham what I want to ask him. She puts a hand on his shoulder sympathetically.

"Any word on the damage?"

He runs a hand over his jaw and nods. "A lot of the vineyards burned, but I'll know more when it's light out, and when they're

CHAPTER 32

Mallory

It's dark outside, but that's the point of a sunrise hike—a little fumbling around with headlamps in anticipation of a warm yellow dawn.

The darkness makes me contemplative, and the steep hill of the hike means I'm not talking. It's strange to walk next to Dash for this long in silence, but he's been wanting us to do this hike for a while, so I finally gave in this morning.

I know why he's been pushing us to come up here—from the top, we have a panoramic view of half the valley, including most of Autumn Lake. He's spend half the hike so far talking about helping me build the vineyards and winery. He's acting like a partner. Like a husband.

It makes my heart swell in my chest, and it makes me feel horribly guilty for not telling him yet that he's free to file for divorce.

"I think you're smart to plant vines slowly over the next

couple years. It will protect you against weather events or fires in any one particular growing season." He points in the direction of Autumn Lake, even though we can't see much in the darkness.

"Yeah," I huff, coming up the hill behind him. How is this man so freakin' fit?

I've spent the past few days in agony, wanting to tell Dash about my meeting with the lawyer. Every time he asked about it, I told him it went fine but didn't elaborate. I couldn't bring myself to tell him we don't need to stay married in order for me to inherit Autumn Lake.

But I have to tell him. I can't just let him stay married to me on a lie.

"You good?" he asks every so often.

"Yup," I huff back.

Then we continue in silence.

An idea has been rolling through my brain for a few days now, and I keep trying to ignore it. But ideas can be persistent, and this one won't let me go...I want to know if Dash is in this marriage to secure land or grapes from me. He's never explicitly said it, but the conversation from the night of the gala still eats at me.

"What if Autumn Lake doesn't sell you grapes for the first year? Do you have other...options? Because I have an idea..." I float the thought quietly as Dash and I hike up a hill at sunrise. Holding flashlights, we're moving quickly, each of us huffing a little bit, trying to beat the sun to the top so we can watch it rise.

Maybe it's not the best moment to broach the subject because I'm too winded to give Dash the rest of my explanation. I have a mostly formed idea on a short-term solution that could work to Buttercup Hill's benefit. And my own.

"What I'm thinking is..." I have to take a breath before I continue up a particularly steep area of the hike, which feels like stone stairs instead of a gentle incline.

Timing is not my strength.

Dash doesn't give me a chance to finish explaining. Halting his movement, he stops, mid-incline. Since I'm hiking right behind him, I nearly slam into his back. Instead, I manage to get my footing on the trail, but I reach a hand out to steady myself.

When Dash wings around to face me, I almost lose my balance again.

"What?"

The sky is lightening by the second, now a serene blue that's somewhere between day and night, but Dash's features are going darker in front of my eyes.

"We have a problem. Or I do. With Felix."

He closes his eyes and takes a deep breath. When he opens them, they blaze hot blue. "If I hear that guy's name one more time…" He seems like he's counting to ten. Or maybe fifty. He paces in a circle, his flashlight beam spotlighting tufts of dried-out mustard plants.

"I'm working to get rid of him, and this is how I can do that." I'm still winded, but the look on Dash's face makes me feel gut-punched at the same time.

"Seriously, Mallory, what the hell?" He says it so quietly that the words almost sound sweet, but they still pierce me in the quiet of the early morning.

I hold up my hands. "Wait. Let me explain."

"You're reneging on our deal now? After all I've put myself through for you?"

Hearing the word "deal" hits me like a slug in the gut. Of course I've known all along that we made a deal to help each other, but we've evolved past that point over the past couple of months. He loves me. Right?

After all I've put myself through for you.

He means our marriage. It's a *deal*. And I'm ridiculous for thinking love would alter the equation.

I finally catch my breath enough to explain. "It's not just about

Felix. Smelling that smoke and realizing how easily our livelihoods can burn to the ground has gotten me thinking. I need a backup plan for my business plan. Maybe that means being less reliant on a single crop or coming up with rental agreements for pieces of our land. Either way, I need to get it right before I start parceling the land and planting vines. It doesn't have to ruin your plans."

The corner of his lip twitches as he tries to maintain his equanimity. "How-how does it not ruin our plans? We need more cab grapes, and I told you that. That was the deal, Mallory. That was the whole point of this fake marriage."

The words sting, so I fight back with my own, even if I know I'm making things worse. "Was it? Because I thought it was about your tarnished reputation."

"Seriously? Fuck all of this."

His words cut me to the bone, but I try to unhear them for now. He's just confused and grasping at something to say.

My ideas tumble out. "There are other growers who can provide cab grapes. Have you talked with Graham? I know for a fact he's overproducing because he offered to sell to me for the first year or so while our vines get established."

"You've talked to fucking Graham?"

"I talk to lots of people, Dash," I say quietly. I don't like the way he's escalating blame here.

"Why didn't you tell me?"

I take a step away from him. It's either that or slug him. "What?"

"I told you the relationship with that guy is tricky. I don't know what he wants. If you're forming alliances with him, it all gets more complicated."

Maybe it's the pent-up love I've been feeling, but right now I'm all emotion. I love Dash and hate myself for not being able to tell him. I'm frustrated and angry and ruining the best thing that's ever happened to me because it feels safer to burn it to the ground than to gamble on love. At least, that's the way it feels at the moment, and I hate that too.

I inhale deeply and try to count to ten before I spew my anger all over Dash's pretty face. I only get to three.

"Okay, first of all, I'm pretty sure he just wants to know his family because you told me that. And second, I had one conversation with him. About business."

The iron mask of Dash's features relaxes a tad, but I'm not done.

"Third, how dare you? I didn't do anything behind your back. I'm meeting with growers all over the area. I've been doing it for months, and there's no reason I wouldn't include someone who's growing exactly what I need."

Dash stares at me, lips pressed together in a hard line. A muscle in his cheek twitches as he grits his teeth.

He's angry? Fine. I'm angrier.

Grimacing, Dash blinks a few times and shakes his head. "You're right. I'm sorry."

I nod, and he reaches for me, but I take a step back. I don't mean to do it, but my body seems to know something my brain hasn't fully absorbed yet. Then it catches up.

That was the whole point of this fake marriage.

The words take their second lap in my brain, and they sting even more this time around.

"I think we should take a little time apart," I say. "You've been through a lot with the fire and the stress of the business, and I'm trying to get myself in order. Let's just...give ourselves some breathing room without all of this"—I gesture back and forth between us—"getting in the way."

"This?" He mimics my movements.

"The attraction. The sex. The...love. I think it's...confusing things, and we both need to take a little break from the intensity and remember 'the point of this fake marriage.' At least I do."

A bird tweets a sweet little three-syllable sound in the

distance, and it's quickly answered by a different bird with a more complicated trill from the other direction. Ordinarily, I'd stop and take the moment to wonder at the rituals of mating and consider the cuteness.

Right now, I want to tune everything out and bury myself under a blanket in a dark room.

Dash's mouth falls open. His jaw works for a moment as though he's trying to produce words, but then he seems to give up.

"Time apart. Yeah, okay. I get it." He clamps his mouth closed in a line and blinks. I never knew a person could express that much emotion in a blink, but I see hurt, anger, and betrayal in his.

"Glad it makes sense."

"Yeah, I'll bet. You probably thought the dumb pretty boy wouldn't be able to grasp such high-level concepts, but I hear you loud and clear."

"Dash, that's not—"

He cuts me off with a raised hand. "No. Don't. I don't want to hear it."

"Okay," I say quietly. "We'll take a break."

He nods. I nod. The only problem is that I have the feeling what little chance we had at a relationship is over now. I'm pretty sure it's my fault. And none of it makes sense to me.

CHAPTER 33

ash

SOMEONE HAS PUT a tray of sandwiches on the big plank table in the old barn where my siblings and I are meeting to come up with a plan. I haven't bothered to investigate the type of sand-wich because I still have no appetite, but something smells like tuna. It makes me want to gag.

Sleeping without Mallory has resulted in not sleeping, and I've been in a shit mood all week. We've made good on our "sleeping in separate houses" freedom since our fight, and I'm still too hurt and angry to talk to her.

But mostly I'm just sad. I miss her and I fucking love her, and that makes every minute of every day depressing at best. Painful at worst.

I have no appetite, so I chew on a paper straw, which gets soggy and disgusting after thirty seconds. "Whoever invented these clearly hates people," I gripe to no one.

So far no one has called me on my mood. I guess my siblings

are distracted by bigger problems like the fact that we still have no guaranteed source of grapes to set us up for expanded production.

"What are we looking at if we can't expand? Is there any chance we can hold shareholders off for another year until we get this sorted out?" Beatrix asks.

"We don't have a year," Jax says. "Investors will go into a full-on revolt if we don't post good numbers in the next quarter, and the only way to do that is by getting new contracts with wine buyers. And the only way to do *that* is to have more grapes than we currently have to take us into expanded production. It's all a promise of the future, but we're out of time."

The general mumbling in the lunchroom tells me no one's happy about it. Just like they weren't happy when I told them we might not be able to rely on Autumn Lake for grapes.

Saying the words made me feel awful on so many levels— letting my family down when our business is on the rocks, falling for a woman who doesn't feel the same way... But mostly, talking about Autumn Lake is a reminder of how close I came to having something perfect. Then I had to fuck it up by flying into a rage.

Swallowing down a lump in my throat, I shake my head at myself. I fucking miss Mallory, and I only have myself to blame.

Jax pours himself a cup of coffee, and Archer puts one of the sandwiches on a plate and sits at the head of the table. His mood is worse than usual, but I don't bother to figure out why. I don't care.

Everyone's bustling about, and Beatrix can't shut up about the sandwiches, which are apparently a new menu item this week at Sweet Butter. "The arugula and brie tastes a little sharper with the clover honey on the bread, don't you think?" she asks through a large bite.

I also don't care about the effects of clover honey, so I sulk and stare into my lukewarm coffee, willing this meeting to start already.

PJ has been standing off to the side, tapping on her phone, so I assume whatever she's doing is part of the holdup. She walks outside and comes in a minute later, accompanied by Graham, who stands slack-jawed as usual with a saddlebag over his shoulder. The conversation in the room grinds to a halt.

"Did I miss something? Why's he here?" I whisper to Archer across the table. He gestures to PJ with a nod of his head.

"You've all met Graham…" PJ says by way of introduction. "He called me with news from the fire marshal, and I thought we should all sit down."

Great. Not only does he now own land bought by our father with Buttercup Hill profits but he's probably also here asking for help after his vineyards burned. We were lucky. Only a small portion of our vines caught fire. If the winds had shifted, the damage would have been far worse. Overall, his property took the brunt of the damage, but I've been too irritable to ask a lot of questions. I have no idea how he fared at the end of it all.

PJ sits down and gestures to a seat next to her at the table. Graham, looking awkward in a straw hat, dark jeans, and a white tee so new it still has creases, sits next to her. Beatrix slides a coffee cup toward him and gestures to the urn in the center of the table.

"I'm good, thanks," he says, turning the cup in his hands. "Anyhow, the fire department just finished their investigation, and they determined it was arson."

"Jesus, really?" Jax asks. "Someone intentionally set fire to your property?"

"Actually, no," Graham says, bending down to take a report from his bag and putting it on the table in front of him. "It was set on your property." He lets his words sink in. It's a good thing because everyone else starts talking at once.

"Wait, what?"

"Are they sure?"

Everyone says a version of the same thing, and after a moment, PJ tells everyone to shut up and listen.

"Yes, they're sure. Yes, it was set on our property. The marshal contacted me after he spoke with Graham. The only thing that saved us was the shift in winds. If not for that, there's no telling how much of our vineyards we'd have lost."

Archer turns to Graham. "How much did you lose?"

"About thirty percent. Not good, obviously, but I'm still in business."

Archer presses his fingers into his temples. "So they're saying someone deliberately set fire to our property. Or tried to."

"Yes, dumbass, that's the definition of arson."

"Super helpful, Jax, thanks. Are they still investigating? Do they have any idea who did it?"

"Do you have cameras on your property?" Graham asks us.

Archer answers. "Yes. We'll check them."

"Investigators will want any footage we have from that night."

"Done," Archer says.

"But the bigger issue, and the reason I invited Graham here, is that someone seems out to get us. Either just us or Graham too, we're not sure. But it seems like we ought to be comparing notes at least and working together a bit more."

An uneasy silence settles over the room as we look from one to another and then down at the table. No one wants to make a suggestion for how to work together when we're still getting to know each other. Trust doesn't come easy.

Graham leans in and fills his coffee cup but doesn't take a sip. He taps a finger nervously on the table. "Look, I know none of you wanted a brother, and the money part…I'm sorry about how it all went down. It wasn't my doing, if that makes it any better."

More silence. Finally, Beatrix clears her throat. "We know it's not your fault, Graham. It's just a lot. A lot for us to process."

He nods. "I get that. And I see why I'm probably the last person you want to work with, but…I'm producing more grapes than I use and need to sell them to someone. I figured I should give you the first crack since we're, you know, family." He says the last word quietly, but it lands loudest.

No one comments, so he continues. "I don't know what your needs are in the short term, but I can make a commitment on cab grapes." We all exchange looks. No one wants to admit that this is a very good solution for us right now.

He's saying exactly what Mallory suggested, and it sticks in my craw because I didn't even give her idea a chance before concluding she was reneging on our whole arrangement, something she never said at all.

I finally pull it together enough to speak. "Maybe in some weird way, this is what Dad wanted for all of us."

"Jesus. You think?" Archer asks, shoving a hand in his hair.

"Thanks, Graham," Jax says. "We can probably make something work here. And yes, if someone is out to sabotage us, they probably won't stop at one fire. We should stick together."

I can hear everyone in the room breathing. In and out. Long, heavy breaths as we digest this new arrangement with Graham Garcia. Guess we'll be getting to know him a little better.

Which brings my thoughts back to Mallory and the idea that she wants what's best for me and for us. I still don't like the way she went about it, but I'm smart enough to know she's right.

"Come on." Beatrix is always barking orders at someone or another, so I don't bother to look up. Then I feel her moving my chair and find her beckoning me with a finger. "Let's go."

"Go where?"

"On a walk."

I don't have the energy to argue, and everyone else is still chatting with Graham, so I follow her out of the barn. She doesn't slow her pace until we've rounded the backside and turned onto a path that winds through a stand of apple trees.

"These should have been picked by now." Beatrix points at the trees still bearing fruit.

"Is that my responsibility too? I'll get right on it." Sarcasm is all I have left.

My sister smacks my shoulder. "You're a pain in the ass, but I love you. Sit." She points at a bench under a particularly full tree. Maybe she's hoping I'll get pummeled by apples. I sit anyway, and she stands in front of me like a lecturing parent.

"I hate seeing you this way, but I love that you're in love."

Shaking my head, I squint at her because she's positioned herself with the sun at her back. She moves to the side, and I can see her face, which is filled with concern, not judgment. It's the only reason I indulge whatever she has to say.

"Glad you're happy," I gripe.

"Whatever happened between you, fix it, Dash."

"There's nothing to fix. It's a fake marriage, and she's out for herself, just like you guys all said." I hate having to admit it. I hate that it's true.

Beatrix shakes her head. "I was wrong about that. We were wrong. From what you told me, she's in a tough spot because of that a-hole ex, but she's trying to do right by you. Mallory loves you, and you need to get over yourself."

I roll my eyes. "Whatever."

"Don't 'whatever' me."

"Trix, when you don't know what you're talking about, you should really mind your own business." My siblings have a lot of nerve, and I'm done with all of it.

"You are my business. And I do know what I'm talking about. Mallory loves you, and if she had to make a business decision, you need to separate those two things."

I hate arguing with Beatrix because she's persuasive and always ends up winning, but I like what she's saying about love. "Why do you keep insisting she loves me? All evidence points to the contrary."

"I saw it in her face on your wedding day. Plus, she told me."

This is news. I perk up for the first time. "She did?"

"Yes, dumbass. She's as helpless in love with you as you are with her, so be the bigger person and apologize for assuming the worst about her."

The words sting. In all my hurt and sadness, I hadn't realized that I'm guilty of exactly what people have been doing to me for years—judging Mallory incorrectly.

I feel awful, but for the first time in a week, I feel something else—hope. If my dad taught me anything, it's that I'm a good judge of character. Only I didn't trust my gut when it mattered, and I took it out on the woman I love more than anyone.

But I can fix this. It's time to stop making life more compli-cated than it needs to be.

CHAPTER 34

*M*allory

IT FEELS good to whack at the soil with a hoe. I don't know if I'm doing the right kind of tilling for the future food garden I have planned for this site, but it's giving my back and arms a workout and my brain a rest.

A lot of dirt is flying in my face instead of staying on the ground, where it belongs. I'm not great with a hoe or any garden tools, for that matter. Ironic, given how much time my parents spent working the land—literally.

Growing up, I never had an interest. Instead of planting a garden, I learned makeup tips. Instead of getting my hands dirty, I got my nails done. And by the end of high school, I couldn't use a hoe, but I did my best to be one.

"So you figured it out." My mom's voice sounds just like mine, only she speaks slightly slower, something that came with age.

"What?"

"How good it feels to whack at weeds with a metal implement."

I turn to look at her, leaning on the handle of the hoe while the business end digs into the ground. "I didn't know you guys were back."

My mom laughs. "That's the beauty of wandering. No set date for return."

Standing here in the field, digging into the soil, I can't believe I never asked her about what motivated her and my dad over all these years. "Why do you do it? What would be so hard about making a set plan and letting the people in your life know what you're doing? Worried they might get the wrong idea and think you care about them?"

I don't mean for the words to come out sounding so harsh, but I guess I haven't fully accepted their choices despite Dash's wise words a few weeks back. Or maybe I'm rejecting his words because he seems to have rejected me. I haven't heard from him at all since we agreed to take a break.

"It was never about not caring. I hope you know that."

I look at my mom. Maybe for the first time in my life, I really look at her. She seems healthy and suntanned in a way that comes from working the land under a broad-brimmed hat. She has more of a glow than a tan. Her light eyes have a sharpness to them, as though observing the tiniest details around her and cataloging them away with delight.

"How could I know, Mom? You were always leaving. Always finding bigger adventures than whatever existed here. Like I wasn't exciting enough to make you stay."

The light dims in her eyes, and she squints at me. "How could you ever imagine that? You…you were what I came back to. You're my touchstone that allows me to go where my heart wants to wander because you're here when I come home. I adore you, Mallory."

So many warring thoughts jockey for attention, but one

shoves its way to the forefront: I'm the reason she comes home, not the reason she leaves. It still doesn't excuse her behavior, but for the first time, I understand her fuzzy logic, at least the way it makes sense in her mind.

"That's not…normal, Mom. Parents don't put their kids in that position. They don't make their kids beg them not to leave just so they can feel valuable when they return."

"I know. I know it doesn't make sense, but it's how your dad and I are wired. We did the best we could. Truly. If we hadn't spent time away, learning from growers and working the land with people who really needed our help, we'd have been far worse parents than we actually were."

"Bull. Shit."

She startles at my words but doesn't disagree.

"*I* needed your help. Me, your own daughter. Life wasn't easy for me, and you weren't there for any of it."

She observes me in the same way she always has, as though I'm an interesting specimen who bears no real resemblance to her. For once, I'm glad we look nothing alike. I don't want to be anything like her.

The longer she looks at me, the more I wonder what she sees. I try to picture myself from her point of view. Ponytail hair with straggling tendrils flopping against my face, dirt on my arms and legs because I'm bad at gardening. She probably sees a farming failure.

"You are amazing," she says. "I've always seen that in you, and I see it now. You're amazing and capable."

"Thanks." I'll take the compliment, even if it comes after I twisted myself into knots to make myself believe it.

She shakes her head. "I don't want you to do it alone. I know you think that makes me sexist, but it's not about that." She stares off into the distance, which is easy since our land is flat. We can see all the way to the mountains from here in both directions.

"I figured it was because you thought I wasn't capable."

"No. You're too capable. You don't need a man in your life or anyone else for that matter, but I hoped for more for you. I wanted you to have a connection like the one I have with your dad. I wanted you to fall in love."

"I did."

Standing there with my hoe, working the land, I think I have it all together, so it surprises me when I burst into tears. They come rolling, accompanied by sobs, and my mom does what only moms know how to do. She holds me and lets me cry it out while she smooths my hair and tells me she loves me.

After a minute, the sobs subside, and my mom loosens her grip. Putting her hands on top of my shoulders, she speaks directly into my face. "I'm sorry for pushing Felix on you. I just wanted you to have some help, and he was here telling us he'd do that for you."

"I hate him."

She nods. "Somehow…I didn't know that. I am sorry."

"Sorry enough to amend the contract and get him out of my life?"

"I don't—"

I cut her off. "It's okay, Mom. I know it's already been signed and executed. It's just a bunch of grapes. It'll be okay."

Underfoot, I feel the earth that I fought so hard to take over, and I feel grateful to my parents for making me work for it even though I didn't understand the method behind their ways. But now, as I stand here, I understand that it's not enough.

It's not enough to plot world domination alone, not when there's a man who loves me and wants to plot it with me.

When I look at my mom again, I find her beaming at me as though she's proud of my hoeing. Which is impossible because I suck. So it must be something else. "What?" I ask.

"You *can* have everything you want. But sometimes you have to loosen your grip a little bit, that's all. If it's the right thing, it'll be yours. That's how it's worked all these years with your dad and me."

Her philosophical advice is opaque, but at least she's staying on brand. I interpret it to mean that if I love something, I need to have a little faith. Maybe even set it free.

I owe Dash the truth, even if it means risking my heart. So I go for broke. Or, in my case, broken glass.

* * *

WALKING THROUGH SUNSHINE FOODS, I can't help but think about the day Dash saved me from crashing to the floor into a sea of glass and pickle juice. I was such a bitch that day, embarrassed and frustrated. I didn't even ask him if he was hurt.

Today, I make a beeline for the pickle display, which is right there on the endcap of an aisle, just begging to be knocked over again. You'd think they'd learn from the past.

I grab one jar of tiny dills and pay for it at the checkout. Then I go home and write Dash a note.

CHAPTER 35

ash

I come home to a jar of pickles on my porch and a sealed
envelope. Inside, I find our marriage certificate and a note that
reads, "Buttercup Hill can have all the grapes it needs. You're free
to tear up this fake document because I love you for real."

CHAPTER 36

$\mathcal{M}$allory

I'm not expecting anyone at my door, but over the past few months, I've gotten way more accustomed to people just showing up. And knocking.

When I look through my newly installed peephole, I see Dash on my porch holding a fistful of sunflowers. I open the door.

"You installed a peephole."

"Someone very smart told me it was a good idea."

He exhales. I take him in, and my heart fills. I reach for him, but he's stiff at first. Then he relents, coming closer so I can circle my arms around his back. The flowers get smushed between us, so he backs away and puts them on the porch swing next to me.

Then he holds up our marriage certificate. "Why would I tear this up?"

"Because we don't need it, and I want you to be free."

I steel myself for whatever happens after I tell him we don't need to be married. Then I unfold the whole story about the lawyer and the contract and thorn-in-my-side Felix.

"Wow, okay."

"Yeah. I intended to tell you everything that day when you took me on that sunrise hike. But then we got into that fight, and after that, I didn't tell you because I love you. I know it doesn't make a lot of sense, but I'm not good at love. I was worried you might be done with me if you knew."

"Done? How could I be done?" His brow creases in confusion and I have the urge to reach up and smooth the lines. Then I get lost in the serene blue of his eyes and almost forget to answer his question. But he deserves the whole truth from me. I promised him honesty, and from now on, I'm going to give it to him.

"The chase would be over. I don't know. Maybe I thought that if we were bound to each other it would give you more time to fall for me."

"Sweetheart, I fell for you the first time I kissed you in that bar." He melts my heart a little bit more and I reach up to take his face in my hands. Leaning closer, he brushes his lips against mine. The soft touch I've been craving for a week. Or really, for my entire life.

A quiet sigh escapes me when we break the kiss. "Can we sit?" I gesture to the porch swing and move the flowers to the slatted wood porch. "I owe you an apology."

"I thought I was the one who owed you an apology." He turns to face me, leaving one leg down and bending the other one. "I behaved like an asshole, and I wasn't fully honest with you about what I'd be getting out of our deal. I didn't want you to feel like I was using you the same way everyone else was."

I nod and put a hand on his knee. "I know. I don't think that. And I'm sorry I wasn't honest with you about…everything."

"Mallory, I want to be with you for *you*. If you want to tear up this marriage license and get married all over again, let's do it because I want to be clear that I'm in it all the way, sweetheart. I want to be married to you no matter what."

My heart swells, and I almost forget what I called him over here to tell him. "I'm in it too. And I don't think we need a new wedding. The first one was perfect."

"It was." He picks up the flowers and plucks one long stem from the bunch. He presents it to me. "Can you accept my apology? I never should have stormed out of here. And I'd have come back or called, but you—"

"I said we needed a break. I know."

"Do you still need time? I don't want to force anything."

"No. I just need to tell you something, though, if you'd stop apologizing."

He makes the motion of zipping his lips shut and throwing away the key. "Okay, you talk."

"That's not zipping it!"

"Sorry."

I press my lips together in mock frustration, and he laughs. But he doesn't talk.

"You wanted to know why I asked you out." I take a deep breath and let it out slowly. "It was because that day we ran into each other at the store…"

He mimes slamming into each other and splatting on the floor, and I laugh. Then I punch his shoulder. "Stop. That day, when you swooped in and caught me and kept me from falling, I felt something…I felt something magical. That's the only way I know how to describe it. I felt like my heart had swelled up in my chest, and it was urging me to cling to you in a way I've never experienced before. My heart was telling me not to let go."

He stares at me, his blue eyes taking me in while he takes in my words. Then he nods. "Me too. I felt it too."

"I was like a zombie for two weeks, only thinking about how I needed to see you again. Like I couldn't even control it. And you see me—I'm logical. I'm focused—this was nothing like me. I *had* to see you."

"And then I didn't respond when you texted me."

I nod. "And I felt crushed, which was ridiculous because I didn't even know you. And now, as I've gotten to know you, my fears just kept growing that once you knew I loved you, you'd be disinterested. I kept worrying about how crushed I'd be now that I love you. And I do love you, Dashiell Corbett. Truly."

He smiles for real this time, and I just look at him. I think about how lucky I am that he's here for me to look at. And to kiss, because now that's what we're doing. I feel exactly the way I felt that day at Sunshine Foods, only more. Better.

"God, I love you. And now I have a confession to make."

"Okay, spill it," I say.

"You said you asked me on a date because you just wanted a hookup. I knew you were lying."

"Yet you fucked me anyway."

"You better believe I did."

"Why?" I ask.

"Because I could tell you didn't see me that way. I knew it might take a while to gain your confidence so you'll tell me the real reason you asked me out. And I decided I was fine with that. I wanted to get to know you better because my heart was already so far ahead of my head. I needed to know you more because I think I already loved you, even then. And now…best decision of my life."

He pulls me close until our foreheads touch and whispers, "Best decision ever."

ash

One Month Later

"I am a spa convert," I say, tipping back on a lounge chair next to our private pool at the Green Meadow Spa.

Next to me, Mallory lounges in a fluffy white robe and sips a blackberry mojito. "Good to know because I will come with you to any spa you want, any time."

It probably doesn't hurt that I kept her up most of the first night of our honeymoon reminding her of all the reasons she loves me. She told me repeatedly, but many of them seemed related to the various orgasms I delivered. I'm going to need clarification on that at some point.

"Gonna hold you to it."

"We honeymoon well. I think we're pros."

"We are. We're pros."

The spa is nestled at the base of the mountains that ring Napa Valley, and it's well equipped with a pickleball court, swimming pool, full service spa and library. But what we like best is our private villa, with its own patio, pool, and outdoor firepit. We've barely left, except to go for spa services and dinner at the restaurant.

Other than that, we've spent two days going between the pool, the lounges, and the bed, not necessarily in that order of importance.

We spend another hour lounging by the pool before shedding our robes and taking a naked dip in the accompanying spa. This place does vacationing right.

Our little villa is a Spanish-styled one-room bungalow with a king bed under fluffy down bedding and a living room with a wood-burning fireplace, where we spent two hours last night drinking wine and doing a tiny bit of a one-thousand-piece jigsaw puzzle of various cereal boxes. Mallory bought it, claiming its connection to the cereal aisle where her cart went awry at the store all those months ago.

I'll do any sort of activity with her, whether or not it's connected to Sunshine Foods or pickles, but she still looks for throwbacks any chance she gets. It's adorable and just one of the many reasons I love her.

Later, I booked us each massage appointments similar to the hot stone massages we had yesterday, only this time they use salt and dry brushes. We're going to walk out of this place smelling like lavender and mint and glowing for days.

The best thing about this resort is the food garden according to Mallory. She's taken about a hundred photos of every fruit and herb growing in it and vows to model Autumn Lake's budding food garden in its image.

"Do you want me to order lunch?" Mallory asks with her eyes closed, sunlight bouncing off the apples of her cheeks.

"In a bit. No rush."

"Okay."

She looks relaxed and content, and I vow to myself that I will do everything in my power to keep her feeling like this for the rest of her life. It's one of many vows that I consider amendments to our wedding vows, much like the Constitution. I keep a list of them on my phone and consider them binding in all fifty states and territories.

When we travel abroad, I supposed I can reassess.

The most significant amendment is the vow to be honest with her. I still intend to do that, but I've added a bit about being honest with myself. If I don't do that, it's going to come back to bite me.

So I'm as honest as I can possibly be when I tell her, "Mallomar, I love you so goddamn much that sometimes it hurts."

Without opening her eyes, she smiles and reaches for me. Her hand lands directly on top of mine like she knows exactly where I'll be.

"I don't want it to hurt," she says. "But I know how you feel."

Truly.

ash

THREE MONTHS Later

I WAKE up to the sound of quiet, insistent beeping in the distance and it makes me smile. It doesn't bother me that it's still dark outside and I really could use the extra few hours of sleep. The trucks backing up in the fields at Autumn Lake offer proof of progress, and I couldn't be more proud of my wife for making it happen.

Without looking to my right, I know Mallory is already awake and out of bed. She gets up before dawn every day when the lights go on in the vineyard. She likes to walk up and down the rows of staked plants and breathe in the scent of soil and morning dew on the vines.

Right now, the Autumn Lake vineyards consist mainly of root stock, the hardy drought-tolerant plants that will be future grapevines. They're taking root and being trained onto trellises. Soon, they'll be ready for chardonnay grapes to be grafted onto the established plants, and Mallory will be on her way to growing her first crop of fruit. I keep telling her that her manager, Jose, can handle the task without her hovering, but she wants to be there when the first buds appear. Like a proud parent wanting to photograph her child's first steps.

Jose is a third-generation vineyard manager who I wanted to hire at Buttercup Hill, but he liked the challenge of building a winery from the ground up—literally. "Are you going to hold it against me?" Mallory asked after Jose made his decision.

"Never." The slight disappointment I felt over not luring him to Buttercup Hill pales by comparison with my pride over how quickly Mallory has taken charge and put her business plans into motion.

And let's face it, I'm so gone for her that I'd offer up the best employee leads to her before bringing them to my own family. Yeah, I'm keeping that fact to myself. For now, I've managed to replace most of the people who were lured away from Buttercup Hill, and with the help of Graham, our finances are stable for now.

"Hey." Mallory's soft voice startles me. A second later, I feel her slip onto the bed behind me and curl her body into mine. She slides a hand over my hip, and I turn to face her. It's too dark to see her face clearly, but I know her gray eyes are sparkling. I know she's smiling.

"Hey. I thought you were out there." I gesture vaguely with my head.

"I was," she says. "But I decided I wanted to be here more."

My eyes start adjusting to the dim light, and now I can make out Mallory's features. Gorgeous as always. I roll onto my back and put my arms behind my head. "Anything in particular you have in mind?"

Her eyes travel to my naked chest and rake over my abs. She's made it clear on more than one occasion what her catnip is and I'm not above using any method at my disposal to get her to out of her clothes.

She laughs. "Yes. I thought we could take a sunrise hike."

At first, I'm certain she's joking. The last time we attempted a sunrise hike, we ended up in a misunderstanding that nearly derailed us. "Not sure that's really my jam."

"Why not? You're the one who bought me a headlamp."

This is true. Maybe I subconsciously want a do-over of that other crappy hike. And as much as I'd prefer to peel Mallory's clothes off and pull her on top of me, I know her well enough to understand that when she's determined to do something, my only option is to jump onboard.

"Hiking, huh?"

"Hiking."

* * *

Twenty minutes later, we're on a trail up the mountain. It doesn't require headlamps because the sun is nearly over the horizon. It means we'll be at the top for sunrise, and we'll have an incredible view of Autumn Lake under bright morning light.

We hike hand-in-hand at a relaxed pace, stopping every so often to take in the view at the top of a rise. From here, I really feel the vastness of Autumn Hill's new vineyards which span out in the distance below us. That's why Mallory likes coming up here—it's gratifying to see the literal fruits of her labor. It's why I like coming up here too.

And hell, I'd follow that woman up any hill she pointed at because I fucking love her. My siblings love her too because our early hikes mean I make it to morning meetings on time. What can I say? She's good for me.

"I'll never get tired of this view," Mallory says, tipping her head against my shoulder. Her long ponytail glides over the skin of my neck and I breathe in the scent of her jasmine shampoo.

"I'll never get tired of you."

Never.

I kiss her temple and pull her close.

We take a minute to look out over the valley from the top of Buttercup Hill, which gave our winery its name. It's the tallest peak in the area, and it's a popular hiking destination. Just not at seven in the morning, which is another reason I don't mind the early hikes.

Today, however, we have company. The heavy breathing of a jogger nearing the top of a steep climb disrupts the quiet. A moment later, we're joined by a tall guy in a backward baseball cap and a long-sleeved workout shirt that has to work to stretch over his chest and shoulders. Athlete, clearly.

He jogs in place at the top of the hill for a few seconds, taking in the view but never taking his earbuds out or stopping to stretch or chat with us.

As he turns around, we make eye contact and I realize I know him. His eyes widen and he extends a fist to bump. We nod at each other before he heads back the way he came.

"You know that guy?" Mallory whispers even though we're a hundred yards away from the guy.

"Yeah. Hockey player."

"That explains it."

"Explains what?" My possessive reflexes spring into action. I suppose they always will around Mallory because she's mine, and I don't care who I need to fight off in order to prove it.

"Relax, caveman." Just as quickly, Mallory settles against my chest and tames my baser instincts. I wrap my arms around her and rest my cheek against her hair. This is what happiness feels like. Good to know.

"That's Dave Calhoun. Plays for the Sailors. Used to date my sister."

"Which sister?"

"Trix."

"Huh. Good on her."

"Yeah. Whatever." I know she loves me, but I'd rather delude myself into believing she doesn't notice other men.

What I don't tell Mallory is that my sister's relationship with Cal didn't end particularly well. She's dated other guys since him, and she doesn't bring him up. But like I've said, I'm good at reading people. I've been with my sister at the Dark Horse more than once when a Sailors game came on the TV and she wasted no time asking for the channel to be changed.

"I think I read something about him. Just bought the Dalehurst winery near Calistoga. Did you hear anything?"

"Nope." And for my sister's sake, I really hope it's not true. Then again, it might not be the worst thing to have Dave Calhoun back in her life. He's the one guy she never got over, and I do enjoy watching people. If he's in town, the two of them will give me something to watch, for sure.

But for now, I swing an arm around my wife's shoulder, and we start making our way down the hill. "I don't have to be at work for over two hours," I say. "Breakfast in bed, Marshmallow?"

Mallory nods. "Anything you want."

"I want you. That's all."

She smiles. "Good. Because you can have me. Forever."

* * *

THANK you so much for reading Dash and Mallory's story—I hope you loved this couple as much as I do. Those golden retriever men get me every time!

For a peek into Dash and Mallory's happily ever after, jump on my mailing list to have a BONUS EPILOGUE delivered right to your inbox! I'll only send you the best stuff—new release info, exclusive sales, and a monthly free romance from one of my author friends.

Ready for Beatrix and Ren's story? You can reserve your copy NOW! Read on for a sneak peek!

ACKNOWLEDGMENTS

Readers, thank you. You make it possible for me to do a job I love —and your DMs while I'm crafting my characters make me smile.

Jesse and Oliver, future heartbreakers—I love you truly, and that will never change.

Thank you to my beta readers Melissa, Leah, Amy, and Meagan for keeping me in line. And Jenny Sims for top notch edits (I still don't know whether to hyphenate that).

Thank you Echo Grayce for the gorgeous covers and for talking me down on the stressy days—I'm so impressed by your work and your kindness.

The team at Valentine PR is lovely and amazing—thank you, thank you.

Bloggers and bookstagrammers—thank you for embracing my books and exposing my writing to readers. I couldn't do it without your help. Glad to have you in my corner.

And to my fellow authors: I know you know. Love you.

ABOUT THE AUTHOR

Stacy Travis writes sexy, charming romance about bookish, sassy women and the hot cinamon roll heroes who fall for them. Keep the coffee coming, and she'll keep writing.

When she's not on a deadline, she's in running shoes complaining that all roads seem to go uphill. Or on the couch with a margarita. Or fangirling at a soccer game. She's never met a dog she didn't want to hug. And if you have no plans for Thanksgiving, she'll probably invite you to dinner. Stacy is the mom of two boys and two poorly-trained rescue dogs who keep her on her toes in Los Angeles.

Facebook reader group: Stacy's Saucy Sisters

Super fun newsletter: https://geni.us/travisNL

Tiktok: https://www.tiktok.com/@stacytravisauthor

Website: https://www.www.stacytravis.com

Email: stacytraviswrites@gmail.com - tell me what you're
reading!

facebook.com/stacytravisromance
instagram.com/stacytravisauthor
bookbub.com/authors/stacy-travis
goodreads.com/stacytravis
tiktok.com/@stacytravisauthor

The Summer Heat Duet

1. The Summer of Him: A Mistaken-Identity Celebrity Romance

2. Forever with Him: An Opposites-Attract Contemporary Romance

The Berkeley Hills Series - all standalone novels

1. In Trouble with Him: A Forbidden-Love Office Romance (Finn and Annie's story)

2. Second Chance at Us: A Second Chance Romance (Becca and Blake)

3. Falling for You: A Friends-to-Lovers Romance (Isla and Owen)

4. The Spark Between Us: A Grumpy-Sunshine, Firefighter, Brother's Best Friend Romance (Sarah and Braden)

5. Playing for You: A Sports Romance (Tatum and Donovan)

6. No Match for Her - An Opposites-Attract, Friends-to-Lovers Romance (Cherry and Charlie)

San Francisco Strikers Series - standalone novels

1. He's a Keeper: A Grumpy-Sunshine Sports Romance (Molly and Holden)

2. He's a Player: A Second-Chance Sports Romance (Jordan and Tim)

3. He's a Charmer: A Brother's-Best-Friend, Forced-Proximity, Sports Romance (Linnie and Weston)

Buttercup Hill Series - standalone novels

1. Love You More; A Single-Dad, Grumpy-Sunshine Small-Town Romance (Jax and Ruby)

2. Love You Anyway; A Small-Town Billionaire-Next-Door Age Gap Romance (PJ and Colin)

3. Love You Truly; A Fake-Fiancé, Small-Town Romance (Dash and Mallory)

4. Love You Too; A Small-Town, Accidental Pregnancy Sports Romance (Beatrix and Ren)

LOVE YOU TOO - SNEAK PEEK

A SMALL-TOWN, ACCIDENTAL PREGNANCY, SPORTS ROMANCE

Chapter 1
Beatrix

I'm running on fumes. Skipped breakfast, as usual, so I fish around in my purse for something with enough sugar and calories to get me through the next hour until I can grab something from the café at Buttercup Hill on my way upstairs to my office. I swear, if we didn't have two restaurants on the property, I'd probably never eat.

My mission is disrupted when the sales clerk returns with my swatches of fabric. "Here we go. I threw in a few extra color palates in case you want to try it a different way." She smiles, tucks her long bangs behind her ears, and adjusts her wire-rimmed glasses so they sit higher on her nose. She reminds me of my younger sister PJ, hard-working eager to prove herself.

"Ha. Yeah, I'll probably come back with a new color scheme after I try the alternates."

"Not trying to make it harder."

"You're not. I love options. You're the best."

Her smile widens and she pulls out a bag from beneath the

counter. It's practically big enough to hold her. And the counter. "Sorry, we only have giant bags for some reason."

"It's okay. I don't need a bag."

I tuck the pile of fabric under one arm and resume the hunt of a snack. Granola bar? Only in my dreams. Tin of mints? The only one I have contains change for parking meters.

I can feel my heart starting to race from the coffee I guzzled earlier on an empty stomach. I don't think I can wait until I get back to the winery to put something in my stomach, so I detour to the bakery at Oxbow. Not exactly a hardship. As I stare at the glass case filled with golden croissants, berry-filled muffins, and little fruit tarts, the only challenge is to choose just one.

"Blueberry bran muffin and a coffee with cream. To go, please." I shouldn't have more coffee, but I rationalize that the muffin will soak some of it up, and I need the energy boost.

I balance the folded white bakery bag on top of the coffee cup and adjust the stack of fabric in my other hand. My purse dangles from a mesh strap on my shoulder, and I navigate past the cheese counter, several people browsing a display of pretty packaged chocolate, and a wine shop with floor-to-ceiling bottles of local vintages.

The owner of the shop hasn't ordered the recent crop of cabernets from Buttercup Hill, but that's a problem for my older brother Archer to solve. I have enough to do managing the restaurants and putting the final touches on the inn before it reopens next month.

I've only been inside for an hour, but the sun has broken through the morning haze and now shines so brightly that I stand outside the market and squint to find my car in the parking lot. I sort of remember where I parked. It was near a tree. At least, I think so.

It's because I'm looking into the distance that I don't see what's directly in my path. Or rather, who is directly in my path.

Not until my knees hit a brown ball of fur and I lose my footing for a second.

Which is all it takes for my bakery bag to topple off the lid of my coffee. "No, no," I instruct, but it obeys gravity instead of me. As I lunge to grab it without spilling the coffee, my purse strap slides off my shoulder, sending the purse toward the ground and dumping its contents. The tin of coins opens and sends rolling quarters in all directions. Tampons fly. Lipsticks scatter.

The ball of fur decides my little catastrophe is a really fun game and begins leaping toward the coins and pawing them to the pavement. "Where's your leash? Who owns you?" I mutter, glancing around. All I see is bright, glary sunlight

I manage to grab the muffin bag before it hits the pavement, but I'm gripping my coffee cup too tightly, so the lid pops off and the life-giving drink sloshes down my arm. The hot coffee burns as I kneel on the hot pavement to put the lid back on the coffee and gather my stuff. Note to self: always carry snacks. Never balance things on coffee lids. Conceal tampons in some kind of a pouch. Advice I will ignore the next time I leave the house.

The furball chooses this moment of vulnerability to charge at me like I've just yelled "go." I lose my footing and roll backward, coffee spilling again. The furry thing, which I'm pretty sure is a rambunctious dog, starts licking my face with glee.

I'd like to state for the record that I am a dog person. I think they're cute. I willingly pet them. I've even toyed with getting a dog. But right now, in this moment, I am not feeling the love. Well, maybe a little bit. The dog's rough little tongue tickles as it laps at my cheeks and chin. It feels like a sort of apology for the chaos. "Okay, buddy. I know. You just want to play. Not your fault your human is a dumbass."

I grab the muffin bag and push it under the dog's nose for a good sniff, and then toss it a few yards away. The dog, predictably, chases after it and I cover my face with both hands to block out the infernal sun for five seconds.

That's when I finally hear a deep shout in the distance. "Truman. Tru! Stop. Sit. Stay."

Even I know that's too many commands for a dog to understand and obey in a single moment, but at least someone seems to be claiming responsibility for the fur monster who accosted me. And then I realize how ridiculous I am because I'm actually a little jealous of the dog and his zest for life. Truman bounces around like he has pogo sticks for legs, his brown curly fur glinting in the sun, tongue hanging out one side of his open mouth.

As flustered as I am here on my back on the pavement, I start to laugh. The whole situation is so ridiculous that it's my only option. Hands still covering my eyes, I take this situation for what it is—a sign that I need to slow the heck down, at least a tiny bit.

Then the air around me grows a few degrees colder. The sun is blocked by a cloud and I wrench my hands from my eyes and open them.

Only it's not a cloud blocking the sun. It's the broad shoulders of a tall man standing over me with a confused expression on his face. With the sun behind him, he's hard to see clearly. "Geez, sorry about that. You okay?" he asks, raking a hand through his hair.

"You really should keep your dog on a leash." I sound like a crotchety old lady, but he needs to be more careful. "Cars barely stop for humans, let alone dogs. Give your guy a fighting chance, at least."

He lets out a long exhale and unfurls a leash from his hand so it dangles in front of me. "That was the plan. But the little trickster escaped before I got it on him." He rubs a hand over his chin, which has a few days' worth of stubble. I still can't get a clear view of his face because of the sun, but something about his voice rings familiar. Probably a local or someone I've run into at Buttercup Hill.

"You sure you're okay?" Something snags his gaze and he spins around to yell. "Tru, what the heck are you doing?"

"I'm good." I push myself to sitting, looking around me at the scattered coins. Looking down, I notice a tampon squeezed in my fist and quickly shove it into my purse. Then a hand comes into my field of vision. It's large, strong-looking, extended toward me. When I look up, I see that the man is offering to pull me to standing. I wave him off.

"Thanks, but I think I'll stay on the ground with my dignity."

He waves his hand, insistent. "Come on. At least let me replace your breakfast."

Grudgingly, I place my hand in his and nearly recoil at the jolt of electricity I feel when I touch his skin. It's jarring because of its intensity but also…familiar.

When I'm on my feet, I look up at the man, who I can now see clearly. From his soft brown eyes, chiseled jaw, high cheekbones, lips that have no business looking as soft as they do.

Guess some things never change. At least not for Dominick Renaldi, star hockey player for the Oakland Oilers. Or Ren, as I called him when we were a couple.

"Trix?" His eyes soften as they go round with disbelief.

Shit.

You know when you want to act like an adult and let the guy who broke your heart see that you're over him? Yeah. I want to do that, really I do. I am over Ren. I have been for years.

I no longer think about him. I barely notice when some picture comes across my social media feed of Ren with yet another beautiful woman on his arm. And when a hockey game is on at the Dark Horse, I never ask for the channel to be changed.

I am over him. And yet…at the sight of him, my heart starts beating like an amateur drummer in a marching band. Loud, discordant thumps that surely can be heard two stadiums away. My face heats with embarrassment—that has to be what it is—

because he found me disheveled and flat on my ass and he looks, well, perfect.

Why does the one man who I planned to never see again have to be so freakin' beautiful? No, not beautiful. Sinfully gorgeous.

I wish that wasn't my first reaction to seeing him.

I wish my second reaction isn't a searing pain in my chest, the combination of regret, heartbreak, and general loathing. Yes, loathing. All the anger I had over the way he dumped me comes roaring back like an untamed waterfall, drowning out any kind feeling I may have toward his adorable dog. I do not like this man, not anymore. He hurt me deeply and I have nothing good to say to him now.

And here he is, looking at me with that amused smirky smile I used to find so damn cute. Dominick Renaldi is as frustrating as he is beautiful. Actually, even more so. I feel my hackles raise and my fists ball into defensive position. I've never slugged a man, but I'd have no problem making Ren the first. It's been ten years coming and it would feel oh, so good.

He's a man I've loved hating ever since we dated and broke up about ten years ago. Now, all these years later, I can admit that hating him was more about heartbreak dramatics than actual animosity. College sweethearts. Young love. Impossible choices.

All the makings for a breakup that left me reeling at the time. Things went from blissful to finished so quickly I had whiplash.

And now…I don't feel much at all after the moment of shock at seeing Ren's face. Maybe a little bit of wistful "what if" lingers in the air because he still looks good. Even if I know better than to trust him with my heart. Never again.

I believe in the power of threes when it comes to relation- ships. If I like a guy enough to spend three hours with him on a date, I'll make plans for a second date. If I can get through three dates and I still like him—which also means I'm hot and bothered and desperate to see what's under the gray Henley the men I like always seem to be wearing—the relationship can probably run for a while.

Three months has always been my barometer for whether we can go for the long haul. It's only happened once, with Ren.

We were hot and passionate for a full year before the wheels came off. Life happened. Real world factors came into play and our romance couldn't survive it.

So many complicating factors got in the way that we never really had a chance. As soon as college ended, he was recruited by a Canadian hockey team and missed graduation because he needed to replace an injured player immediately. I moved to Napa to help out at Buttercup Hill, but I never intended to stay so close to my family. Would I have followed a hockey boyfriend to Canada? Back then, sure.

Now, I'm far too rooted in my feminist ideals to follow anyone anywhere. My career is my identity, and I wouldn't follow a guy like Ren across the room, let alone across the country. He showed me his true colors when it mattered and I'll never forget it.

All of these thoughts hurtle toward me at lightspeed. Just seeing him in front of me produces a rip inside my chest. The same feeling of a deflating heart that I felt all those years ago, but now it's tinged with pissy irritation that he's here. Now. In my territory. With a dog who's clearly as poorly behaved as him.

He's got a lot of nerve.

-v-

You can preorder LOVE YOU TOO now!